DESPERATE HOUSEDOGS

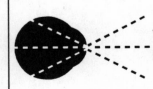

This Large Print Book carries the
Seal of Approval of N.A.V.H.

DESPERATE HOUSEDOGS

SPARKLE ABBEY

THORNDIKE PRESS
A part of Gale, Cengage Learning

Detroit • New York • San Francisco • New Haven, Conn • Waterville, Maine • London

GALE
CENGAGE Learning·

LIBRARY OF CONGRESS CATALOGING-IN-PUBLICATION DATA

Abbey, Sparkle.
   Desperate housedogs / by Sparkle Abbey. — Large print ed.
     p. cm. — (A pampered pets mystery series) (Thorndike Press large print clean reads)
   ISBN-13: 978-1-4104-5278-8 (hardcover)
   ISBN-10: 1-4104-5278-6 (hardcover)
   1. Dog owners—Fiction. 2. Animal behavior therapy—Fiction. 3. Murder—Investigation—Fiction. I. Title.
PS3601.B359D47 2012
813'.6—dc23   2012031050

Published in 2012 by arrangement with BelleBooks, Inc.

Printed in the United States of America
1 2 3 4 5 6 7 16 15 14 13 12

This book is dedicated to our husbands,
our children, and grandchildren.
Tim and Steve
Justin, Candice, Aaron, Isaac, Eliana,
Joshua, Kelli, and Evie
Joshua, Sarah, Jeremy, Colleen,
Rachel, and Seth
You all are "Best in Show"
and we love you.

CHAPTER ONE

I don't normally break into people's homes, but today I was making an exception.

Not wanting to make the burglary too obvious, I'd parked my car down the street and fought through the bougainvillea hedge to the back of the house. In southern California the bougainvillea blooms every-where, luxurious but tough, like old starlets wearing too much pink lipstick. Determina-tion thumped in my chest but I was still as nervous as a long-tailed cat in a room full of rockin' chairs. Glancing left and then right to make sure none of the neighbors were around, I flipped up the sand-crusted mat and grabbed the key that lay under it.

My cousin, Melinda, always kept her spare key in the same spot. This particular mat said, "Wipe Your Paws."

Mel's place was nice. Not posh, but very nice even by Laguna Beach standards. Not at all like the open spaces we'd grown up with in Texas but nothing to sneeze at. Palm trees and Jacaranda trees surrounded her patio and morning was already warming the ocean breeze. I unlocked the door and slipped inside. If I were lucky I'd find my target right away and get out quick. If I were really lucky, it would be a few days before Mel realized the brooch was gone.

I stepped into her sunshine-bright kitchen and noted the stack of dirty dishes. I truly wished the girl wouldn't leave dishes in the sink. Here in the semi-desert you run the risk of bugs. Bugs the size of cocker spaniels.

Eww. I shivered, shaking off the thought like a wet dog shaking off summer rain.

First, I checked the freezer. Not a very original hiding place and not a very effective one either, as I myself had discovered. I'd tried freezer paper and a label that said "Pig Hearts" but Mel had figured it out.

Okay, nothing in there.

Missy, Mel's bulldog, lumbered into the kitchen, her only greeting an eye roll that said, "Oh, it's just you."

I reached down and scratched behind her ears. She leaned into the ear rub. "If only you could talk, sugar. You'd tell me where Mel put it, wouldn't you?"

Missy gave a low, snuffly bark and butted my hand, effectively sliming it. Bulldogs are pretty darn loyal. Could be she wouldn't give up the hiding spot even if she knew. She waddled back to the living room and her spot by the picture window, as if to say, "You're on your own, girl."

"Fine, Missy. You're as stubborn as your mama." I wiped dog drool on my jeans and got back to the task at hand.

Hmmm . . . where would my beautiful (but devious) cousin put the thing? Like a bad Texas summer heat rash, irritation prickled.

Geez Louise, Mel, how long would it have taken to clean up after yourself?

I ran water in the sink and started stacking plates in the dishwasher.

See, that was the problem. Mel's not a bad kid, and only a couple of years younger than me, but she's so dang impulsive it seems I'm always cleaning up her messes. Take Mel's fight with the zoning board over not getting a permit for her new patio or her on-and-off again relationship with Grey Donovan.

Grey is a prince (in the metaphorical sense) and is caught in the unfortunate position of having befriended two headstrong southern women with a competitive streak. We'd inherited it — the competitive streak, I mean. Our mamas had both been

Texas beauty queens and we'd both lived the pageant life — for a while.

That's to say, until we rebelled. We'd each defied our mothers in our own unique way. Mine a little pushier, but straight-forward. Mel's a little wilder and out there. But then that kinda sums up everything y'all need to know about the two of us.

More about that later. Right now I had some searching to do before my cousin came home or her *lovely* neighbors called the cops.

I tried her bedroom, the study (junk room in Mel's case), the bathroom (I was happy to see she was still on her allergy meds), the closet (smaller junk room) and still came up empty-handed. Now, I was back to the kitchen.

Stumped, I stood and looked around, hands on my hips, arms akimbo, mind on hyper drive. It was a funky kitchen but decorated more for fun than utility. Mel's cookie jar was in the shape of a golden retriever. It was just flat adorable, the dog in a playful ready-to-pounce position. I wondered where she'd gotten it. If we were speaking, I'd ask her. But we're not.

I couldn't help it. I shook my finger at the cookie jar. *Melinda Langston, you should not be living on junk food and sweets.*

Her freezer'd been full of microwave dinners and her refrigerator completely devoid of any healthy fruits and vegetables. Probably living on processed food and sugar.

Still, Mel had always been a fabulous cook. She just didn't necessarily follow a recipe. The girl was a bang-up baker though, and cookies were her specialty. My mouth watered. One cookie would never be missed.

Don't mind if I do, cousin. I lifted the dog's butt to help myself and plunged my hand in the cookie jar.

Well, for cryin' in a bucket! Was the dang thing empty?

I couldn't believe I'd made the decision to indulge in empty calories only to be thwarted. I rooted around the inside of the cookie jar, my fingers only touching smooth pottery.

Wait. What was that?

Instead of cookies, my hand connected with metal. Grandma Tillie's brooch. She'd put Grandma Tillie's brooch — *my* brooch — in a cookie jar.

I pulled it out, brushed off the cookie crumbs, and turned it over carefully to check for damage.

Grandma "Tillie" Matilda Montgomery's brooch is the ugliest piece of jewelry you've ever laid eyes on. A twenty-two karat gold

11

basket filled to the brim with fruit made from precious stones. Diamonds, topaz, emeralds, rubies. It is beyond garish.

Garish and gaudy, but significant. In her will, Grandma Tillie had left it to her "favorite granddaughter." I knew she meant to leave it to me. Mel was just as convinced she'd left it to her.

I prodded it with my finger. One of the emeralds might be a teeny bit loose. Promising myself I'd check more thoroughly for damage when I got home, I tucked the brooch in the outside pocket of my handbag and gave it a little pat.

Back with me, where it belonged.

I finished stacking the dishwasher, turned it on, called good-bye to Missy (who ignored me), and let myself out the back. I was just replacing the key when my cell phone rang.

"Hello." I answered in a low tone. No need to alert the neighbors. I'd made it so far without drawing any attention. Making my way to the front of the house, I walked quickly toward my car.

"Hey, Caro, this is Kevin. Kevin Blackstone." He sounded frantic. But then I'm used to frantic clients. "I need your help."

Oh, I don't think I mentioned it, but I'm Caro Lamont, and when I'm not breaking and entering, I'm the proprietor of Laguna Beach's Professional Animal Wellness Specialist Clinic. (The PAWS Clinic for short).

I'm not a dog trainer. Tons of other folks are more qualified in that arena. I basically deal with problem pets, which as a rule involves dealing more with the behavior of the humans than the pet. If I suspect a medical problem I refer pet parents to my veterinarian friend, Dr. Daniel Darling.

I could hear the deep barks of his two German Shepherd dogs in the background. It sounded like Kevin had a problem.

Kevin lived in the exclusive Ruby Point gated community just off of Pacific Coast Highway (fondly referred to as PCH by the locals).

With all the noise, I couldn't hear what it was Kevin needed.

"I'll come by in a few minutes."

I think he said, "okay" but it was difficult to tell over the chaos on his end.

Extremely pleased with myself over the successful retrieval of my inheritance, I climbed in my silver vintage Mercedes convertible. Humming, I thought about the brooch, *my* brooch, safe in my handbag.

It was turning out to be a beautiful day in lovely Laguna Beach.

Life was good.

CHAPTER TWO

The dogs were desperate and so was Kevin.

He was clearly at the end of his rope. Or would that be leash?

Kevin's two German Shepherd dogs circled and barked and circled and barked while the television blasted above the din, and Kevin Blackstone shouted at me.

"They've been at this for two whole days."

That was Kevin.

"Bark. Bark."

"Bark. Bark."

That was the dogs.

"Come in for the spring clearance sale at Orange County European Motors."

The TV announcer.

It had been going on since I'd arrived at Kevin's and it was enough to make *me* desperate.

"I've tried everything to get them to stop. They continually run to the patio doors but there's nothing out there." Kevin was a

14

good-sized guy and had a strong grip on their collars, but clearly the dogs were distraught. Kevin looked like he hadn't slept in days.

"Bark. Bark."

"Bark. Bark."

"Breaking news: The body of a man found at Crystal Cove State Park has not yet been identified. Authorities are releasing few details but TV 10 News will talk with hikers who discovered the body."

Kevin continued shouting over the clamor. "I tried letting them outside thinking it was maybe a squirrel or something but at first they wouldn't go. They just stood in the doorway and growled."

I didn't approach the dogs just yet. "Tell me about what's been going on? Has anything changed in their routine?"

Shepherds aren't a nervous breed. When they bark, they're barking at something.

"No, nothing has changed."

Or at least I think that's what Kevin said.

Between the bark, bark and the "Now we go live to . . ." from the television, I could hardly hear myself think, let alone carry on a conversation.

"Kevin, sugar, would you mind turning the television off?"

"What?"

I pointed toward the super-sized wide screen TV.

"Oh." He released his hold on the dogs, picked up a manly remote, and clicked the TV off.

I sighed. At least one din-producing item down. The dogs continued to bark, but the noise level was a bit more tolerable.

Okay, where were we?

I'd worked with Kevin's dogs before. About a year ago they'd had a problem with chewing up his new furniture. The doggy therapy seemed to have done the trick. At least the furniture I could see from my vantage point appeared to be intact.

"Tell me again, when did this start?" I asked.

"Two days ago."

"Tell me specifically when you first noticed the dogs' behavior problems."

"Well, I'd been at the gym. I came home and they came to greet me like they always do. No jumping up."

He saw my raised brow.

"Then they just started going bonkers. Running to the patio door and then back to me. Patio door — me. Patio door — me." Kevin flung his arms back and forth for emphasis. "I let them outside and they ran out there. They ran around and barked and

16

then ran back to me. I finally had to bring them inside for fear Mandy next door would turn me in to the homeowners' association for noise pollution."

Ruby Point was way over the top about their association rules. Apparently Kevin had gotten sideways with Mandy Beenerman, his next door neighbor, a few months ago over a non-conforming mailbox he'd put up. It had been LA Lakers purple and gold, and Mandy, who was a former Celtics cheerleader turned super-snob, had turned him in.

I thought it probably had more to do with spite than good taste. But I could see where Kevin Blackstone might occasionally need a reminder.

To tell you the God's honest truth, I wasn't sure what Kevin Blackstone did for a living, but the same could be said for a lot of my clients. None of my business, you know. All I knew was he lived alone in his huge, multi-level, modern contemporary mansion, and he asked me out at least once a month. I turned him down just as regularly.

While the house was tastefully decorated, I'm certain it had been professionally done with little input from Kevin because he, today as most days, sported really bad plaid shorts paired with a loud orange-colored polo. Who knows, maybe the guy was color-blind.

And me? Who was I to judge? I guess today I sure didn't look like I knew Dior couture from the Dollar Discount store. It would drive my mama insane, but then pretty much everything I did drove her bananas.

Anymore I dressed more for comfort than fashion. Jeans, t-shirt, tennies. My vocation often required rolling around on the ground with puppies or crawling behind ten-thousand dollar couches to retrieve recalcitrant kitty cats. I loved to get gussied up on occasion but lately those occasions had been few and far between.

Kevin raked a meaty hand through his reddish hair. "They're always such good dogs. I thought maybe they were just stir-crazy so I took them for a walk, but drama princess Shar was outside with her dinky dog. She claimed 'her baby' was being traumatized by Zeus and Tommy Boy, and told me if I didn't get my dogs under control, I'd 'be sorry.' Woo, Shar, I'm so scared." Kevin held up his hands and did a fake frightened look.

His neighbor a few mansions down the street, Shar Summers, had a tiny Chinese

Crested named Babycakes. For those of you who aren't familiar with the breed, they are delicate, very needy pooches that look more like small alien creatures than dogs. Easily traumatized. A toy poodle would do it, let alone Zeus and Tommy Boy and their bark-fest.

Bottom line, Kevin's housemates were out of control and if the barking continued there was the distinct possibility someone (probably Mandy) would lodge a neighborhood complaint and Laguna Beach Animal Control could impound the dogs. In lieu of an explanation, we'd start with behavior modification.

"Bring me their treats." I'd been ignoring the dogs. The last thing you want to do when dealing with bad behavior is inadvertently reinforce it. Unfortunately that's exactly what a lot of pet owners do under the mistaken impression they're comforting the animal.

Kevin returned with a box of Bowser Treats from my cousin Mel's shop, the Bow Wow Boutique. Their favorite.

"Okay, here's what we're gonna to do." I picked up one of the treats, closed my hand over it, and turned my back on the dogs.

When they stopped barking, I spun around and gave it to them. It worked only for a moment and then they were back at it.

After a few more tries, I handed the box to Kevin. "You try."

He mimicked my ignore/reward method and eventually the spans between barking spates increased.

After an hour of working with Zeus and Tommy Boy (and Kevin), I felt like we'd made some progress. I bent and hugged the two dogs, partly to assess their tension and partly because I sincerely liked the guys.

Initially, the times they weren't barking were very few, but eventually there were longer gaps. I tell you, I've worked with a bunch of barkers and I'd never seen anything quite like it.

"You said you let them out on the patio?"

"I did the first day," Kevin said. "I thought maybe they'd smelled a wild animal or something. But there was nothing. Nothing I could see, anyway."

"Well, let's try it again." Maybe there was a dead bird or squirrel and they'd picked up the scent. Could be it was the nose thing. Their super nose is why German Shepherd dogs make such great police K-9s, sniffing out drugs at airports or during traffic stops.

Kevin opened the door and the dogs were out like a shot. They loped around the pool and after a circle or two, tramped through his flowers, and then headed down the side yard. We followed and got to the edge of the house just as the dogs galloped through the open gate.

I looked at Kevin.

He shrugged his line-backer shoulders in denial. "I didn't leave it open."

If the dogs were running loose, there was an even better possibility they'd end up in doggie jail. I started after them, thanking my lucky stars I'd worn my running shoes instead of the really cute Marc Jacobs sandals I'd just bought. Still, Kevin got to the front of the house before I did.

I could see the dogs halfway up the street and took off after them. A landscape worker, or, I suppose in Ruby Point he would be called a "horticulturist," worked in one of the brick planters that lined the boulevard. Zeus and Tommy Boy were headed his way.

I yelled, "Stop those dogs."

He looked up.

"The dogs." I gestured so emphatically it's a wonder I didn't dislocate something.

He continued to stare.

Sheesh. How dense can you be?

Zeus and Tommy Boy ran up to him. Each grabbed a pant leg and held on.

He swung his shovel at them, narrowly missing the two furry heads.

Oh. No.

Zeus growled and adjusted his hold on the guy. Judging by the look on his face, dog teeth had reached flesh this time. He continued to swing the shovel.

Kevin was within earshot and used the commands we'd practiced.

"Zeus, Tommy Boy. Off."

The dogs released the worker, but looked disappointed. I didn't really blame them. I mean, seriously, what would you do if someone came after you with a shovel?

I finally caught up with them.

"Are you okay?"

"Are you an idiot?"

Kevin and I spoke in tandem. His was the voice of concern, mine the ill-mannered one.

Hey, I'm from Texas and we don't cotton to stupidity. Especially where it concerns our horses or our dogs.

The guy had crawled up onto the planter. Clearly not a dog person and these were some big dogs. Okay, so maybe he'd reacted out of fear but still — a shovel?

Zeus and Tommy Boy sat at attention but continued to eye him with interest.

"Are you hurt?" I addressed the man but rested my hand on Tommy Boy's back. I could feel the tension in his body, but both dogs stayed in place.

The guy was young and wiry. His spiky black hair and multiple piercings suggested a latent punk rocker look. The legs of his blue jeans were ripped but I think they might have been before his encounter with Zeus and Tommy Boy. He jumped down from the planter and rubbed his leg.

"You need to keep your killer beasts under control." His dark eyes were hard and his posture tense.

If the dogs *had* actually broken skin and he went to the emergency room, it would definitely be the canine slammer.

"Well for cryin' in a bucket, let me take a look." I reached for his leg.

He jerked backward as if he thought I might bite, too.

"I'm fine." His voice was as tight as a fist.

Zeus and Tommy Boy both growled a deep rumble.

I looked at Kevin hoping he understood the seriousness of the situation. "Do you have a first aid kit at your house?"

He nodded.

"Let's take the dogs home and I'll grab the kit." I turned to the gardener. "You sit and catch your breath. I'll be right back. Then we can take a look at your leg."

The guy continued to glare. With his dark,

23

spikey hair, he kind of reminded me of one of those Texas horned lizards that puff up so they're all spiny when they're upset.

Kevin gave the command for the dogs to follow and the four of us trouped back down the street toward his house. The dogs periodically glanced back as if to make sure the guy was staying put.

It took very little time for Kevin to find his first aid kit and for me to head back to where we'd left Mister Angry Pants, but by the time I returned to the planter, the landscape worker was nowhere to be found.

What a fruitcake. I guess he must have been okay or he would've stuck around. Heading back to Kevin's to gather my things, I looked for one of the landscaping company's trucks, but didn't see a vehicle of any kind. On second thought, in such a fancy schmancy community they don't often leave the maintenance trucks out in plain sight. Maybe he'd needed to move on to another area of Ruby Point.

The morning had warmed up. I stopped back in at Kevin's and reminded him to keep up the behavior modification. I felt sure it would eventually work. Sometimes dogs can get into a barking cycle and you have to break that cycle. I left with a promise to Kevin I'd check in tomorrow to see what kind of progress he'd made.

I pulled out of the drive and drove a short ways down the street to my friend, Diana's, house. Er, castle.

Diana's showcase abode dwarfed Kevin's, and her graceful flower-filled front entrance always made me think of the magic and glamour of a bygone era in Hollywood. The era that brought us stars like Elizabeth Taylor, Sophia Loren, Katherine Hepburn and yes, Diana Knight.

You might recognize the name. Diana Knight had been a perky heroine in a series of big screen romantic comedies a few decades ago and, though it turned out her leading man had been gay, the public still loved her. In fact, there had been a recent nostalgic resurgence of interest in her movies. She was still perky, at least in the personality sense.

In the physical sense, not so much.

Diana was a widow, I believe for the fourth time, having out-lived a college sweetheart, a fellow actor, a banker, and finally a business tycoon. She'd recently been keeping company with a local restaurateur though she claimed it wasn't serious. She no longer acted but now used her considerable celebrity to advance her first love — rescue animals.

We'd met because Diana volunteered at the Laguna Beach Animal Rescue League, and I did, too. We were in the throes of planning the annual "Fur Ball" which was a "cough-up some cash" black-tie affair for the ARL. Diana had chaired the event for the past few years, and somehow this year I'd been roped into being her co-chair.

Being a co-chair with Diana meant there really wasn't much heavy lifting involved because she had it down to a fine science. She and I had spent a day last week calling corporate sponsors and setting up the advertising, which in most cases Diana'd been able to get comped. It was near impossible to tell this woman no.

Since I was in the area, I decided to drop off the final ad copy I'd picked up the day before from the graphic designer. I thought it had turned out great.

The picture was a handsome Doberman in a tux waltzing with a classy Siamese in a ball gown under a title that said: "Fur Ball — Cough Up Some Cash for the Laguna Beach ARL" and then gave all the details of the event. It was a picture the graphic designer had manipulated via magic software, you understand. I can assure you no animals were embarrassed in the making of this ad.

I was sure Diana would love it but still this was her big event and so I wanted to run it by her.

I rang the doorbell and her housekeeper answered the door.

"Hello, Bella. Is Diana here?" I asked.

"No, I am sorry. She is not in at the moment. Can I give her a message?" The dark-haired beauty raised her soft musical voice to be heard over the cacophony of barking in the background.

Diana often took the more difficult rescue cases and at times had up to a dozen dogs in the house. Canine chaos.

"Bella, honey, I don't know how you do it." I patted her arm. "Would you give her this, please?" I handed over the ad copy.

Bella took the folder and promised to see that Diana got it.

"Tell her I'll give her a call tomorrow."

Back in my car, I waved at the Ruby Point guard, and then left the gated community. I turned in the direction of Main Beach. Heading down Broadway, I made a quick stop at Whole Foods, and then pointed myself toward home.

My home is an eclectic blend of styles. It's nothing like my mama's house, which is always ready for a feature spread in *House Beautiful.* My house is hardly ever ready for its close-up. Not because I hadn't been raised right but because I basically didn't care about fancy things. It was clean, it was comfortable, it was mine.

I walked in and kicked off my shoes.

Dogbert, my rescue mixed-breed mutt, bounded across the room to greet me. He's part Spaniel, part Terrier, and parts unknown. He's the most adorable mutt alive.

Always faithful, always thrilled to see me. He is the love of my life.

I sat on the floor for some serious puppy hugs and flipped on the TV.

I have an incredible view of the Pacific out my patio doors and an open floor plan that takes full advantage of it. I'd paid a pretty price for my gorgeous view but I'd never regretted it.

Promising a long walk later, I gave Dog a final tummy rub and got to my feet. The television in my family room is visible from my kitchen, allowing me to monitor what's happening in the world as I prepare dinner. I use the term "prepare dinner" loosely.

I unpacked the organic mayonnaise I'd just purchased and opened a can of tuna. Sad, I know. Here I am within view of the ocean. You'd think I could get some fresh fish.

I was soon swarmed by Thelma and Louise, my two cats. I dumped half the tuna into a bowl and set it on the floor. Dogbert hurried over but was too late.

"None left for you, boy." I smiled at his resigned sigh. Upstaged by the felines again.

National news shifted to local news and I listened for an update on the weather as I stirred some fresh cilantro and mayo into what was left of the tuna.

"Police are on the scene of what officers are calling an 'unexplained death' in the upscale gated community of Ruby Point."

That got my attention.

Not just Diana and Kevin but practically all of the residents of Ruby Point are clients or acquaintances of mine.

A female reporter, in a long-sleeved business suit that was much too warm for Southern California, and a hairdo that was much too big for this decade, gave the live report.

"The body was found this afternoon and police are at this time going door to door speaking to residents. Officers have not yet identified the individual, but the investigation centers around the house you see behind me."

I tried to see the home behind Big-Hair but couldn't quite make out the property. The homes in Ruby Point are all so different and individual that if I could get a glimpse I might recognized it, but I just couldn't see enough to tell.

The pounding on my door startled me. "Well, for cryin' in a bucket! I'm coming and by the way I have a doorbell." I stomped to the door and yanked it open.

The doorway was filled with the poster boy for *People*'s Sexiest Man Alive. I'm not often speechless, but short of asking if Christmas had come early, I was at a loss for words.

"Carolina Lamont?" His voice had a deep serious-as-a-heart-attack timbre.

"Yes."

"Detective Judd Malone."

Uh-oh. I was pretty sure this was about my earlier break-in. I wouldn't put it past Mel to call the police. But for the Laguna PD to send a detective? Really?

"Do you have identification?" I asked.

He hadn't offered a badge or an ID and though I didn't truly think serial killers looked like Brad Pitt's brother and stalked pet therapists, you just can't be too careful.

He reached inside his jacket pocket and handed me a card.

Apparently business cards had replaced badges.

"May I come in?" He spoke awfully proper

for a tough guy detective but, hey, I'm from Texas so it always seems to me that folks are puttin' on airs.

I opened the door a bit further and he shouldered past me.

Judd Malone smacked of attitude. He wore black jeans, a black leather jacket and a chip on his shoulder. He scanned the room, his baby blues taking in my over-stuffed couch, easy chairs and crowded bookshelves. Thelma and Louise, perched in the windowsill, replete with tuna, each opened an eye and then, unimpressed, went back to their beauty sleep. Dogbert climbed from his doggie bed, trotted over for a sniff, but then also dismissed Malone and went back to his nap.

"Can I get you something to drink?" Some southern hospitality is automatic. Even when you have an unannounced guest. Even a guest who might arrest you. "Coffee, coke, iced tea?"

He shook his head and continued his scan.

"Well, then. What can I help you with, Detective Judd Malone?"

"I understand you visited Kevin Black-stone today?"

Okay, maybe not about the brooch. "Yes, I did. What about Kevin?"

31

I had a really bad feeling about this.

"Kevin Blackstone is dead."

CHAPTER THREE

"Oh, my God. How?"

"Cause of death has not yet been determined, ma'am."

Well, okay, Mr. Literal. I understood that but surely they had an idea whether he'd been in a car accident, had a heart attack, or if he'd been shot dead in a home invasion. You know, just the general category.

I didn't have to ask how they knew I'd been to see him. You have to check in with the guard when you enter Ruby Point. I'm sure it was noted for the record, so I didn't go there.

"Zeus and Tommy Boy?"

He looked puzzled.

"The dogs?"

I'd ruled out the home invasion idea. I couldn't imagine how anyone could get past the guards at Ruby Point, or if they had how they could've gotten close enough to Kevin to harm him. German Shepherds can be ferocious protectors and are fiercely loyal to their owners.

"Are the dogs okay?"

Detective Malone looked a little confused. "The dogs?"

"Yes, Kevin Blackstone's Shepherds. Are they alright?"

"I guess so."

"Well, dammit, Detective, are they or aren't they?"

"When I arrived at the residence the dogs were shut out on the patio. They were pretty agitated but they appeared to be alright."

Well, of course, they were agitated. Their human, who in their minds they'd been charged to protect and serve, was dead.

"What are you doing about the dogs?"

"Excuse me, ma'am. You seem much more concerned about the dogs than the man." The expression on his face was still no-reaction-cop-neutral but a little tic over his left eye gave away his irritation.

I suddenly realized just how bad it sounded. I hadn't inquired anything about Kevin — other than how he'd died — all of my concern had been for Zeus and Tommy Boy.

"Well, of course, I'm concerned about Kevin but it sounds like concern for him would be wasted at this point."

34

"I believe animal control was en route and the dogs were to be taken to the Animal Shelter."

Detective Malone wanted to know why I was at Kevin's, how long I'd stayed, and when I'd left. I recounted the details as well as I could and he listened. I thought he should take notes like all the television cops but he didn't seem inclined to fit my stereotype.

I called the shelter as soon as Detective Just-the-Facts-Ma'am Malone was gone. I got the answering service. Not to be deterred (I had cell phone numbers), I called Don, one my favorites of the group of full-time volunteers. He confirmed that Zeus and Tommy Boy were there.

"So I can stop by and check on them, right?"

"Sure, Caro. In fact, we were hoping you would." Don Furry (I swear that's his real name) was a good friend to me and a great friend to the animals of Orange County. "But if you don't mind it'd be best to wait until tomorrow. The dogs were pretty worked up and we've only just got them settled down for the night."

I knew Don was right and he and the others at the shelter were taking good care of Zeus and Tommy Boy. I thanked him and promised to come by in the morning.

What had happened to Kevin? He was way too young for heart problems, but the guy hadn't necessarily been a health nut. You heard all the time about people who seemed perfectly healthy, athletes even, who just dropped dead. But the news had said "unexplained death." And then there was the fact that a homicide detective had been the one asking the questions. Looked like Kevin's death might not just be unexplained.

What if he'd been murdered?

By dawn the next morning, I hadn't slept much. As I showered, the events of the day before played like a crazed recording in my head. There were too many unanswered questions.

It was still unbelievable that Kevin Blackstone was dead. What if there was a murderer running around Ruby Point? And now what would happen to Zeus and Tommy Boy? Who would take the dogs? I wondered if Kevin had relatives in the area. I tried to picture whether I'd seen family pictures anywhere in his home and couldn't remember any.

I dressed for the day and gathered the materials to get the Fur Ball flyers printed.

I started my car and hit the garage door button. It slid open and southern California sunshine rolled in. I reached in my bag for my sunglasses and settled them on my nose.

Once downtown, I dropped the flyer off at Quick Print and then pulled into a parking spot in front of "Glitter," my favorite jewelry store.

"Well, good morning, Caro." Grant Trask looked up as I entered. "Quite the business out at Ruby Point, huh? I guess the police are thinking Kevin Blackstone's death wasn't natural causes."

"Really?" Seeing as I'd been visited by a homicide detective, that made sense. "What do they think happened?"

"Nobody seems to know. Or at least the police aren't saying."

"Wow." It still boggled my mind. Yesterday, I'd been talking to the guy. Working with him and the dogs. Today he was dead. "I guess you just never know when your number is going to be up."

"Guess so. But enough about bad news, hon." Grant leaned on the counter. "What can I do for you today?"

I attempted to gather my wits, which were definitely ungathered. "I'd like to get this cleaned and the setting checked out." Reaching into my purse for Grandma Tillie's brooch, I came up empty-handed.

"Certainly." Grant waited, his brows raised in question.

I began pulling items from my handbag. My wallet, cosmetic case, several tissues, a leash . . . no brooch.

"I had it." I continued emptying my Coach bag. "I swear I did."

"Your grandmother's brooch?" he asked.

The ongoing battle between my cousin and me for ownership of the antique pin was no secret among our close friends in Laguna Beach. Grant specifically knew about the brooch because Mel and I had each had it appraised for insurance purposes.

I nodded faintly, a sick feeling spreading through me like a flood. There could only be one place I'd lost it because I'd only been one place besides Mel's.

Kevin Blackstone's house.

Holy Guacamole. Now what?

I'd just have to go there and retrieve it. That was what.

I piled everything back into my purse, thanked Grant, told him I'd be back, and headed toward Ruby Point. I prayed Kevin had not changed the security codes, and that Detective Judd Malone was chasing other law-breakers.

CHAPTER FOUR

Kevin's house stood still and silent. No police. No crime scene tape.

That was good. On the drive there, I'd considered that the house might be sealed off as a crime scene with what I'd just heard, but it wasn't. Perhaps Grant was wrong and Kevin really had died of natural causes.

It appeared whatever they'd decided, the police were done with Kevin's house. I didn't waste any time. The entry wasn't clearly visible from the street, but I didn't want to have to explain myself, either to the neighbors or the police. I just wanted to retrieve my grandmother's brooch. I punched in the alarm codes, eased open the door, slipped in, and reset the alarm.

Inside, I surveyed the room.

Zeus and Tommy Boy's rawhide bones, their "Howlickin Beer" rubber chew toys, and other squeaky playthings lay strewn around the room. As I walked through to the kitchen, their food and water dishes sat half full on the "Hund 1" and "Hund 2" placemats Kevin had commissioned for them.

We'd worked with the dogs on German language commands and he'd thought it was clever to have Dog 1 and Dog 2 in German. The dogs never paid much attention to which one was which, they would both eat out of one and then both switch to the other. The house seemed hollow without them and their master.

I didn't know where Kevin had actually died. The detective hadn't said, nor had Grant, but for some reason I pictured it in the entry way or perhaps the living room.

I had no idea where to start looking for the brooch. I stood still and tried to think.

I'd only been in the living room with my handbag. I'd dropped it by the door when I'd arrived and hadn't picked it up until I'd left. Since the brooch wasn't anywhere on the floor, I had to assume either the police had found it and thought it belonged to Kevin, or Kevin had found it and realized I'd lost it. If so, I wondered why he hadn't called me about it.

Well, duh, Caro. Maybe because he was dead?

If I had something, like a piece of jewelry I was holding onto until I could return it to the owner, I'd put it in my underwear drawer. Probably different for guys though. Where would a guy put a god-awful-ugly brooch he'd found in his living room?

Maybe the best place to begin was to look for it in plain sight. I checked all shelves, all tables, all counter tops. Nothing.

Fine. On to a deeper dive.

I started with the kitchen and pulled open a drawer and peered in. Nada. Next, the refrigerator. Nope.

I had a terrible thought. An awful, awful, terrible thought. What if it *had* been a robbery and whoever broke in took it?

Don't go there, girl.

It's here. Keep looking.

The cupboards were full of mismatched dishes and the pantry full of junk food. This was worse than Mel's. Chips, candy bars, even several boxes of those powdered sugar donuts. Oh, and then a big bottle of vitamins. Like ingesting the junk food wouldn't negate the health benefits.

While the high-priced LA decorator had given Kevin's house polish and class, the refinement was clearly only skin deep. I methodically worked from one side of the room to the other, opening drawers and doors, but finding nothing.

I moved to the living room checking every nook and cranny. A desk was empty — more show than function. The entertainment center housed only electronics. Although it was a big room, there were few places where an item could be tucked away, so it didn't take long.

The house was too quiet. I couldn't help but make the comparison between yesterday's noise and today's silence.

I hesitated at the foot of the stairs. I'd never been to the second floor of the house. Working with Zeus and Tommy Boy had never involved Kevin's bedroom.

Thank God.

I needed to get on with it before someone spotted my car. Even though I'd parked down the street, I didn't want to be found in the house and have to explain to Detective Malone, who already seemed to think I was a couple of sandwiches short of a picnic.

I tiptoed up the stairs, not exactly sure why. I tried the first door. Sure enough, it looked like a master bedroom. The curtains were drawn so I flipped on the switch. Music and light flooded the space, which illuminated a king-sized bed draped in black satin. Mood lighting threw shadows on the wall and a red lava lamp flickered on.

Holy mojo, baby. What was up with the Austin Powers theme?

Moving quickly, I searched through the drawers of Kevin's man-sized dresser. The last drawer I opened held Kevin's underwear — and my grandmother's brooch wrapped in a fluffy yellow kitchen towel.

Nice of Kevin to keep it safe for me. I sent a thank-you heavenward and curled my fingers around the brooch. Suddenly I realized along with the towel I'd also picked up a pair of silk boxers and a tiny black book.

I quickly dropped the boxers.

Opening the book, I flipped through several pages of notes and my eyes landed on *my* name.

Suddenly I heard a sound downstairs. The barest click. I stopped and leaned toward the doorway listening.

I heard a creak.

Panic rose in my throat. It sounded like the front door, but I couldn't be sure. I quietly closed the dresser drawer, scooted across the room and turned off the lights.

My heart pounding, I realized I couldn't go back down the stairs so I headed in the opposite direction.

Just as I reached the end of the hallway, a shrill screech blasted through the house.

CHAPTER FIVE

The awful screeching continued. Whoever had entered the house had set off the alarm.

I ran down the back stairs and stumbled outside. The door I'd come out looked to be the delivery entrance. There was a narrow alleyway behind the houses, and I started in what I thought was the direction of my car.

"Whatcha doing?" A bedraggled man, his long coal-black hair in a pony-tail, popped up out of nowhere.

I nearly let loose my own screech and backed up a step.

"S'matter, luv? Are they after you?" He reached up and inched his sunglasses down a notch, the ginormous rings he sported on every finger glinting in the sun. His bloodshot eyes said he'd either started the party pretty early today or had continued it from last night.

"No." I finally choked out. "I'm lost. I'm

trying to get back to the street."

I'd thought at first he was a homeless person. Even Laguna Beach with all its wealth has its share. But if I was any judge of bling (and I was) those weren't exactly Cracker Jack rings.

"Oh, smashing! Come this way then." He motioned me toward a doorway I hadn't spotted before.

I hesitated.

"S'all right. It's too early in the day for me to ravish you, tho' 'tis tempting." He guffawed at his own joke and staggered toward the doorway.

The sound of Kevin's alarm in the background outweighed my fear. I followed. The door led to a walkway protected on each side by a tall hedge.

"This way, luv." He motioned again.

Dark hair, dark glasses, a black t-shirt under a black leather vest, and black sweat pants. The guy almost blended into the shadows between the hedges.

Suddenly we rounded a corner and we were in the shockingly brilliant California sunshine. It was like stepping from an Alfred Hitchcock black and white flick onto the set of *Blue Hawaii.*

I stopped in my tracks.

A kidney-shaped pool was surrounded by

lush tropical plants. My eyes drank it all in — a tiki bar in one corner, a telescope pointed skyward in another, a white bench draped in beach towels in a secluded nook. I looked back at my guide hoping either a) this was his backyard or b) we'd keep moving through really fast.

Mystery man placed one be-ringed finger to his lips. "Shhh . . . everyone else is asleep."

He opened the French doors and invited me in.

An older black Labrador loped towards us. I couldn't resist and stopped for a moment to scratch the dog's neck.

"That's Elvis." My friend also stopped to pat the dog.

I could see how Elvis had ended up with his name. The dog had what must have been a mouth injury or defect and was left with a permanent lip curl.

Thank-you. Thank-you, very much.

He was a handsome guy.

The dog, not my newfound friend.

I barely had time to glance around as we continued through, but what I could see of the house matched the patio. More of the same opulence. I also realized "everyone else is asleep" must have meant the many dogs littering the multiple leather couches in the living room.

There had to be ten or more.

He unlatched the front door and swept his arm toward the opening. "No worries, luv. I've no bloody idea what you were doing next door, but I won't tell a soul I saw you."

"Thanks."

I stepped to the street and hot-footed it to my car.

As I glanced over my shoulder, I could see a blue and white Laguna PD patrol car sitting empty in Kevin's driveway.

I thought I was going to pass out. I gulped back my fear and kept going.

Once in my car, I finally stopped holding my breath.

Breath in. Breath out, Caro.

Close call.

I unclenched my fist, admiring the glint of sunlight on my precious recovered treasure. Grandma Tillie's brooch.

I started my car and slowly made my way down the palm-lined street and to the Ruby Point exit gate. Arranging my face in what I hoped was an innocent looking smile, I waved at the guard as I passed.

Deep breath.

At that very moment, the realization hit me. I held the brooch in my hand, but at

some point I'd dropped the fluffy yellow
kitchen towel and Kevin's little black book.

CHAPTER SIX

I sure as heck couldn't go back and look for the items I'd dropped, but I mentally retraced my steps. Down the stairs, out the back, scared out of my wits by the man in black, through his house, out the front. I remembered having the towel when I got to the alleyway but not afterwards.

Wow, I hoped the pet therapist gig worked out for me, because turning to a life of crime was not a possibility. I was a pretty dang inept burglar.

Turning my car onto PCH and then into the Village section of Laguna Beach, I entered the canyon and headed for the Animal Rescue League to check on Zeus and Tommy Boy.

It was a short trip to the ARL but the drive through the valley on Laguna Canyon Road gave me time to think. I'd had only a few minutes to peek at Kevin's little black book before the alarm had sounded, but even at first glance it didn't appear to be contact info, dating or otherwise.

Thinking through what had just happened, my escape from Kevin's and the bizarro trip through the house next door, I snickered to myself. Okay, I admit it was a snicker that was a little on the hysterical side.

Still, the neighbor guy had been funny. I'd just been too freaked out to appreciate it at the time. I wasn't sure if he was on something or the stoned-out attitude was the lingering fog of too many drugs when he was younger.

Still, thanks to him, my search at Kevin's had gone undetected.

What a knight in shining leather, huh?

That Kevin was dead still seemed surreal on a lot of fronts. Part of what made it seem even more unreal was Grant Trask's intel that there was some question about whether it had been natural causes. If so, that meant someone, not something, had killed Kevin.

I couldn't imagine it. He'd been an affable guy, well-liked in the community. Except for the run-in with Mandy Beenerman. But I hardly thought the mailbox dispute was a killing offense. Besides that had been months ago.

Also, if it were true someone had killed

him, Kevin had been offed not in a risky situation of any kind, but behind the secured gates of a guarded community.

Hard to comprehend.

The bells on the ARL door gave a distinct jingle and the smell of disinfectant and pets greeted me. Don Furry looked up from the paperwork he was working on at the counter.

"Hi, Caro." His sun-crisped face crinkled in a friendly smile. He didn't seem to notice the racket that came from other parts of the complex, and I knew from my volunteer experience you got to a point you tuned the noise out. "Here to see the boys?"

"I'd love to."

He stacked his paperwork, set it aside and opened the gate to let me in the backroom.

"How are they doing?"

"Much better than yesterday." He led the way to a large dog run area. "They're still wound up a bit, but not as wild. Quite the deal. Kevin Blackstone dying, I mean."

"Yeah, quite the deal." I took a moment to compose myself and then entered the area calmly.

The dogs were happy to see me. Zeus and Tommy Boy barked in greeting, but seemed to have dropped the nervous bark-bark-bark we'd dealt with yesterday.

Sheesh. Was that only yesterday?

Don scratched Tommy Boy's head and then leaned over to pat Zeus. "I didn't know much about the guy, but he wasn't that old for a heart attack or anything sudden like. Always gave a decent donation for our annual fundraiser."

With Don, like Diana, it was always about the animals. Kevin could've been a mafia don, but if he was good to his animals and contributed to the cause, he qualified as a good guy.

"I know you usually have to keep them for a period of time, but I didn't know what the rules were if the owner was deceased." I looked around for the box of dog toys usually kept near the fenced exercise space. "I'd be happy to take them until we can find a good home for them. Hopefully someone who will be willing to take them both."

Don handed me the box of toys, which had been hidden by a mound of newspapers.

"We contacted the German Shepherd Dog rescue organization this morning about getting word out regarding potential adoptions, but it sounds like we may not need them. Kevin's next of kin apparently contacted the police department."

"Next of kin?" I fished out some dog toys.

I'd never heard Kevin mention family and I'd not seen any family pictures in the pretty thorough search I'd just done of his house.

I didn't mention the search to Don.

"Yep, that's what they said. A brother, I guess. I don't know if he'll want the dogs or not, but we're kind of on hold until we hear one way or the other."

"Wow. I didn't know Kevin had a brother."

"I guess nobody did."

While we talked I threw some tennis balls and the dogs chased them down. Don and I chatted about the weather, the potential for flooding this year, and the upcoming Fur Ball fundraiser.

"I don't know what we'd do without people like you and Diana who volunteer so much of their time." Don shook his head.

I waved his comments off. I volunteered once a week and helped exercise the dogs. I also worked with any who had problem behaviors, but most often exercise helped the most. Being cooped up with lots of time on your hands isn't good for man or beast.

"There are a lot of people who give of their time and money. I just hope we can get a whole bunch of them to part with their money at the Fur Ball. The numbers from last year were great. I'm hoping we can top them."

"Oh, I have no doubt you will. I've heard you and Diana have been out twisting arms for some pretty snazzy auction items."

"We do have some great offerings." I gathered the toys and put them away. Zeus and Tommy Boy seemed to be doing really well. They were actually in better shape than the last time I'd seen them. At Kevin's house.

"I'll see you Thursday at the usual time."

It was hard to leave the dogs behind but I knew they were being well cared for until Kevin's family could take them.

Next I was headed to check in at the office and catch up on some paperwork. I'd retrieved Grandma Tillie's brooch, Kevin's dogs were being well cared for, and I was hopeful Kevin's brother would turn out to be a dog lover and want to take Zeus and Tommy Boy home.

The thought the two dogs had been so agitated yesterday nagged at me. What had set them off? It probably wasn't a coincidence that they had been so upset just before Kevin's death. Something or someone had to have disrupted their routine, most likely something or someone who had ended Kevin's life.

CHAPTER SEVEN

My office was in the same building as a real estate broker, an accountant and a psychic. Only in Laguna Beach.

PAWS was located in a downtown but off-the-main-drag shops area. We shared a receptionist whose name was Paris. Besides having the same moniker as the hotel heiress, she also echoed her bleached blonde bob and her fake-bake tan.

I rarely needed her help as I saw very few clients in my office. In most cases, the issues I dealt with had to do with where the animals lived and played, so I had to see them in their home environment. But Paris collected the mail for all of us in the office building and parceled it out, kept the office equipment going, and greeted the occasional visitor.

I was alternating between paperwork and obsessing about what kind of a trail I'd left at Kevin's when the intercom on my phone buzzed. I jumped.

"Detective Malone to see you." I could tell from the breathy way she pronounced his name she was drooling on her lip gloss.

"Send him in." I attempted to compose myself. I sincerely hoped this had nothing to do with my stop at Ruby Point this morning. If it did, I'd just have to confess. What I'd done was wrong but I could explain my motives. I'd throw myself on his mercy.

Throwing myself on Malone's anything brought up an entirely different image that had nothing to do with justice. I pushed away my distracting lustful thoughts.

Detective Judd Malone was again dressed casually. Jeans, another plain dark t-shirt, black leather. Malone's black leather told a different story than my earlier rescuer.

I'd not run into Malone around town and, except for the tourists who bloated our numbers during the season, Laguna was a pretty tight knit community. Maybe he lived in one of the surrounding areas. Many who worked in Laguna did given the high price of local real estate. Even the tiniest dump cost a pretty penny.

"Ms. Lamont." He gave a terse business-like nod.

Malone had changed his clothes but not his attitude.

"Please call me Caro." I indicated one of the plum-colored leather chairs in the open area next to my desk.

He sat.

His long legs reached out onto the black and white paw-print rug I'd placed in front of the chairs. I could see him taking in the surroundings and mentally cataloging.

It wasn't unlike what I did when visiting a pet home for the first time. The space, the furnishing, the setting told me a lot about the people. And with dog behavior modification, the more information you had, the more likely your success. I imagined the same was true with murder investigations.

I took the matching chair opposite his and waited.

And waited.

I broke the silence first. No power play necessary on my part, he could be the alpha dog. "What can I do for you, Detective? The word on the street is that you believe Kevin did not die of natural causes."

His intelligent blue gaze moved to mine. I noted a flicker and then we were back to face neutrality.

His voice was very even and calm, his body almost motionless.

"That's true. It seems from our preliminary investigation that Mr. Blackstone may have been the victim of a murder."

I mentally flinched. I thought I'd been prepared for the possibility but it was still a shock to hear it confirmed.

"Ms. Lamont, I have some questions for you."

"Caro, please," I reminded him.

"Caro." The corners of his mouth tugged upward reluctantly as if the friendly expression was an effort. "We've done a little background work-up on you but I need to fill in some blanks."

Of course, they'd done some poking around in my background, and it was pretty easy to dig up the dirt.

"Hey, my life is an open book." I kept my expression neutral, too.

"How long had you known Kevin Blackstone?"

"I'd met him before around town, but just knew him in passing. I'd been working with him and his dogs for about the last year. A problem with chewing. The dogs, I mean."

"Is that why you were there yesterday?"

"Yes, Kevin had called me. But not about chewing this time."

"Walk me through your time at Mr. Blackstone's house."

I covered my arrival, the dogs' behavior, our discussion, and the limited success of my behavior modification exercise.

I could have gotten my file and used my notes on Zeus and Tommy Boy, but I didn't need to. The afternoon at Kevin's was burned into my memory.

Still, as a psychologist, I knew memories were often faulty and the more we rehearsed certain details in our minds the more we became convinced those details were fact.

Detective Malone was most interested in when and where I left Kevin, and I did my best to be accurate.

"Did you stop anywhere?"

"Yes, at Diana Knight's home, which is just a couple of houses down the street."

"What time was that?"

"I'm not sure, but I'd say around four o'clock."

We were quiet for a while. I was lost in thought. Malone waited me out.

Again I wasn't playing the power game. "How do you think Kevin died?"

"Taser."

"What?"

"A —" He started to repeat himself.

"Got it." I'd heard what he'd said but was just shocked (no pun intended) about the method. "I didn't think a Taser would kill a person."

"Normally doesn't."

"How do you know it was a Taser?"

"Marks on the body."

I could tell he was impatient with my questions by his shift in the chair, but his expression remained dispassionate. I decided to go for one more question.

"What kind of marks?"

"Puncture marks."

Okay, I could see by his terseness he was done. That and the don't-make-me-take-you-downtown glare. I waited for him to continue.

"Ms. Lamont . . ."

"Caro," I corrected again.

"Caro." Again the unwilling smile. "What time did you say you left Kevin Blackstone's house?"

"As I said, Detective, I'm not sure." Gosh, I hated to be one of those, I-have-no-idea sort of witnesses, but I truly had no idea. At the time I hadn't known it was going to be an important detail.

"Can you give me a range?"

"Well, like I told you yesterday. And again today." I fixed him with my best I-know-what-you're-trying-to-do stare. "I left Ruby Point, stopped at the grocery store, and then went home and fixed myself a tuna sandwich. No one but Thelma, Louise, and Dogbert to collaborate my story."

"Who?"

"My dog and two cats. You've met them."

"I have." He got to his feet.

I stood also. Very few men make me feel tiny. I'm a tall girl. Tall and with beauty pageant posture. No slouching allowed. Still, Detective Judd Malone had a way of making me feel petite.

I walked him out and returned to my office.

Some of Malone lingered after he was gone. I tried to put my finger on what it was about the guy.

His arresting good looks filled the room for sure. But there was also this aura of danger. Was that because he was a homicide detective or was that because my hormones went on high-alert every time we interacted?

I got back to my paperwork and tried not to think about it.

The intercom buzzed again and I jumped for a second time. This was getting ridiculous.

"Diana Knight to see you." Paris was again breathless and I could tell she was just a tad bit impressed the former movie star turned animal activist had come to see little ole pet therapist me.

"Hello." Diana breezed in.

I was always amazed by the amount of

energy the woman exuded. At eighty-something (no one knew for sure), she had not slowed down one iota.

Her once vibrant skin was weathered by her time in the California sun but her smile hadn't dimmed, her bright blue eyes sparkled with good humor, and she still had that signature bounce when she walked. Her shiny silver hair was perfectly coiffed as always.

"Thought I'd stop by with the update on the sponsors for the Fur Ball," Diana chirped, her words spiked with enthusiasm. Mr. Wiggles, a rescue puggle puppy Diana had adopted, was tucked under her arm.

Normally a pug-beagle hybrid would be highly sought after and not be found on puppy death-row, but Mr. Wiggles had a non-regulation ear. He was the sweetest natured dog you can imagine and I thought the tipped ear gave him character.

But he'd been constantly passed over for other more "perfect" puppies, and finally Diana had taken him home. It was a good thing she had because I'd been leaning toward adopting him myself and Diana had tons more dog space.

I gave Mr. Wiggles a scratch behind the ears and a pat on the nose. True to his name he wiggled in Diana's arms.

"I can't believe the Fur Ball is in three weeks." When I'd committed to co-chairing the event, it had seemed a long ways off, but now we were down to the wire. "It looks very good in terms of sponsors and advanced ticket sales."

"Well, here you go then." She shifted Mr. Wiggles and handed me some papers, but didn't move to leave. I could tell she had something else to say but was hesitant. Very uncharacteristic for Diana.

"The police came by to talk to me about Kevin Blackstone." Diana's voice lacked its usual lilt.

"I suppose they talked to everyone in Ruby Point."

"Well, I guess they probably zeroed in on me because they think someone killed him, and some idiot told them about my little tiff with Kevin over his dogs."

"Little tiff? Diana, hon, you smashed the window out of his Jag."

The incident had happened in the Whole Foods parking lot. Kevin had run in for something and had left the two dogs in the car with the window cracked open. He claimed he hadn't been gone more than five minutes. Still a car can heat up very quickly in the southern California sunshine.

Diana had seen the dogs and wasn't taking any chances. She used a tire iron out of her Bentley to break his window.

"Well, he shouldn't have left the dogs in the car on such a hot day," she huffed.

"Can't say I disagree. If I'd been there, I'd have probably helped you."

Diana looked sheepish. "I didn't think you told them."

"Of course not, sugar." I gave her a hug.

"I was just thinking what if the person who really did Kevin in, if someone did, might tell the police something like that to throw them off the scent."

"You know, that's a distinct possibility." I hadn't considered the idea but it did seem reasonable. "I can't imagine how anyone got past the Ruby Point guard."

Diana was silent for a couple of minutes. "Or else they didn't," she leaned toward me and whispered, "and it's someone inside."

Well, geeze Louise. I felt a shiver zip up my spine.

That was a scary idea.

Diana shook her head as if to get rid of the thought. "Okay, Caro honey, I've got to run. Let me know if you need anything else from me on the Fur Ball. You've been the best co-chair I've ever had for this event. You may have a lifetime commitment."

"Oh, no, no. You made it easy." I'd done

the majority of the legwork but it truly was the community's love for Diana that had made everything work so slick. "Do you have plans tonight?"

"I do. I have a date with Dino." An impish smile danced across her well-worn face.

"Ooh la la, girl, this is getting to be a regular thing." I walked with her to the lobby. She was just so darn cute.

Dino Riccio, a local restaurateur, had a major crush on Diana and was oblivious to the fact she was mainly after his doggie bags. It wasn't about the handsome Italian. It was about the animals. With Diana it was *always* about the animals.

Still, it was kind of sad the eighty-year-old with crow's feet had a date and I didn't.

As if she read my mind, Diana paused. "You're welcome to come along. You know Dino loves you, and he's always a fan of eye candy."

Oh, no. We were not going there. I was not so pathetic that I needed to be a third wheel. Not even with people I adored as much as I did those two.

"Thanks, but I've got a date with a bad boy."

"Alright, but if you're making that up, I'll find out." She waved over her shoulder as she left.

I wasn't making it up. I did have a date with a bad boy. A bad-boy out-of-control Akita named Varmit.

Completing the paperwork on the clients I'd seen and sending out my billing took very little time. I emailed the invoices and closed down my computer. You've gotta love technology.

I had a moment's pause when I put away the file on Zeus and Tommy Boy.

The office was quiet. It sounded like everyone else had gone home. Our building usually emptied out early. The real estate lady, Kay, had irregular hours at best. The accountant, David, came at eight and left promptly at four-thirty, except during tax season when he came at dawn, stayed late and had a steady stream of clients who all seemed to wait until the last day. Suzanne, the psychic, wasn't in every day. The office next to mine was vacant. We used to have a sales and marketing firm in that spot but they'd been gone for a while.

I pulled out a pad of paper and wrote down what I remembered about Kevin and the day he died, and then slid the piece of paper into Zeus and Tommy Boy's file. If I thought of additional information, I'd add it later.

I checked my cell phone messages and saw

I had missed a call from my mother. It was a rambling please call the-one-who-gave-birth-to-you or else kind of message.

I also could see I had a bunch of emails I needed to answer but nothing looked urgent. Four of the emails were also from Mama. Some things are best left to deal with when you have a clear head.

Next I made my list for the next day. Go on, laugh at me if you like, but I'm into planning ahead and I've found list making calming. Tomorrow I had three appointments, a pedicure, and I would drop Grandma Tillie's brooch off at the jewelry store.

I tucked the note in my bag and headed out the door. My world was back under control, even if Kevin's death left me feeling unsettled.

CHAPTER EIGHT

The next day, I headed inside the rarified walls of Ruby Point once again for two of my pet house calls. I enjoyed the short drive with the top down on the convertible. It was early and the streets of Laguna were illuminated with the wash of the morning sun. The Highlanders, as they were called, up in the hills had been feeling its touch of gold for a while, but we mere mortals in the Village part of town were only now feeling the warmth. My guess was many inside Ruby Point weren't even up yet.

I stopped my car at the stone and iron gate that separated the *über* rich and privileged Ruby Point residents from the rest of us Laguna Beach riff-raff.

Checking in was part of the usual routine, though I didn't recognize the uniformed guy who stepped out of the guard shack looking very official. Most days I just got waved through but I imagined the recent excitement had everyone on high alert.

Mr. Homeland Security walked to my car window and sized me up. His ocean blue eyes flicked from the top of my red hair (I like to call it Irish Setter auburn), to my Donna Karan jacket, to my Save the Whales t-shirt, then dropped to my ripped at the knee jeans, and my Hello Kitty watch.

He looked confused.

I have that effect on a lot of people.

Clearly part of his guarding-the-rich-and-privileged training had included fashionista brand identification and he was having trouble typing me. Then, of course, there was the car. Was I driving a classic because I loved it, or could I not afford new?

He hesitated and I leaned forward to read his name badge.

"Good morning, Tucker." I smiled. "My name is Caro Lamont and Mr. and Mrs. Beenerman are expecting me."

Tucker checked his clipboard and must have located my name.

"Through here and to your right. Fifth drive." He stepped back into the hut and opened the iron gate.

I knew the way. It was, after all, right next to Kevin Blackstone's.

The Beenerman's dog is a Lhasa Apso who'd already been through a couple of sessions. I truly thought we'd dealt with his anxiety issues, but when I'd gotten the phone call that morning telling me Nietzsche wouldn't leave the house, I knew he'd lost ground.

I followed the curve of the palm-lined curbs and turned in. The Beenerman home was tucked in among more palms and greenery. I parked my car and got out, grabbing my tote from the backseat. I'd brought along a variety of doggie helps, not sure exactly what I might need to coax Nietzsche out of hiding and hopefully outdoors.

Mandy Beenerman opened the door, then turned and went in, leaving me to follow. Her bare feet made no noise on the gleaming marble floor of the entryway.

Mandy was typical southern California beautiful. Tall, tan, and toned. I'm no shrinking violet but Mandy had a couple of inches on me and also had a lithe workout sculpted body that she displayed for maximum effect with pink spandex workout pants and a midriff-baring top. No matter where she went.

Granted it was her stock in trade. She's a fitness guru with studios in six southern California locations. *Mandy's Place* was the local hot spot for yoga or Pilates. I took a class at the Laguna Beach studio twice a week myself.

But back to the dog.

"What seems to be the problem with Nietzsche?" I asked.

"He hasn't left the house since Saturday." Mandy shook her shiny blonde locks. "I've put him on the leash but he just locks his legs and refuses to budge."

Mandy led the way through the formal living room to the massive great room at the back of the house. Nietzsche sat in his specially made leather lounger looking out the window like a brooding Heathcliff.

The Beenerman's dog was a perfect specimen of a Lhasa Apso, the Tibetan breed who once served as the guardian of Buddhist temples. Lhasas are intelligent, strong-willed, often even obstinate, and resemble a big white mop. Nietzsche turned his head from the window, eyeing me. Or at least I think he was. It was a little hard to tell under all that fur.

"We weren't sure what to do." Mandy twisted her hands as she spoke. "We've been doing the training exercises you recommended but suddenly Nietzsche decided he didn't want to do them."

Part of working with dogs who have issues is working with the owners. Let me rephrase that — most of working with dogs who have

71

issues is working with the owners.

In this case, it wasn't difficult to deduce that the royal floor mop had sensed weakness on the part of his keeper and was taking full advantage of it. Mandy's uncertainty was working against her.

The key clue was, "Nietzsche decided."

"When did this start?" I dropped my tote on the floor and stood back to observe the dog. Lhasas' long white fur is legendary and the Beenermans did a great job of keeping Nietzsche groomed. I could only assume either the agoraphobia had just started or the groomer made house calls because otherwise his fur would have been a matted mess.

"On Monday." Mandy flipped her long blonde hair over her shoulder and I had the fleeting thought about dogs and their owners looking alike. "We tried to take him out for a walk in the neighborhood and he refused to go."

Nietzsche tipped his head with seeming interest.

"Then yesterday he decided he wouldn't even go outside to do his business. When I tried to force the issue, he actually nipped at me."

Nietzsche growled low in his throat as if disagreeing with the accusation and then put his head back down.

"He's been going in the house?"

She nodded and pulled her hair back with both hands. Her beautiful face framed by the action.

I stared at Mandy.

For the first time I noticed there was a fine dusting of white powder on her nose. Not a lot, grant you, but I wondered if the health freak was into drugs to keep her weight down.

It wouldn't be the first time I'd seen the phenomena. Back when I was counseling people instead of dogs, I'd had more than one client who'd started with food issues and ended up with drug issues. Cocaine addicts can go for more than a day without being hungry. The habit does often make you thin. Of course, it wrecks your life at the same time.

I looked for other signs, dilated or bloodshot eyes, burns on her hands, but saw none. Hmmm. Maybe Mandy had been baking and it was flour, but somehow I didn't think so.

"Mandy, is everything okay?" I had to at least open the door for a conversation in case there truly was a problem.

"Sure." She looked at me like I'd lost my mind. "Except for Nietzsche. He's got to get over not being able to leave the house."

I retrieved my bag and got out a toy and some treats. What to do with an agoraphobic Apso? We'd try coaxing with the dog treats. It had worked well before and hopefully it would again.

I opened the package and Nietzsche raised his head from his paws. A bit of interest. Talking to him in a quiet voice, I got closer so he could smell the organic dog biscuit I'd brought. It was barbecue chicken flavor.

His favorite.

I waited. Don't try fooling me into thinking you're all high-class, Mr. Canine Philosopher. You may have Tibetan royalty bloodlines but I know you've got Texas barbeque longings.

He finally made his way to where I was sitting on the floor, crawling toward me all hunched over, like he was doing some sort of military field exercise.

I took it slow and let Nietzsche dictate the pace.

Eventually he took the treat and stayed with me. I moved further away, closer to the door. Then a few steps outside and then back into the house. Then back out and staying on the steps for a while. Each time waiting until he relaxed. We finally got him to the curb.

The technique is pretty effective but takes tons of patience. Also, you need to be able to read when you need to push and when you need to back off and give the dog time.

I hoped Mandy had it in her. To her credit she had stayed with us through the whole exercise.

I explained how to read the dog's body language. The lowered tail, lowered ears, the "C" shaped crouch that means he's afraid and wants to escape. I left Mandy with the treats and instructions on how to continue to work with Nietzsche.

The dog still seemed somewhat tense but so did Mandy. We didn't talk about Kevin, but I imagined I would be tense, too, if my neighbor had just been tased to death. Even a neighbor I didn't like.

The next stop in Ruby Point was to work with Huntley, a Cavalier King Charles Spaniel, who belonged to Davis Pinter, a retired newspaper tycoon who lived in a very nice Mediterranean style home at the western edge of the development. It had one of the best views in Ruby Point.

The two greeted me at the door.

CKC Spaniels are beyond cute and Huntley was no exception. The adorable guy was a well-behaved pooch, and I didn't think he truly needed my services anymore. Initially, Huntley had some problems staying with his owner and barking at other dogs.

As those of us who have dogs know, even a friendly bark can get the whole neighborhood howling. That's not usually a serious problem in a dog-friendly community, but it could become an issue.

I'd previously worked with Davis on some simple training techniques for their daily walks, and Huntley had soon curbed his barking habit. I'd just been doing periodic check-ins and things seemed to be going well.

But Davis had called yesterday and said Huntley had been barking frantically on walks. He asked me to stop by.

Something was for dang sure going on in Ruby Point. Kevin's dogs had gone nuts. Nietzsche was too scared to leave his house, and Huntley, normally so well-behaved, had been acting up.

Or maybe Davis, though he'd never admit it, was probably a little bored and lonely, and it was just my over active imagination finding patterns that were no more than coincidence.

Laguna Beach, with its artsy-fartsy crowd, was a long way from the hustle and bustle of the newsroom. Davis Pinter was a bit of a legend in the industry, having won a Pulitzer in his rookie days for his story about a young woman who refused to take her husband of one day off life support despite the wishes of his family. Davis had been retired for a couple of years now but hadn't really adapted to the concept.

I imagined my own daddy would be the same way. He had his routine and I don't know what he'd do if he couldn't go into the office. And besides, if Daddy didn't get out of the house every day, Mama would drive him bonkers.

We took Huntley for a walk and chatted. The dog seemed a little hyper, at least compared to his usual sweet, calm nature, but no frantic barking. As we circled back towards his house, Davis brought up the topic of Kevin Blackstone's death.

"I hear the police believe he was killed with a Taser." He had a good handle on Huntley's leash and we'd established a nice pace.

"That's what I'm told." I didn't say who told me.

"Something was off with the guy." Huntley spotted another dog across the street and stopped but Davis easily got him moving again.

"Great job." I complimented both the

owner and the dog. "What do you mean, something was off?"

"I don't know exactly, but mark my words, there's a story in Kevin Blackstone's life. I don't know what it is, but there's a story." Davis' dark eyes sharpened and I saw the shadow of what must have been a strong and stubborn dog-with-a-bone investigative reporter.

After I left Huntley and Davis back at their house, I thought that maybe Davis was right. Kevin had seemed to me to be much like the rest of the crowd in the gated community. I didn't know a lot about him but he'd seemed to be like a lot of my other dog parents. A bit over indulgent with his dogs, often more money than sense, but I'd seen nothing to create the kind of suspicion Davis seemed to have about the guy.

As I opened the car door my cell phone rang. I prayed it wasn't my mother. I knew I owed her a phone call and I reminded myself to put it on my to-do list.

I glanced at the phone but didn't recognize the number. "Hello."

"Is this Carolina Lamont?" I didn't recognize the voice either.

"Yes, it is. Who is this?" Many clients called my cell number rather than the office number and I hadn't discouraged the practice. It was the easiest way to reach me.

"My name is J.T. Blackstone and I believe you knew my brother, Kevin."

No wonder I hadn't recognized the voice.

"Oh, my, yes, of course. I'm so sorry for your loss." Don Furry had mentioned Kevin's brother, but I hadn't expected to hear from him.

"Thank you." I could hear a little hint of a regional accent in his voice but couldn't place it.

"Is there something I can do to help?" I couldn't imagine why he'd call me.

"This is a little awkward, Ms. Lamont, but I wondered if maybe Kevin had given you something to keep for him."

"What? No, Kevin didn't give me anything."

"You're sure?"

"I'm sure." I had been responsible for losing the little book and the yellow towel, but he couldn't mean those things.

"Is there something missing at Kevin's?"

"No, not really. I don't know. I'm going there this afternoon. The police think they'll be able to release the house so I can get in."

"Mr. Blackstone, you know Kevin had two dogs, right?"

"Yes."

"They're wonderful German Shepherd

Dogs and are currently being kept at the ARL. Do you think you'll be interested in taking them?"

There was a pause.

"I haven't thought about it."

We said good-bye, and I tucked my phone away and started my car.

What a bizarre conversation. Why on earth would Kevin's brother think Kevin would give me something to keep?

I gathered from his reaction about the dogs that he was not going to be taking them home with him. I wondered how much time we had to give him to make up his mind. I'd tell Don to continue working with the German Shepherd Dog rescue.

I had some time before my next appointment and decided this was a good time to swing by the jewelry store. Now that I had Grandma Tillie's brooch back in my possession, I wanted to get those loose stones checked out right away.

Grant Trask was behind the counter again. A tall blonde young man in a white shirt and a clumsily knotted tie stood nearby. His at-full-attention stance made me think he might be a trainee.

"Hi, Caro." Grant motioned the young man up beside him. "This is my nephew,

Zane, who is staying with us for a while. He's going to be working part-time at the store."

"Nice to meet you, Zane."

Zane smiled showing what would someday be a beautiful smile. Currently it was a work-in-progress with a mouthful of shiny silver braces. He shook my hand.

"Nice to meet you, too."

"Let's take a look at that brooch, Caro." Grant laid a cloth on the counter in readiness.

I handed over the jeweled pin.

Grant placed a jeweler's loop to his eye and examined it, poking with his fingernail at the stones.

"As you suspected, one of the emeralds is a bit loose. Twenty-two carat gold is very soft and so often settings on vintage pieces like this one have to be checked."

I wasn't sure whether he was explaining to me or to Zane. He put the loop back to his eye.

"Hmmm. Possibly one of the rubies, as well."

"I didn't notice that one."

"Caro, it's excellent you brought it in before any of the stones were lost. These are extremely good quality stones and they would be difficult to replace."

81

I was glad I'd noticed the loose emerald.

"We'll get this repaired and call you when it's done. It shouldn't be more than a week at the outside." He reached under the counter and pulled out a large envelope, jotted some notes on the outside, and slid the brooch inside.

"Okay, thanks, Grant. Sorry to be such a flake yesterday. I really appreciate it."

Once out on the sidewalk, I breathed a sigh of relief. One thing I could cross off my list. Grandma Tillie's brooch was safe and sound and any problems were being fixed.

After the last couple of days, beach time and some exercise would be a great break from thinking about all that had transpired. I hooked up Dogbert to his leash and headed toward Main Beach.

We stepped around the posted dog rules sign and onto the sand. Dogs had to be leashed and were only permitted on the beach at certain times, depending on the time of year.

Dogbert was excited about the idea of a run on the beach and we kept a steady pace for a while. Eventually we had to stop for a breather, both of us panting like crazy. At least I tried to keep my tongue in my mouth. I love running along the coastline but if the sand was wet, like now, it was like running with a bulldog clamped to each ankle. Definitely a workout.

I took in the salt air, exhaled, and gazed down the boundless beach. We'd come a long way from where we'd started. I twisted my neck left and then right, loosening the knots of tension, and then turned, admiring the saturated turquoise of the water and the endless horizon. For me, the ocean sort of puts everything in perspective.

It's a big world out there. Too big to focus on the small stuff.

Stuff like irksome detectives and neurotic mothers.

Even stuff like family heirloom battles.

Breathing better, I turned back to the beach and stretched forward, feeling the tug in my hamstrings.

"Ready to go?" I patted Dogbert, shook some of the sand off my shoes, and readied myself for the run back.

That's when I spotted him.

Oh. Wow. I was suddenly breathless again.

Muscular and fit, he pounded toward me with a smile as if we were long lost friends. As his strong legs brought him closer, his warm brown eyes sent a tingle through my body. Mesmerized by his perfection, I didn't realize he was headed right for me until the last second.

The *very* last second.

As in too late to move.

I let go of the leash as he hit me, so at least poor Dogbert wasn't tangled in the mess.

The smile never left his face as the hugely handsome Border Collie smacked into me, and we both went tumbling into the soft sand. I tried to get up but he held me down and licked my face.

"Stop, sugar. Stop it, now."

I, of all people, knew it would take a commanding voice to get his attention, but unfortunately I couldn't stop laughing. Both at the dog and at myself.

Like a fool, I'd just stood there mesmerized and let the big dog bowl me over.

"Name is Mac, after John McEnroe."

Clearly the dog wasn't talking, right?

I looked up from my soggy spot in the sand. Until that moment, I hadn't registered the leash or the fact there should have been a human at the other end. My focus had been on the dog.

The human, like the dog, was gorgeous, his pedigree clear in his attitude, his posture, his perfect smile.

"Well, no wonder he has control issues

then." I stroked the canine's silky fur and struggled to get to my feet, the wet sand making me about as graceful as a goofy rodeo clown.

"Sam Gallanos." Mac's human offered his hand and his assistance as introduction. "I'm sorry Mac mowed you down. His enthusiasm gets out of hand at times. Especially on the beach."

"Caro Lamont." I accepted both the assist and the apology. "Well shoot, darlin', I'm pretty enthusiastic about the beach myself."

Finally upright, I attempted to dust the worst of the wet sand off my backside. The two canines were busy sniffing each other's butts. Doggie speak for "Hello, who are you? What've you been up to?" I looked down at the masculine hand I still held. Thank goodness we humans settle for a handshake.

"You from around here?"

He didn't look like a tourist but you never know. It was still off-season, meaning the big influx hadn't begun, but we get visitors year round.

"At the moment."

Well, what the heck kind of answer is that?

I wasn't interested in playing twenty questions with the guy, attractive or not. I gathered my wits and my dog's leash and turned to go. "Come on, Dogbert."

"Nice to meet you, then." I couldn't resist one last stroke of the Collie's fur. "You have a handsome dog."

Placing my hands on each side of the dog's big head, I leaned down and gave him a squeeze. "You watch where you're going from now on, Mac." The dog's brown eyes looked up at me with adoration and he leaned into my caress. I gave him a nuzzle.

"I think I've just been upstaged by my dog."

I looked up to find Sam Gallanos staring at me. I got the impression he didn't get ignored too often.

I'm not much for pretty boys but his somewhat mussed dark brown hair was an attractive contrast to what otherwise might have been a too-perfect face.

"Y'all take care." I gave the dog one last pat.

"Hope to see you around." Both Sam and his dog had easy-going smiles and seemed friendly. But either my natural suspiciousness where men were concerned or the events of the past few days made me wary.

Dogbert and I started our run back to Main Beach. I dare say both of us were intrigued by the new acquaintances we'd just made. Still, I think Dogbert probably gained more from his butt-sniff introduction than I had from my conversational encounter.

CHAPTER NINE

The next morning started off just fine. I did some laundry, minor cleaning, straightened up my desk, took care of paying some bills. And you know me, I made my list for the day.

The sun streamed in and warmed the room. I'd pulled up the blinds at the window next to my desk. Even paying bills seems easier when you've got a breath-taking view of blue sky and breakers. I decided to take a little break to lavish some affection on the critters.

Thelma, Louise and I had adopted Dogbert as a puppy, so they didn't seem to realize dogs and cats weren't supposed to get along. I wasn't sure if Thelma and Louise thought they were part canine, or if Dogbert thought he had feline blood, but in any case they definitely acted like family.

Ahh . . . family.

That's when I opened my email. Mama

had been at the computer early it appeared.

Now, as you've probably already figured out, I'm not the helpless type. Caro Lamont takes care of herself and anybody else who needs saving. But when it comes to dealing with my family, my mama in particular, I confess I'm a dang wimp.

Mama had gotten it into her big, bouffant, hair-sprayed head she needed to come to Laguna Beach for a visit. And she was planning to stay with me.

Yeah, that was *not* going to happen.

If Katherine Lamont, "Kat" to her friends and Mama Kat to me, came to stay with me for more than say, fifteen minutes, it would be my undoing. I guarantee no matter how put-together I looked, she would have something to say about my weight (too much), my make-up (too little) and my social life (pathetic).

I tried my stepdaddy's cell number. Maybe I could get Hub to call her off. As I listened to the rings, I felt more and more panicky.

I left a message. If Hub didn't call back soon, I'd try my brother next. Mama would do just about anything for "Perfect Boy." Sure I'd owe him, but it would be worth it.

Mama could *not* come here.

I had a dead client, a distrustful detective,

and a business that was suddenly booming. The last thing I needed was a visit from the Queen of I'm-Just-Tryin'-to-Help-Honey.

My cell phone rang in my hand. Startled, I fumbled and dropped it. Grabbing it from the floor, I pushed the button without even looking at the screen.

"Hub?"

"No." The male voice on the other end was not Hub, but was unfortunately all too familiar.

You know when you tell yourself, things could be worse? This was worse.

"Hello, Geoff." Worse was Geoffrey Carlise, my ex-husband. Pronounced just like the regular old "Jeffrey" but spelled in a fancy way. That should have been my first clue.

"How are you, Carolina?" His rich, cultured voice was free of Texas twang, a testament to years of expensive diction lessons.

I was over him. I really was, but still I felt my pulse rise and ping through my body at the sound of his voice. Old habits die hard.

My brain knew anything to do with Geoff was bad news.

How was I?

Fine. I was fine.

Super.

Great. Better than great, I was busy. Busy

with my new life.

"Good." He didn't wait for my answer. How like him. He continued without waiting for any acknowledgement on my end. "Say, I'm clearing out the office and I need your new address to ship some of your books and papers."

I couldn't imagine it was anything I needed but I supplied the info and said good-bye. Dang it all, just when you think a hurt is healing, somebody comes along and rips off the scab.

Geoff and I had met at college. I adored college. After being involved in the beauty pageant scene, it was a relief to be someplace where no one really cared what you looked like. Well, some did, but you didn't have to hang out with that particular crowd. I ate pizza, got pimples for the first time in my life, drank beer, and discussed politics, ethics, ecology and philosophy with a group of people who, to this day, I consider my friends. With the exception of one.

That one I married.

I was dazzled by his intellect and his charisma. He was dazzled by my adoration. We both were psych majors and both planning on a counseling practice, which we ended up starting as a husband and wife team. Less than a year into the venture I found out that Geoff needed more adoration than one woman could supply.

I'd suspected he was having an affair long before I had proof. What I hadn't suspected was that he was having an affair with one of our clients.

In what turned out to be a very nasty and public vetting, we both lost our licenses to practice. In my mind, he should have lost much more.

After what Mama refers to as "The Big Mess," I'd needed to find a new career and get out of Dodge. So I'd come up with this plan to work with animals. I'd been doing a bit of that kind of work already. And I seemed to have a talent for it.

More talent, at least, than I had in picking husbands.

Laguna Beach came to mind because I'd always loved it and because it's such a pet friendly community. Eleven thousand dogs — more dogs than kids.

All I needed to do was cash in some stock from my trust fund, buy a place, and set up my business. I'd done that about four years ago and business had been barking at my door ever since.

The feeling of contentment I'd started the morning with shattered, I picked up my list for the day and tucked it in my bag. I intended to get on with the morning and would continue trying to call in reinforcements to derail the Mama-train.

The rest of the day was a blur of house calls with misbehaving pets and misguided pet parents. I'd found myself in the midst of plans for Spanky's birthday party and Bark Mitzvah. Spanky was a Japanese Shiba Inu who was a lively and playful guy but didn't always love hanging out with other dogs. I suggested a limited guest list for his big event.

Varmit, the Akita I'd mentioned earlier, was still out of control and not only creating chaos in his own household but terrorizing the neighborhood when his owners or their dog walker tried to take him on walks. They'd purchased the treadmill I'd recommended for the dog so he didn't have so much pent up energy. This visit I pointedly noted that just like exercise equipment for us humans, the treadmill only works if you use it.

At my next stop, teen dog owners, Trina and Erikka, were in the throes of planning a "Whole Enchihuahua" pool party with their Chihuahuas. Godiva, a chocolate, was Trina's and Livi Tyler, a long-hair, belonged to Erikka.

Exclusive invitees included twelve other Chihuahuas and their owners. The event was to have poolside pet massages, a mariachi band, salsa dance lessons, and a special chef preparing Godiva and Livi's favorite foods. Only Chihuahuas were invited to attend. I know it seems a bit discriminatory but, hey, they didn't ask for my advice on the party planning. Only on the behavior issues.

I really love Chihuahuas. As a breed they're bold and spirited. Big dogs in little bodies. But I've warned both Trina and Erikka that babying their pooches can create problems. The dogs are friendly and respond well to positive reinforcement, but an owner has to be careful to pay attention and send the right signals. The girls seemed to be getting the message.

My final call of the day was a stop at the ARL to look in on a Lab they'd just taken in. The poor thing had been a companion dog and her owner had been taken to a care center that didn't allow dogs. She was a beautiful old girl but clearly depressed by the separation.

I talked to Don about the situation and we made some phone calls. There were several foster families who might be possibilities. If they'd agree to take the dog to visit the care center that would be a wonderful outcome for all concerned. If they didn't, well, Diana and I were the backup plan.

I looked in on Zeus and Tommy Boy who were thrilled to spend a little play time with me. I knew Don and the others tried to get everyone the exercise they needed but some days were overwhelming and they could use all the help they could get. I scheduled a regular dog park outing for the two on Thursday.

I left the ARL feeling like I'd had my workout. I'd dealt with all I could for the time being. Some people drink to cope, some shop. I find a good dog romp helps me clear my head. Zeus and Tommy Boy were great dogs. Energetic. I smiled as I brushed the dog hair from my jeans. Yep, the dog park it was. They'd be perfect for Kevin's brother if he had the space and the right household. If not, we'd need to look for a forever family who had a lot of energy and enjoyed being active.

I left the ARL and turned the Mercedes onto Laurel Canyon Road. The past few days had been crazy and, with a clearer head, I thought about the last time I'd seen Kevin alive.

Wait a minute. How could I have forgotten the guy working on the landscaping and how oddly the dogs had behaved? The guy had disappeared.

But what if he'd shown up at Kevin's, robbed him, and during the robbery had tased Kevin, killing him? The detective had said the dogs were shut outside when they arrived. I'd mentioned the dogs escaping, but the way the dogs had acted toward the guy had been worth noting, and I hadn't stressed that fact. It had been clear to me it was odd, but it might not be to someone who didn't know the dogs. Sometimes you forget others don't know what you know.

I had to call Malone right away. I pulled over, fished his card out of my bag, and placed the call. Voicemail. I left the information.

Wowza. What a day.

I was so happy to be home. There were times I found it a bit lonely to live alone, but today wasn't one of them. Dogbert met me at the door. He must have heard me pull in the garage. Thelma and Louise were busy sunbathing in the picture window but stretched in welcome. Then, as if suddenly realizing they hadn't eaten in the last fifteen minutes or so, they bounded to their feet and rushed to circle my ankles.

I replenished everyone's water. Filled the dog food dish and shooed Thelma and Lou away from it to give Dog a chance. Then I opened a bag of special cat treats for them.

Next I poured a glass of Pinot Noir for myself and opened a bag of dark chocolate, the human version of pet treats. I tuned the sound system to some smooth Miles Davis, kicked off my shoes and settled into the couch.

My whole décor was based on comfort. Dog, cats, people should have a place to eat, a place to sleep, a spot to rest and feel safe. I closed my eyes, took some deep cleansing breaths, and a sip of my wine.

Wonderful.

For the rest of the evening I wasn't going to think. At all.

Not about loving but wacko pet parents who mean well, but mess up their pets with too much excess and too little exercise. I wasn't going to think about my own loving mother who also meant well, but needed to stay in Texas. I definitely wasn't going to think about Kevin Blackstone being zapped with a Taser.

I was going to veg. Maybe have another glass of wine. Maybe watch an old movie. Maybe do absolutely nothing.

Pound. Pound. Pound.

I shot up, splashing wine on my couch and myself.

Hell bells, people. Can't I have one dang evening?

And I *do* have a working doorbell.

Déjà vu all over again. Oh, no. No, it couldn't be. But it probably was.

"Coming. I'm coming." I scrubbed at the couch with a paper towel.

Oh well, that's why my couch was navy and tough fabric. Then I scrubbed at my blouse. Not navy and not so tough but it would probably come out in the wash.

Pound, pound, pound.

"Oh, for cryin' in a bucket. I said, I'm coming." I pulled the door open and sure enough there he was again. Detective Judd Malone.

And no friendlier than the last time I'd seen him.

"Come in." I continued to scrub the front of my blouse and his eyes traveled from my face to my chest. Then back up.

"You startled me, Detective. I spilled wine on myself. And my couch."

"Sorry." He seemed a bit flustered. Unusual for him.

"Make yourself at home." I gestured toward the living room. "I'm going to change and put this to soak."

He started for the couch.

"Don't sit on that end."

I left him figuring out where to sit and retreated to my bedroom to change clothes. When I returned to the living room he was still standing.

"Okay, sugar, I assume you're here about my voicemail." I'd changed into a dark-colored top just to be safe.

"What voicemail?" He apparently hadn't checked his messages.

"About the dogs." I waved him toward one of the chairs. "Sit. So, why are you here?"

He made no move toward the seating. "We had a report that you were at Kevin Blackstone's house yesterday."

"I was. Why?"

"That property is a crime scene."

"Well, darlin', it wasn't a crime scene when I was there." I drank what little was left in my wine glass, carried it to the kitchen and set it on the counter. "There was no crime scene tape."

"That's because someone took it down, wadded it up, and put it in Kevin's mailbox."

"It was nowhere in sight when I arrived." I refilled my glass.

"I didn't say *you* removed it. In that place it could have been any number of people."

99

The frustration was apparent in his tone.

I held up the bottle of wine in offering but he shook his head.

"In *most* places the police department puts up crime scene tape and it stays put. But in places like Ruby Point it seems there are folks who don't think the rules apply to them." Malone's movements were still restrained but I had the sense that if he could get ahold of whoever had messed with his crime scene, he'd like to shake them silly.

"Hmmm."

"What were you doing there?"

"I'd forgotten something at Kevin's house and I just went back to pick it up." I set my glass on the coffee table.

"What was it?"

I guess the guy believed in direct.

"A piece of jewelry." I didn't think I needed to say anything more.

"Why didn't you tell me about your trip to Kevin's when we talked earlier?"

Oh, man. I should have. Now it looked really bad.

"I should have." I dropped onto the couch, unconcerned that I sat in the wet spot. I picked up the glass I'd just filled with wine and drained it. "I don't know why I didn't. I guess I thought it would look bad. Especially after you told me Kevin hadn't

100

died of natural causes."

"It looks bad *now*," he noted. "Where all in the house did you go?"

"The entry, the living room, the kitchen, the master bedroom." I ticked them off on my fingers.

"The master bedroom? You'd left a piece of jewelry in the master bedroom?"

"No, I did not, but nevertheless that's where I found my grandmother's brooch. Kevin had put it in a drawer."

"Jeez, Caro, what is it with you and your cousin and this brooch?"

Seemed our secret battle over Grandma Tillie's bequest wasn't much of a secret.

I sighed. "It's a long story."

"I've got plenty of time."

"Sure you don't need a glass of wine?"

"No, just the truth. The whole truth this time."

My heart pounded.

"Nothing sinister, Detective. I apparently lost my grandmother's brooch when I'd been at Kevin's helping with Zeus and Tommy Boy."

He crossed his arms.

"If it had been a crime scene, I wouldn't have gone in, but it wasn't cordoned off, and I have the codes to Kevin's alarm system. So I just let myself in, located the brooch, and left. In and out."

"Except you traipsed through most of our crime scene in the process."

Well, I did kind of feel bad about that. "I'm sorry."

"This brooch. You carry it around?"

"No, I'd planned to take it to the jewelry store to be checked for damage."

Tell him about the book. Idiot! Tell him about the book.

The voice in my head wanted to do the right thing, but I didn't know what had happened to the book.

And until I could make sure I wasn't about to make public something that would ruin someone's life, I didn't really want the whole world searching for Kevin's book. Still, if the police had it maybe it would be helpful in their investigation.

Maybe they'd be careful with the information.

Yeah, and maybe Detective Malone moonlighted as a standup comic.

In the end I couldn't do it. I'd been there. It was a terrible thing for the sordid details of people's mistakes to be aired and judged in the court of public opinion.

"We've narrowed Kevin's death to between four o'clock and five o'clock. That places you at the scene at the time of death."

"It does?"

"It does."

"Diana Knight's housekeeper confirms you were there before four but you could have gone back to Kevin's after that. The guard doesn't log visitors out, only in. You came in around two. I talked to you here at six."

Great.

"Wait." I suddenly had an idea. I hoped it was a good one.

He waited.

"I went directly from Ruby Point to Whole Foods. I think they have a date and time stamp on their receipts. If I still have my receipt that would give you a timeframe, right?" I jumped up and retrieved my Coach bag, which I'd dropped on the floor when I'd gotten home.

I hoped the receipt was still in there and hadn't fallen out like Grandma Tillie's brooch. You'd think I'd learn, wouldn't you? I started pulling things from the satchel.

"Ah-ha. Here we go." I unfolded the crumpled up receipt and searched the lines of print. "Three-thirty-eight it says. That's what time I was there. So, I'd just left Kevin's at that point. Maybe ten minutes to drive to the store. Wait." I thought through the sequence.

Again, Malone waited.

"I left Kevin's, stopped at Diana Knight's house, she wasn't home, left some stuff there for the Fur Ball, and then went to Whole Foods. So, maybe fifteen to twenty minutes."

"Fur Ball?"

"Yes, Fur Ball. Diana and I are co-chairs for this year's event to raise money for the ARL." Apparently our advertising to date had not reached Malone.

"Fur Ball?" He repeated.

"Yes, Fur Ball." For cryin' in a bucket, was the guy totally dense? The event was held every year. Maybe he was new on the Laguna Beach force. "The annual 'cough up some cash' fundraiser. It's a play on words," I added for clarification. He seemed to not be getting it at all.

Still, I guess when your job is investigating the seamy side of life you might find something like a Fur Ball a bit frivolous.

"What was it you called me about?" He changed gears.

"The dogs' reaction to the strange landscaper who was working in Ruby Point." I was glad he'd remembered. I'd completely forgotten what with all the talk about why I'd returned to Kevin's, what I'd touched, and how to prove I hadn't had time to kill him. Never mind the guilty conversation I was having with myself about the book I'd inadvertently picked up, and then accidently lost.

The police had surely searched the premises and found it. That was it.

"What?" I jumped when Malone touched my arm. My attention hadn't been on what he was saying but rather on worry about what I was withholding.

"I said, wouldn't they have acted aggressive with any stranger?"

"No, they might be wary with a stranger."

"But you said, the landscaper waved a shovel at them." Malone stepped back and looked at me like I was making a mountain out of a molehill.

"Right. What's more significant is their reluctance to back down. They stayed tense."

"Well, I'd be tense too if someone swung a shovel at me."

I could see Malone wasn't buying my insight and, in fact, those had been my own thoughts at the time.

"We'll check it out," he said, moving toward the door. His words said one thing, but his tone said another. "And we'll check this out." He tucked the Whole Foods receipt in this pocket.

I had no confidence he and his fellow investigators would follow up. I'd have to ask around myself the next few days, when I had house calls in Ruby Point, and see if anyone else had encountered the guy.

CHAPTER TEN

You know how sometimes things seem dire and then you wake up the next morning and they don't seem so awful? Yeah, not the case this time. It was a new day but Kevin was still dead. I was still a murder suspect. And my mother was still coming to town.

I opened my eyes, moved a dog and two cats, and made my way to the kitchen for coffee and toast.

Malone had called and requested my presence at the police station for fingerprinting. Since I'd been all over Kevin's house touching things when I was searching for Grandma Tillie's brooch, they needed to "eliminate me as a suspect" by matching my prints with the others they'd found at the crime scene.

I was pretty sure that was cop-speak for "we think you did it and we'd like your fingerprints to prove our theory."

I'd had no reason to off Kevin Blackstone,

and I prayed the receipt also proved I hadn't had time.

I decided to tackle the second problem. Hub would help me with calling Mama off which would also give me an opportunity to talk to a sane person. Hub was absolutely the sanest person I knew. He also always managed to make me feel saner.

I pulled up his office number on my cell phone.

"Lamont and Landry," a soft west Texas voice answered.

"Hi, Nancy. It's Caro, is Daddy in?" Nancy had been with the firm for as many years as I could remember. She was in Hub's words, "the one truly running things."

"He sure is, honey, but he's with someone." As she talked I could picture her. Perfectly styled white hair, crisp navy-blue suit, a single strand of pearls. "It sounds as if they're almost done though. Could you hold for a little while? Or would you like me to have him call you?"

"I'll just hold, Nancy, if you don't mind."

"Okay, honey, I'll let him know you're waiting."

The hold music clicked from whatever it had been playing to an instrumental rendition of "Sweet Caroline" and I took that as a good sign. I hummed along as I waited.

Hub had always supported the big choices I'd made in my life. For instance my move, five years ago, to Laguna Beach. I don't know how, growing up outside land-locked Dallas, I'd developed such a love for the sea, but I had. Once I'd experienced it, the ocean drew me. When I moved to Laguna, I felt like I'd finally moved home.

People call it the Laguna Beach bubble because it seems we move at a different pace here. It's not L.A. with the glitz, the glamour, and the big business, big stores, and big stars. And it's not New York — that's for sure. Nothing against New York, you understand. I've been there and there's much to commend it. I love nothing better than a trip to the Big Apple. The people, the theater, the museums, and yes — the shopping. But I'm from the south, and though we're hard-working people, we just don't rush in the same way as New Yorkers.

Laguna Beach is a microcosm of ages and backgrounds and interests. Old money, new money, artists and art collectors, surfers, and dog lovers. The dog lover part is the main reason I moved here. That and the ocean.

The Montgomery clan is Texas oil money from way back when Texas was known for oil. Then my granddaddy got interested in real estate and that's how the Montgomerys ended up with a second home in the little seaside town of Laguna Beach. We spent at least a month in Laguna every summer from the time I was a child. Usually August, which in Texas is unbearably hot.

Let me rephrase that. August, which in Texas is as hot as Hades.

Mama was a debutant and a beauty queen, and as I was blessed with all the requisite equipment it was expected that I would be, too. I had other ideas, and, thank the Lord, a stepfather who when push came to shove supported them. I did the pageant thing like an obedient daughter until I was seventeen. Then one day, things changed.

I'd come home from yet another back-biting, stress-inducing competition. I reeked of hairspray and gossip. All I wanted to do was saddle up my horse and get away from the noise.

As I walked out the door, Mama said, "Don't you mess up that manicure, missy."

And with the self-involvement that only a seventeen-year-old can muster, I replied, "Bite me."

She's a very fast woman. And I mean that in a lot of ways.

When she slapped me, her obscenely large

diamond grazed my cheek.

Blood dripped down my cheek and off my chin onto my riding jacket.

"Oh, my God, look what you've made me do," she snapped.

"It doesn't matter." It didn't hurt and I didn't care.

"Yes, it does. Get back here. We've got to call Dr. C right away."

Dr. C was Mama's plastic surgeon. She had him on speed dial.

Turned out the cut wasn't that bad and didn't even need stitches, but it was at that moment that I realized Mama's single-minded focus on my winning beauty pageants was not about me.

Now don't get me wrong. I love my mother, but the woman has enough issues to start her own magazine stand. Chief among them was being the runner-up with my birth father, who contributed the DNA but not much else. Vic Howard was a movie-star-handsome rodeo cowboy who didn't see a family in his future. My grandfather had offered him a large amount of money and an in with a rodeo promoter, and Vic had headed off into the sunset.

That caused a bit of a scandal for the Montgomery family.

Mama eventually recovered sufficiently to

marry a wealthy widower, Hub Lamont, who I adored. Hub raised me as his own and together he and Mama had Nolan, my half-brother. To my delight he was just a miniature little Hub.

Anyway, most of the time Hub bowed to Mama's wishes on things.

Things like beauty pageants. Mama made no bones about the fact that her goal for me was Miss Texas and then Miss America. She'd been robbed of the crown by a silver-tongued distraction who played her and left her. It didn't help that Vic had gone on to fame and fortune on the rodeo circuit, winning the Professional Rodeo Cowboys Association's All-Around World Championship Title.

In fact, he won it a record (at that time anyway) five times. She, on the other hand, had to settle for runner-up in the Miss Texas competition, unable to go on to Miss America where she could have wowed the nation with her talent and beauty. She became an also-ran in Vic's life as he went on to a string of rich and beautiful starlets, playmates, and models.

I was her only hope.

So when I walked away from the pageant scene, Mama Kat was devastated. Now, after years of training as a therapist, I understand that better. But, of course, then I was just a seventeen-year-old bundle of hormones and attitude.

We were civil, but it was better for both of us that I lived several states away. It was better for me if Mama Kat didn't come for a visit in the midst of all of this insanity.

A beep in my ear signaled that Nancy was back on the phone so I pulled my brain back from the trip down memory lane.

"He's free now, Caro. Let me put you through."

When Hub answered, he was so happy to talk to me that I felt guilty calling to ask for such an incredibly self-serving favor.

"Hello, how's my favorite girl?" Hub's voice boomed through the phone.

"Great, Daddy. How are you?" I'd always called him "Daddy." He was the only daddy I'd ever known. I had no interest at all in finding Vic. In fact, I hoped I never ran across him in this lifetime.

Hub took me in like I was his own and, like I said, he'd taken my side when it mattered.

"We miss you so much, honey. I do and I know your mama does, too."

"That's kind of what I'm callin' about, Daddy."

He chuckled. "I thought you might be."

113

"Do you think there's any convincing her not to come out here?"

"I'll do my best, but she's got her heart set on it."

"I emailed her that now is not a good time." I filled him in on a little bit of what was going on.

"You be careful, Carolina." His voice was gruff which meant he was truly worried. "I know you don't like to be told what to do, but please be careful."

"I will."

"How's our girl, Melinda?"

"Uhm . . . I don't really know," I hedged. "We haven't talked lately."

"Still feuding about that damn pin, aren't you?"

"Yeah. Well, partly that anyway."

"Caro, it's just a piece of jewelry. It's not like you to be so materialistic."

"No, it's not. But Grandma left it to me."

"Your grandmother was never one to show favorites so I can't think what she was up to. But the lady was a Montgomery woman through and through, so I know she was up to something."

I didn't know either, but I knew for sure Grandma Tillie and I had shared something special. She never would have betrayed the relationship we had. Not that she didn't love

Melinda equally. Of course, she did.

I'd even have been willing to share possession of the brooch, but Mel wasn't one for half-measures, and then there'd been words. About a lot more than just the brooch. And then it was game on.

"About Mama . . ."

"I'll do my best."

"Thanks, Daddy. I owe you one."

"You sure do. I'll expect you home for Christmas." He paused. "And I'll expect that you and Melinda Sue will have sorted things out."

"I'll be home for Christmas. You can take that to the bank." I assured him. I wasn't making any promises on figuring things out with Mel.

A truce like that would take two willing parties.

In the meantime, I had bigger issues to deal with. Now that I'd done what I could to get help diverting my mother, I could get back to trying to figure out what had gone on in Ruby Point after I'd left Kevin and his dogs.

I hadn't mentioned to Hub that the police seemed to think I was somehow involved. He would have worried. I was always the responsible one in the family. Still I'd entered a crime scene, or *contaminated* the crime scene according to Malone, in order to retrieve Grandma Tillie's brooch, and in so doing cast suspicion on myself. I only hoped the receipt I'd provided would clear me once and for all, and the detective would figure out the real killer. On top of all that, Diana's worry about the potential for the killer being someone inside the walls of Ruby Point was unsettling.

Maybe I was chasing my tail, but I was even more convinced it had something to do with the landscape worker who'd disappeared. At the very least, he might have seen something. At the most, he was involved.

If the police weren't going to track him down, I'd do it myself.

CHAPTER ELEVEN

Laguna Beach had gone to the dogs many years ago. Very few Laguna restaurants don't allow dogs, at least for patio dining, but there were a few. Unfortunately Diana had picked one of those few for our lunch meeting. However, the owners and wait staff at Zino's were pretty lenient with pet owners like Diana whose dogs went everywhere with them. That's to say they pretended not to notice handbags and totes that wiggled and yipped.

The hostess seated us by the open window. I glanced around the crowded bistro and then scooted my chair so I could enjoy the beautiful ocean view.

Was it my imagination or had the room quieted?

The bistro was casually decorated but sported starched cloths on the tables and colorful seascapes on the walls. I nodded to a couple of clients I recognized.

Angie Westrum nodded back, her micro teacup Chihuahua, Cassie, sound asleep in her silver Kwigy Bo carrier. Angie tucked her platinum locks behind one ear and leaned forward to say something to her lunch partner.

The comments may have been about the eggplant sandwich on her plate, but somehow I didn't think so.

I was used to getting a bit of attention when out and about with Diana but this seemed different. People were looking at me as much as Diana, and that could only mean word was out that I was a suspect in Kevin's murder. What was the Oscar Wilde quote? Something about curiosity. Oh, I know. "The public have an insatiable curiosity to know everything, except what is worth knowing." I'd been the target of that truth back in Texas when my marriage and my practice went belly up. Everyone was interested in knowing my business. Seemed like I was under the same kind of scrutiny again, and I didn't like it any more than I had then.

Our waiter was quick to supply mineral water for Diana and iced tea for me. I pushed aside the discomfort about what other people were thinking and saying. I knew better than to get tied up in knots over something you couldn't do a plumb thing about.

I ordered the blackened salmon salad as I was saving room for dessert. Diana ordered the *Boeuf Français* aka the French Dip as she was planning for a doggie bag. As we ate we chatted about the remaining details of the Fur Ball. Her Honor, Mayor Teri, had agreed to be the auctioneer. We had several great auction items that would add to the take and thus to the coffers of the Animal Rescue League. I was betting Mel would bid on the safari or the sky-diving package. I was hoping the whale-watching was within my price range.

While we talked I pretended, along with the wait staff, not to notice that Diana appeared to be feeding her handbag. Mr. Wiggles was very quiet, as if he knew he needed to be on his good behavior.

"Grey has donated a lovely piece of art for the auction." Diana's rose-painted finger slid down the names on our list. "But I've not heard back from Melinda on a donation from The Bow Wow Boutique. I don't suppose you'd like to give her a call."

"I'd rather not." I tensed as I flipped through my folder of ticket receipts.

"It would be good for you girls to make up."

I glanced up to see Diana looking at me pointedly. Had she been talking to Hub?

"It would, but I'm not sure either of us is ready. You know, I apologized for what I said to her. I'm still waiting for her apology. However, Diana, sugar, I'm sure the donation just slipped her mind. Mel is stubborn but not spiteful. At least not where animals are concerned."

Her cornflower blue-eyed, do-the-right-thing stare continued.

I sighed. "I'll call her."

"Good girl."

"What about entertainment?" I took a big bite of salmon and swallowed. "Did you hear back from your friend?"

"He says Sarah McLachlan is already booked. He knows a lot of other people in the business though. He'll find someone for us." Diana continued to take a bite and then slip a morsel to Mr. Wiggles.

"Great. Just let me know if there's something I need to do."

"Oh, that reminds me. I've got something in the car for you. Don't let me forget."

We finished our meals and, though I'd promised myself a dessert, it turned out I didn't have room after all.

We'd parked nose-to-nose in the parking lot and as soon as we arrived at Diana's car she released Mr. Wiggles from the confines of her purse. He seemed happy to stretch. She reached in the backseat of her Bentley sedan and handed me a wicker basket.

"What's this?"

"It's from my neighbor, Oliver Hembry. I didn't know you two knew each other, but he asked that I give this to you the next time I saw you."

I peeked inside.

The basket contained a bunch of tasty looking, and even better smelling, cookies. Fancy ones.

Sugar cookies dusted with big crystals of sugar and a group of what appeared to be chocolate chip, cranberry, pecan cookies.

Yum. I wasn't sorry I'd given Zino's dessert menu a pass.

Then I noticed they were nestled on a familiar fluffy, yellow, kitchen towel. The very towel I'd accidently taken from Kevin's house.

"Does this neighbor of yours happen to be a drugged out rocker who dresses in black leather and has a houseful of dogs?"

"That's the one!" Diana smiled. "Oliver is a fabulous cook. And I don't think he does drugs anymore."

"Maybe not. Could be it's just booze." I wasn't sure it was just booze, but Diana liked to believe the best of everyone.

"Caro, honey, I'm pretty sure he's given all that up. He does have to take some prescription drugs. For his back injury you know. And Ollie may have the occasional glass or two of wine. But I wouldn't hold that against him. He's a very nice young man." Diana patted my arm.

"Uh-huh." I was sure my skepticism showed on my face.

"He is." Diana was earnest in her support of him. "And his dogs are simply wonderful. All rescue animals. All well taken care of and well-behaved."

"Yeah, I did notice the dogs." The whole pack of them.

"He doesn't leave the house. His assistant walks them but they do get walked. He doesn't neglect them."

"Wait." I was still thinking about Ollie and baking and wasn't exactly tracking. "He doesn't leave the house ever?"

"No, not at all. He has that disease people have where they are afraid to leave home." Diana shook her head. "Arachnophobia or something."

"I think you mean agoraphobia. Arachnophobia is fear of spiders."

"Oh." She paused for a moment. "I don't think he's afraid of spiders, although he might be, poor man. I think it's just the other."

Ah, now I got it. It had seemed an unlikely friendship, but Diana can't resist the wounded. Human or animal.

"I guess he used to be in some big rock band." Diana reached in the car to pat Mr. Wiggles' head as she talked. "That's how he made all his money and can afford such a nice home. It's very nice. But he apparently was pretty wild in his day and his wife left him and took their two lovely children back to England with her. Now he has sobered up but they won't come back."

"Diana, I'm not convinced he's sobered up."

"Oh, Caro honey, you're such a cynic."

"Yes, I am. And for good reason." I smiled at her concern. "Let's get you on your way. Mr. Wiggles is getting impatient."

I questioned Diana about the landscaper, but she didn't remember seeing him at all. With that, Diana and Mr. Wiggles were off to take care of their afternoon errands, and I climbed in my car and headed back to the office. I wanted to pick up some files and then I had my own afternoon appointments.

There were two more calls from Ruby Point residents. Seemed like there was a whole spate of pet problems in the enclave.

Or perhaps a whole spate of snoopy pet parents who were wondering what I knew about the investigation into Kevin's death.

That would be one short conversation. What I knew was — nothing.

Still the appointments gave me ample opportunity to ask a question or two about who and what my clients might have noticed the day Kevin died.

I took the basket of cookies in with me and placed them on my desk. I was pretty sure it was safe to eat the cookies, but Diana was right. I am truly a total cynic.

Paris was at the reception desk again today. I noted the blonde bimbo look she favored and wondered if any ambition at all lived inside her. Then I felt bad for my stereotyping. Sort of.

I walked out to the desk.

"Paris, hon, I have a question for you."

"Sure, Caro." Her surfer girl hair flipped over one shoulder as she turned.

"Have you ever heard of Ollie Hembry?"

"Sure, absolutely everyone has. He's lived in Laguna like forever."

"Really?" I must have missed the memo. "What do you know about him?"

"Well . . ." Paris laid one French manicured finger on her tanned cheek. "He used to have really wild parties. Major, major, like epic big rockers would come and there'd be, you know, like sex, drugs, and famous people. The police would have to go and tell everyone to chill and calm the neighbors. Then his wife left him and he went bonkers. Crazy. He's crazy now, ya know. No one ever sees him." She stopped. "Maybe he's dead."

"What?"

"Do you think he's dead?"

"No, no, I'm sure he's not dead." I backed away and returned to my office and stared at the basket of cookies again. "No, I'm sure he's very much alive. A bit wacky but very much alive."

I lifted the towel out of the basket careful not to lose any cookies or pieces of cookies.

Holy crap.

There nestled in the bottom of the wicker basket was the black book I'd found in Kevin's drawer. I didn't have to read the entire book to know it truly belonged to him. The first page was filled with notes in Kevin's flamboyant handwriting. The same handwriting on the checks he paid me with every month or so.

I flipped through, noting names I recognized, looking for my own.

Ahh, there it was. I knew I'd seen it.

Carolina Lamont, fmr ms tx, scdl clsd psych

prtc, LB 4 yr, ho. Well, hell, that wasn't hard to interpret. Former Miss Texas. (I was.) Scandal closed psychology practice. (It had.) I wasn't sure about the LB four-year reference but I imagined it could mean Laguna Beach because I'd been in Laguna for four years. Actually working on my fifth year.

I turned the page and looked at some of the other entries. It was a little more difficult when you didn't know the person's history.

I finally found another whose history I knew intimately.

Melinda Langston, fmr ms tx, disqual ms am, eng Gry Don, LB 4yr, ho.

Again I could pretty easily decipher the entry about Mel. Also a former Miss Texas, she was disqualified in the Miss America pageant. (A story she'll have to share with y'all. Not mine to tell.) Mel was engaged to Grey Donovan (today anyway, as far as I knew), and she and I had been in Laguna about the same amount of time.

The "ho" after each of our names I wasn't sure about but I didn't think Kevin thought we were "hos" in the money for sex connotation. We were former beauty queens from Texas, not hoochie mamas from Hoochistan.

There were other entries:

Ollie Hembry, rck lgnd, sep w-fam, Rhde, arrst 1998 HK, LB 10yr, ho

KR, cub gy dgr, frm SFB, so fk id, LB 2yr, rtr

Mandy Beenerm, yga ldy, frmr chldr, swt dn, LB 6yr, ho fcls

Mr. Mandy, inv fm, brk, aff SS, LB 6yr, ho fcls

Sharmin Summers, schwartz, tvstr, frm neb, nt 17, LB 3yr, ho

Mona Michaels, btch Fluffy, sep dh Cliff, ck inv, LB 19 yr, rtr

I flipped through the pages and recognized many of the names. Most of them were known to me, and many were clients. Some I didn't recognize at all. I tried to interpret other entries based on what I'd been able to figure out regarding the notes about Mel and me. Then there was a section at the back in another language. I wasn't sure what language.

There was one spot in the book where I could tell a page had been torn out. I wondered if Ollie had done it, but his page was still in there. Who else, besides Kevin, had seen the book?

Maybe someone had a secret worth killing for.

But why not take the whole book?

I glanced at my watch and seeing the time

tucked the book in my briefcase to look at later. Maybe with fresh eyes I'd be able to figure out Kevin's shorthand notations.

Maybe I needed to call Malone and fess up about the book.

Okay, no "maybe." I needed to call Malone and hand over the book.

I picked up the files I'd pulled on my repeat offenders, and grabbed my notes on a new client, Hilda and her new puppy, a Saluki. Business was booming. I hated the idea that somehow my business was profiting from such a horrible incident almost as much as I hated people thinking I might have killed him.

My cell phone rang as I was headed to my car. It was my friend, Walt, reminding me we were meeting for dinner that evening. We always met once a month for either dinner or a movie.

Before you get your hopes up (you and my mama) this isn't exactly date night. Walter Cambrian was a friend, a former photojournalist, and he had been my stepfather's college roommate. He'd been a great help to me getting my company started, I enjoyed his company, and we had similar tastes in movies and restaurants.

Walt was retired and always knew what was going on in the community. Maybe he'd heard something. Now that Kevin's book had surfaced, I also had other avenues to investigate, avenues I hoped would lead far away from me.

It'd been another busy day so I'd had to rush to get home, change clothes, and get to Riccio's on time. Walt was already there by the time I arrived. Dino Riccio's restaurant was known for its Italian fare and tonight it was packed. I was glad we'd made reservations.

When I'd made my stop at home, I'd reviewed the pages of Kevin's book again for any insights, but without understanding his shorthand it was difficult. He had only left out vowels and shortened words, but without a context, there were too many possibilities for most of it. My best bet was using the entries about people I knew.

I looked for one about Walt.

Got it.

Walter Cambrian, aw pht, blgr, wdr, snp, LB 23yr, ho

I jotted it down. I didn't want to be seen with the notebook in case anyone recognized it.

As soon as we'd ordered, I filled Walt in on my adventures since we'd last gotten together. I began with Kevin and how wild his dogs had been, then moved on to Detective Malone and his insinuation that I was somehow involved in Kevin's death. I recounted my adventures in retrieving my Grandma Tillie's brooch and ended up with the basket of goodies from Ollie that had Kevin's book hidden inside.

Walt shook his head. "You, child, lead an exciting life." His tone was gruff but I could tell from the suppressed line of his mouth he was trying not to laugh.

"I'd rather have boring."

"Hell, Caro, boring is for old age."

The waiter appeared and placed our salads in front of us. "Anything else you need right now, folks?"

We both shook our heads.

As soon as the waiter left, he continued. "What do you think he was doing with the information he kept on people?"

"I don't know." I took a bite of the greens. Perfect as always. "It could have just been a weird obsessive thing Kevin did. Keeping track of people. Or rather their secrets."

"Could be," Walt agreed.

"You know, like my daily list. Only my list-making obsession impacts me, not others."

"So what does the note about me say?"

"Here." I slipped him the piece of paper where I'd written it down.

"Pretty easy to interpret."

"Most of it. Award-winning photographer, blogger, widower. I think the number after LB means you've lived in Laguna Beach for twenty-three years. Is that right?"

"Exactly right."

"And I'm not sure but I'm wondering if the 'ho' notation means home-owner because all the notes either said 'ho' or 'rtr' or 'fcls.' "

"Makes sense." Walt continued to stare at the paper. "Most of us own or rent. And unfortunately lately there are a good number of people who would fit the foreclosure category."

"Yes, sad but true."

"I don't know what 'snp' means." Walt handed the paper back to me.

"Hmmm. Not sure." I thought it probably meant "snoop" but I wasn't about it tell Walt that.

Our dinners had arrived and we dug in.

"I'm not sure why the police think Kevin's death is anything more than a home invasion." Walt tasted his manicotti.

"Good?"

He nodded. "Seems more likely that Kevin would have tased the invader instead of the other way around if it was just a robbery."

"I agree." I nodded. "I'm still bothered by the encounter with the landscape guy and how the dogs acted. I've been asking around about him." I took a bite of my chicken piccata. It was incredible. "He seems to me to be the best bet for someone, besides me, who interacted with Kevin the afternoon he died. Though the police don't seem to think so."

"I'll keep my ear to the ground for any rumors or innuendos involving Kevin Blackstone," Walt promised. "Useless police. Waste of our taxes."

We spent the rest of our dinner chatting about other things and only came back to the topic of Kevin as we walked to our cars.

"Thanks for a great evening as always, Walt." I kissed his rough cheek.

"Can't come here often." Walt groused. "Food's too good. I don't get enough exercise to handle the calories."

I laughed. "Leave it to you to find something bad about good food." I turned to open my car door. "We didn't even have the tiramisu."

He put a hand out to stop me. "Caro?"

"Yes, Walt." I turned to face him.

"You know I try hard not to tell you what to do. Figure you already have too darn many people doing that. But my advice on this notebook of Kevin's is that you need to turn it over to the police. Right away."

Danged if I didn't know Walt was right.

I started toward home. I wanted nothing more than to go home, sit out on my patio, and enjoy the view. But Walt had nailed it. I had to get Kevin Blackstone's little book of secrets to the police.

Sooner, not later. I needed to quit being wishy-washy about it.

I don't know what I'd been thinking.

Well, what I'd been thinking was of all the people who might be hurt if the information were mishandled. I'd operated under the assumption it would be mishandled because that was what had happened to me.

During "The Big Mess" every embarrassing detail of my life was splashed all over the news. Reporters stalked my friends, they questioned my hairdresser, they made my life a living hell. Geoff and I had been a whole section in the *Dallas Morning News Sunday Edition.* Super-stars in their feature on high-profile ugly divorces.

But the information in Kevin's book wasn't mine to keep.

Still I wasn't going to give up on figuring it out myself. So, before I turned it over I would make a copy. Kevin's shorthand code was making me crazy, and I was determined to crack it.

I changed direction and headed toward my office instead of home.

There might be something in the information Kevin had noted that would help to figure out who had killed him. I knew these folks *way* better than the police did. And after all, it might help to dissuade them from the idea I was somehow involved.

I parked in front of the office rather than in the back. My key slipped easily into the lock and I opened the door. Offices always seem a little creepy when there's no one there, and I suddenly wished I'd waited until morning.

But once I get my mind set on something, I just push forward. It was a blessing and a curse. Now I was feeling a little funny about being alone in a deserted office.

Interesting how murder in your sleepy little community will do that do to a person.

Our reception area held a circular wooden desk. The copier had been turned off to save energy, so I had to wait a bit for it to warm up.

The real estate developer's office was closed and locked. A few years ago when the housing boom was at its height I'd come in and find her here all hours of the day and night. Now I knew she was barely hanging on. In fact, she'd had to downsize her own real estate.

The accountant had a steady business, busier during the tax season, but stable the rest of the time.

The office beside him was always locked up. I'd not asked any of the others about it but I was a little afraid it was a front for something not quite legal. You know, one of the types of companies where *60 Minutes* or one of those news programs comes in and everyone says they never saw anyone there, and the cameras go in and it's just empty space used as a front to rip people off.

The next office was the psychic's. Now I know you've got a picture in your head of long gypsy skirts, bare feet, scarves and bangles. But this lady dressed more like your average business woman. Usually a pantsuit with a nice pastel blouse, low sensible shoes. I didn't put any stock in psychics myself, but she seemed to have a steady stream of clients.

The copier finally warmed up and I carefully copied each page, laying the book flat and making sure that I had a legible copy of each of the notations.

There were twenty-seven pages in all. Most of the names I recognized but there were a few who were unfamiliar. There were also some other notes in the back, also in code, that seemed unrelated. I copied those, too, just in case.

Once done, I slipped the book and the copies in my purse, locked the office, and climbed back in my car.

I had animals to feed and a dog to walk. Tonight I would call Malone, and regardless of how angry he might be, explain how I had unintentionally picked up Kevin's book when I had retrieved my grandmother's brooch.

Before I made that call I needed to figure out how I was going to explain the fact I'd intentionally omitted that information from our previous conversations.

I wondered who I could count on to post bail.

CHAPTER TWELVE

I called and got Malone's voicemail. I said, "I have information about the case." Now *that* ought to merit a return phone call.

I hit the sack. I felt, if not exactly great about facing the detective, then good about doing the right thing.

The next morning it was another day, another dog. Life in the fast lane for your intrepid pet therapist to desperate house pets of every kind. Today it was a depressed Dachshund, a headstrong Basset Hound, and a kvetching Savannah kitty cat.

I'd been up early. Taken Dogbert for a short walk. Promised him a longer one later and headed out the door.

My first call was a little different from the usual. It wasn't really a therapy call. Lydia Custler was out of town. Most of my clients were so attached to their furry friends they always figured out a way for Fido, Fluffy, or Figaro to go along. But Lydia was a hot-shot ad agency stylist and her specialty was food styling. You know, those beautiful mouth-watering shots of fresh peaches, piping hot biscuits, and juicy, calorie-oozing barbeque ribs. Good grief, I made myself hungry just thinking about it.

Well, on-site food jobs and Eleanor Rigby, Lydia's very spoiled Cardigan Welsh Corgi, did not play well together. After a disastrous photo shoot where Eleanor ate the client's foie gras and then puked it up on said client's expensive Italian shoes, Lydia had decided to make other arrangements.

She could have boarded Eleanor at the vet's (you remember, Dr. Daniel Darling, right?) luxurious digs or at the Laguna Dog Ranch, but no, that just wouldn't do. She'd hired an in-home sitter. One who didn't yet have a driver's license. This way Eleanor would have all her own things around her so she wouldn't miss Lydia so much. See "very spoiled" reference above.

So, I was on my way to pick up Eleanor at the groomer. I'd had to double back to my house because I'd forgotten the dog car seat Lydia insisted on, and now I was running late.

Just as I pulled out of my driveway for the second time my cell phone rang.

I could see from my caller ID it was Walt.

"Hey, Walt." I headed my car toward the highway.

"Hello, Caro, I have a clue for you." His voice was a raspy whisper. Raspy because he used to be a smoker and a whisper, I could only assume, because there were other people around.

"What kind of clue?" I didn't tell him I was behind the wheel because I knew what Walter thought about cell phone conversations while driving, even hands free, and I didn't want to incite a lengthy lecture.

Or face the possibility of my picture ending up on his "Beach Bum" blog. In my head I called it the "Grumpy Old Man" blog but I'd never in a million years tell him that. Walt delighted in catching people doing stupid things and then posting their photos with pithy comments. Most times it was pretty darn funny. If you weren't the one in the picture.

"I can't tell you over the phone. Can you meet me at the Koffee Klatch?"

I thought the Koffee Klatch was one of the least private places he could have picked, but after dealing with Queen Doggie, I was going to be ready for some caffeine.

"I'm fixin' to pick up Lydia Custler's Eleanor at the dog spa and drop her off at home, but I could probably make it by nine."

"I'll meet you there then." Walt hung up without saying good-bye but then that wasn't really unusual for him. When he was done talking, he was just done.

I pulled into the lot at the Divine Dog Spa and parked. I checked the doggie seat, making sure it was secure so it would be ready when I got Eleanor to the car.

When I walked into the spa, things were all abuzz with tails and tongues wagging. And a few of those were even the dogs. In Laguna Beach, the doggie spa is more of a gossip haven than any beauty shop in Texas.

"Hey, Jade." I waved to one of the senior groomers. She was Eleanor's favorite and I hoped to heck she'd had the pooch's appointment today.

"Hey, Caro," she waved back. "I'll let Kendall know you're here for Eleanor." She patted the Labradoodle she'd been playing fetch with and said, "Hold on for just a moment, Hugo. I'll be right back."

Jade went through the swinging doors that led to the grooming area, and within minutes a groomer who I'd never seen before burst through the doorway carrying Eleanor. Tall and dark, with obvious Latin bloodlines, the guy pranced across the room

140

like he was showing at the Westminster Kennel Club.

He stopped in front of me, looked down his hawkish nose and nailed me with dark flashing eyes. "This little bitch bit me." He held the Corgi at arm's length. He didn't appear to be badly hurt, but I noticed he did have a towel wrapped around his right hand.

I also noticed something else. The folks who worked at the Divine Dog Spa were generally casually dressed. Like me, they knew when you're dealing with rambunctious canines you're not going to stay all neat and tidy.

Not this guy. He was decked out for an eighties disco party with tight retro bell-bottoms in a Dalmatian-patterned fabric (where did he even find those pants?) and a black ruffled shirt open to the waist. The *pièce de résistance,* though, was the pair of sequined platform shoes in what must have been at least a size twelve.

Eleanor whimpered, but I wasn't sure if she was bothered by the accusation that she'd nipped him or by his fashion sense. Or lack thereof. I felt a little like whimpering myself.

I reached out to take her and he gave up the dog without hesitation.

"I'm sorry to tell you but Eleanor was a bad, *bad* girl." His voice was a bit nasal and feminine but not really unpleasant. His attitude was cordial in spite of his initial outburst.

Eleanor nuzzled my hand and I rubbed the back of her neck. She was rarely temperamental and had never had a problem with biting, but it was possible something had set her off.

"Was there another dog nearby who might have caused her to feel threatened?" I considered it my duty to try to get to the bottom of her behavior.

"No, no other dogs even in the room." He shook his head. "I'm Kendall, by the way. I don't believe we've met."

When I shifted the Corgi and reached to take Kendall's hand, Eleanor let loose a deep growl. A warning growl. A get-your-hand-away-from-me-give-me-some-space-or-else growl.

Kendall yanked his hand back and swung his arm behind his body. "No, you don't, girlfriend!"

As he moved, I caught a whiff of fragrance. "What cologne are you wearing?"

"Oh, this?" He sniffed his wrist, started to offer it to me to smell and then thought better of it. "I have my *eau de toilette* made especially for me at this little shop in Palm Springs. It's called 'Kendallicious.' Do you like it?"

"I don't mind it, but I'm afraid Eleanor finds it objectionable." I could smell a hint of spicy pepper in the fragrance. I wasn't sure if the scent had caused her to react but it sure seemed like it. "You might want to skip it when you're around the dogs."

His handsome face fell. "You don't think the doggies like it?"

"I don't think they like or dislike it, but many dog breeds are driven by their noses. Perfume and dogs don't always mix."

Kendall appeared crestfallen by this information. His shoulders slumped and the ruffles on his disco shirt drooped.

I'd spent longer at the spa than I'd intended and didn't want to keep Walt waiting so I moved toward the front desk.

"I'll get you signed out then." Kendall clomped his way to the reception area, those size twelve platforms sparkling in the morning sun. I could almost hear "Disco Inferno" playing in my head.

"Great. You can just put it on Lydia's account and she'll settle up when she's back in town."

"You're not Lydia Custler then." Kendall was torn. I could tell he wanted to retrieve

Eleanor until he was sure I was authorized to pick her up, but on the other hand — well, he didn't want to provoke another nip.

"No, I'm Caro Lamont and I'm on Eleanor's approved list."

Kendall stopped in his very large tracks and turned. His lip-glossed mouth formed a surprised "O." "You're the pet therapist."

"Right." I nodded, still keeping the little Corgi a distance away.

"The one who . . ." His voice trailed off.

"I'm the one who what?" I was losing patience with Kendall and his drama. I just wanted to get Eleanor home and get to my meeting with Walt at the Koffee Klatch.

"The one who was the last person to see Kevin alive," he whispered.

Kevin knew a lot of people, but I couldn't, in any scenario, picture Kevin and Kendall together.

In fact, Kevin had never even mentioned knowing a dog groomer. I'd thought he usually took Zeus and Tommy Boy to a no-nonsense dog wash place in Dana Point in the spring and summer. Shepherds blow their coats twice a year and shed a lot. Other than that it was just nail trims, and I thought Dr. Daniel did those. Not much grooming needed.

Besides, you couldn't have gotten much

more "guy" than Kevin, and, unless I was mistaken, Kendall wasn't into macho.

"How do you — did you — know Kevin?" Sometimes it was best to just ask.

"We were friends." Kendall looked down at the floor and then away.

Jade picked that moment to re-appear. "Is everything okay?"

"Yes, fine." There was a wobble in his voice and the flamboyant groomer still hadn't looked me in the eye. "Jade, honey, would you please check out Ms. Lamont and Eleanor for me? I've got to see to this." He indicated his towel wrapped hand.

Without waiting for a response, he disappeared through the swinging doors and out of sight.

Noting my expression, Jade was quick to reassure. "Don't worry. I don't think it's a much of a bite, but we have insurance."

I signed Eleanor out and gathered her things. I didn't think the bite was serious either. I'd received a nip or two from time to time myself. Goes with the territory in my line of work. But somehow I had the idea that Kendall's quick exit had nothing at all to do with a dog bite.

The Koffee Klatch is a great coffee drinking and people-watching spot downtown, right

145

on PCH. Walt and Millie were taking full advantage of their primo observation seat as locals, shopkeepers and tourists passed on the sidewalk and came through the attached patio walkway. Walt was viewing the world through his ever-present camera lens and Millie was viewing the world through her ever-present ADD.

Before you get the wrong idea I should mentioned that Millie is Walt's Norwich Terrier.

His dog, not his wife. A wife would never have put up with all the things Millie endured with good humor. Walt had lost his wife, the love of his life, over twenty years ago, and he'd been alone ever since. Millie had been with him the past five years and while she hadn't completely softened Walt's hard shell, she'd made a crack.

Millie was clever, scrappy, and lively but I honestly believe she was ADD. She can't focus on anything for any length of time, and in spite of my best efforts, I've not seen much improvement.

Didn't matter. Walt loved her just the way she was.

"Hi, Walt." I'd picked up a sugar-free hazelnut latte and a croissant as I'd come through the Koffee Klatch. I slid my cup onto their table just as Walt snapped a shot of a lanky teen on a wave board. I could only imagine the caption it would have when it appeared on his blog.

He lowered his camera and eyed my croissant. "Now, that's real healthy."

"Don't start with me." I took a big ole bite, and the butter and jam dripped onto my fingers. I resisted licking them. Barely.

Walt's deep chuckle belied his disapproving words. He raised his camera and snapped another picture, this one of a silver Jag running a red light. "You suck at driving," he pronounced in his gravelly Sam Elliot voice.

"What kind of clue do you have for me?" I was already halfway through the croissant. And okay, I admit it, I was licking my fingers. (I do, however, want to point out to y'all that I had not had any breakfast.)

"The best kind." Walt actually set his camera down and gave me his full attention. I knew just as with Millie, it was limited. "Do you know who Kevin Blackstone was making whoopee with?"

"Making whoopee?"

"Yeah, whoopee or whatever you young folks call it these days. Hanky panky, gettin' busy, doing the horizontal hustle, parking the Plymouth —"

"Oh good golly, Walt. Stop!" My ears

burned with the euphemisms, and I did not want those pictures in my head.

"You're the one who was all curious," Walt pointed out, his craggy face creased in a rascally grin.

"I know." I took a sip of my latte. He had a valid point.

"Your dead guy, Kevin," he paused for effect, "and Ms. Hot Yoga Burn were dancin' in the sheets."

"Mandy Beenerman?" Several heads turned our way. I lowered my voice. "Mandy? Really?"

"Really." Walt nodded so vigorously I thought he might lose the Angels ball cap perched on his salt-and-pepper hair. Walt was a handsome scoundrel at sixty. Bet he'd been a heartbreaker back in his day. It sounded like he'd been a one-woman man, though, and I admired that. There were too few of those.

"I just don't see it, hon. I didn't think they even liked each other."

"Not a requirement for the four-legged frolic."

"Walt, stop it." I held up my hand. "Now you're just trying to torment me. Did you look those phrases up on the Internet?"

Walt chuckled under his breath. "Just tryin' to keep up with the times."

I'd have to check Kevin's book and see if there was anything hinting at something special between him and Mandy Beenerman. "How do you know they were . . . you know."

"I heard it at the grocery store." He grinned. "In the cracker aisle. There were two women talking about Blackstone and one said, 'everyone knows he was having an affair with his neighbor.' Beenermans on one side. Oliver Hembry's on the other. Don't think Blackstone had a thing with old Ollie."

"No, but it could be someone else in Ruby Point, Walt." I took a sip of my latte and tried to remember any references Kevin had made about Mandy. And vice versa. "It doesn't have to mean his next door neighbor."

"The ladies mentioned Mandy by name. I tried to get closer to hear better, but then they stopped talking altogether, and I had to just get my box of Triscuits and go."

"Wow, Walt. Thanks for the tip. I'll check it out." I gathered my cup and dish to drop off inside the coffee shop. "I'm off to the office. You and Millie have a good day."

"Hmmpf. Hey, did you give the police that book yet?"

"I called. Couldn't reach my detective buddy."

"Don't forget about that." Walt picked up his camera again as a huge Lincoln Town Car pulled up and stopped by the curb in what was not a big enough parking space. The large vehicle extended over the yellow lines. "You suck at parking."

"Love you, hon." I patted his arm, slipped Millie one of my special dog treats, and headed back to my car where *I* had parked properly between the lines.

CHAPTER THIRTEEN

Business was truly barking at my door. Paris handed me a stack of messages and I spent at least an hour returning phone calls. There continued to be a lot of calls with misbehaving pets from Ruby Point residents, and I figured those house calls would give me the opportunity to ask about the phantom landscaper. And now about Kevin and Mandy.

One of those calls had been from television star, Sharina "Shar" Summers. Shar had been mentioned in Kevin's book but was one of the entries I'd had no success in figuring out. Since I had some time this afternoon, I decided to work her into my schedule.

Shar's house was the smallest home in Ruby Point, but that's not to say it was any slouch. The sunny yellow two-story boasted wisteria climbing up the trellis on the wrap-around porch, and it had an honest-to-goodness turret.

I'd run into Shar when I'd been out working with other pet parents in the gated community, but I'd never worked with her Chinese Crested, Babycakes. Shar's dog was the Hairless variety and they can be sensitive to cold or sun, so when they were out walking she often had the pooch dressed in a doggie outfit to prevent sunburn. Usually something frilly.

That should have been a hint about Shar's taste.

Gypsy Rose Lee (yep, the "let me entertain you" one) was an ardent breeder of Chinese Cresteds and helped to publicize the breed. Most Crested kennels can trace their dogs' ancestry to one of two lines, the Gyspy Rose Lee line being the most famous. Since I'd started working as a pet therapist, I'd done a lot of research. In addition to the random animal trivia, my head is also filled with pet particulars so I hunted my brain files for what I knew about the breed.

I knew the dogs could be a touch high-strung if not properly socialized, but they're extremely affectionate. Still, Shar had told me on the phone the little dog had become so nervous she couldn't have friends over. If anyone made the slightest move toward Shar, Babycakes nipped.

I knew from experience when pet owners said "nipped," if you talked with the nip recipient, they often reported it felt more like a "bite" to them.

Shar had handled Babycakes's bad behavior by simply not having friends over. According to her phone call, this had been going on for a couple of weeks and she'd decided to take action.

When Shar answered the door, she held Babycakes in her arms. The dog and the girl were cuteness defined. Babycakes was petite and the silky fluffs of fur around her pixie face brought out her fine features. She wore a pink satin polka-dot jumper and a stunning crystal collar. My guess would be Swarovski. Her bright almond eyes looked me over with interest.

The human girl was pretty in pink, too. She was attired in a sundress with pink lace daisies. My guess would be Lily Pulitzer. Atop her blonde curls was a pink paisley baseball cap with the name of her television series, "Bibbidi Bobbidi Boo," embroidered across the front. All the "i"s were also crystals.

They were both in full bling mode.

I suddenly felt underdressed and ancient at thirty-one. Not only underdressed and ancient, but also humongous. Both the dog and the girl were tiny.

"Hi Shar, I'm Caro."

"I'm so glad you could fit me in." Her voice was high and girlishly breathless. "We've got to get this little girlfriend under control. She's been a vawy, vawy, bad puddy dog. Haven't you itty, bitty Babycakes?"

I hoped the baby talk was just a temporary thing. I know I may be in the minority, but I'm not wild about baby talk to animals, no matter how cute they are. But then, come to think of it, I'm not all that crazy about baby talk to babies, no matter how cute they are, either.

Shar escorted me into her living room and I think I probably took a step backward. At least mentally I know I did. I have never in my life seen so many frills, so much lace and so much pink in one room. It felt like I'd accidently stumbled into the princess castle at Disneyland. Or fallen down a rabbit hole.

"Would you like something to drink?" Shar offered. "We're going to have a widdle dwinky, aren't we, Babycakes?"

"Sure, I'll take a wid . . . er, water or whatever you have." I wondered why she didn't just sing out a "bibbidi bobbidi boo" and make it appear.

"I'll be right back." Shar swished out of

the room, her tiny legs power-walking to what I assumed was her kitchen.

I continued to look around in amazement.

I guess decorating a house like this would be a challenge for anyone. I mean look at the help Kevin Blackstone had brought in to assist him in figuring out his manly style. Shar was all of seventeen or eighteen, and had scads of money. She hadn't yet developed to the point of having a style of her own.

So she had ended up with this. I hoped she liked it.

I didn't know a lot about Sharina Summers. I knew she'd been a huge success on a television series about three girls who performed magic. On the show, they were triplets. In real life, they were all her. It seemed to be the hot show to watch with the little girlie-girl crowd, and I'd heard it had been picked up for another season. I believe it was on its third or fourth year but whatever year it was on, the show certainly had afforded little Miss Summers a very grand lifestyle for a teen.

I looked around the room again.

Wow.

The staircase was a lacy white wrought iron. And there were — I kid you not — butterflies and hearts painted on the wall that followed the curve of the stairs.

I took a seat on a white Victorian couch. It looked like a prop. I hoped it was okay to actually sit on it.

Shar was back and handed me a glass of what else, pink lemonade. "I thought you might like some lemonade. It's really, really refreshing."

"Thanks." I took the crystal goblet, hoping she hadn't added any magic potions to the drink. I needed all my wits about me.

Taking a sip, I asked. "How long have you been having a problem with Babycakes?"

Shar plopped down beside me on the couch, folding her tiny tanned legs under her, still holding the little dog who was by now shivering.

"Let's see. I think it was a couple of weeks ago it started." She twirled a blonde curl around one finger as she spoke. "I guess it was mostly this past week. Baby's always been a little timid, but she started getting really frazzled. I mean more than usual. But then, you know, I've been like all frazzled myself with taping the show, and wondering if the network is going to renew, and all the stress."

She finally took a breath and I took the opportunity to interrupt. "You said something on the phone about her nipping at

156

some of your friends?"

"Yes, I had some girls over for a little girls' night get-together. A 'tini party." She looked at me as if she wasn't sure how much to confess.

I knew by 'tini she didn't mean tiny. She meant martinis.

"Alcohol-free martinis, you know." She'd apparently decided I was ancient and an old stuffed-shirt who just might turn her in for underage drinking no matter how famous she was.

I tried to focus on her and the dog, ignoring the swirls of cotton-candy pink surrounding me. It was difficult.

Easing a little closer to her and the Chinese Crested, but not touching either the dog or Shar, I kept my voice low and calm. "It was then you had the problem with Babycakes nipping at people?"

A little rumble had started in the dog's throat and the warning got louder the closer I got. The important thing was to stay very calm and to let Babycakes know the situation was under control. It was often insecurity or an unstable situation that caused dogs to bite . . . er, nip.

The technique I liked to use was not to challenge the dog since that could create more fear, but to let the animal know it was safe and the person was in control. You did that with your voice and your body language. I was about to explain the technique to Shar when she lifted the pooch in front of her face and gave her a little shake.

"Now, listen here, sweetie peetie, that's not a vewy nice way to talk to our guest," she scolded. "You better be a good girl or no sweet potato puppy treats for sweetums."

Shar looked at me for approval, bobbed her pink sparkly head, and plopped the dog down on the couch.

Babycakes promptly ran over and bit me.

Chaos ensued. Shar screamed and ran around, and the dog barked and ran around.

I was afraid I was going to drip blood on the white couch so I jumped up and ran around trying to locate something for my hand. I tried to calm the other two and maintain my sanity.

Of course, it was at that exact moment the doorbell chimed.

I don't know if Shar didn't have house staff or if they were afraid to wade into the chaos, but no one answered the door.

Shar was still running around trying to catch Babycakes. Babycakes was still running around barking. I'd decided to staunch the blood with the hem of my favorite Akris Punto top. I knew I'd regret it later but there was not a rag, tissue, or paper towel in sight, and I figured if I tried to find the kitchen, I'd leave a Hansel and Gretel blood trail behind me.

The doorbell pealed again.

And again.

And again.

Finally, I walked to the door and pulled it open.

On the other side was, of course, Detective Judd Malone.

That's the kind of day I was having.

He looked at the chaos going on, looked down at my bloody hand, and stepped into the entryway. A screaming Shar jumped up and down. A barking Babycakes ran out from behind the princess couch and charged toward the detective.

"Quiet!" Malone ordered and then reached down and picked up the little dog.

Babycakes promptly bit him.

To say the detective and I formed a blood bond might be putting it too strongly, but Malone and I definitely had the most civil conversation we'd ever had as we stood together at Shar Summers' kitchen sink, rinsing our wounds under her fancy gold faucet.

"Make sure you rinse it really well," I

159

cautioned as I reached over and pulled his hand back into the flow of warm water. "You want to be sure it's clean so you don't risk infection."

His raised brow said he was tough and wasn't scared of any silly little infection, but he let me hold his hand under the water and pump another dab of antibacterial soap into the puncture wound.

Holding Malone's hand in mine, I realized that while I'd admired his tough guy looks from afar, I'd never been this close before. Looking up at him, I decided his long dark eyelashes were just as attractive up close as they'd been from across the room. And the five o-clock shadow . . . yeah, scruffy was a good look on him.

"So why —" We spoke in unison.

"You go first." He shook the water from his hand and looked around for a towel.

I spotted one on the kitchen island, retrieved it, and handed it to him. I had no idea where Shar had gone, and I still hadn't seen any staff.

"I was here working with the dog. Shar had been having some issues when she had friends over."

"Let me guess. Biting kinds of issues?" Malone's posture still said bad boy, but I think there was the barest hint of a snicker

160

trying to break through.

"Yeah, biting kinds of issues."

"Still some work to be done," he noted.

No Shih Tzu, Sherlock.

"Yes, more work to be done." I let go of his hand and stepped away looking for another towel. He handed me his.

"You?" His appearance at Shar's door had to have an explanation.

Malone stared at me. I felt the intensity of his gaze like the hot California sun.

There are some men, just like dogs, who can't really be domesticated. They'll still be part wild, and no matter how tame and housebroken they seem, when push comes to shove, they'll revert to their wolf nature.

Detective Judd Malone was one of those breeds.

"I stopped by to talk to Ms. Summers."

"Someone broke into my garden shed out in back." Shar surfaced and was holding Babycakes wrapped up in a pink fluffy blanket. "I don't know when it happened, but my dad said I should turn it in to my insurance company. And when the insurance guy came out, he said I needed a police report."

"And they sent a homicide detective?" Something about that didn't quite add up for me.

161

"Given recent developments, I decided to come by and take a look first. I believe you left me a phone message about some information you have regarding Kevin Blackstone's death?"

I nodded. This was the perfect time to explain about Kevin's notebook and hand it over. Maybe he'd be a little more sympathetic since we'd shared injuries.

"I don't want to hear any more about death!" Shar pulled the fluffy blanket up off the dog and over her head like a pair of giant pink earmuffs. "Kevin was such a sweet man. Wasn't he, Babycakes?" She touched noses with the little dog who was back to shivering.

I couldn't let the misrepresentation go. Shar had an entry in the book. Maybe she had something to hide. "I thought you had a run in with Kevin this week over his dogs."

Shar's head swiveled toward me. "Who told you that?"

"Kevin did. Said you told him if he didn't get his dogs under control, he'd be sorry."

"Oh." Shar held Babycakes against her pink lace daisies. Her small hands patted the delicate head. "His big dogs scared Babycakes. That's all. I told him their barking frightened her."

Malone looked at me as if to say it all

162

seemed reasonable to him.

I took Malone's hand again and looked at the puncture. He resisted a little. "I think the soap and water has cleaned the wound pretty well, but better safe than sorry."

I turned to Shar. If I could get her out of the room, I'd tell Malone about the book. "Do you have any alcohol?"

"Like vodka?"

I guess those 'tinis were vodka martinis.

Malone and I looked at each other, and this time I thought he really was going to crack a smile. His resistance to the humor of the situation was far greater than mine.

I snorted.

"No, like rubbing alcohol to use as an antiseptic on our matching dog bites." I held up my hand.

"Oh, no. I don't have anything like that."

Detective Malone's cell phone buzzed and he stepped outside to take the call. But not before telling me, "Don't go anywhere."

I could see him walking the perimeter of Shar's backyard. He stepped into the shed and then stepped back out. He disappeared around the corner of the house. Then came inside and chatted with Shar for a few minutes in the kitchen. I gathered my belongings and waited for him by the front door. As difficult as it was to reach him, I wasn't going to let this opportunity pass.

Malone walked back into the living room, a stark contrast to all the girly frills, his tall, dark, and dangerous good looks making a swath through the pink. He seemed surprised to see me waiting. Had he forgotten he'd ordered me to?

"Thanks for waiting." He reached past me to open the door, and I could see the puncture from Babycakes was still bleeding a bit.

We walked toward my car. *Okay, deep breath. Best to get it over with.*

I reached into my bag, pulled out Kevin's notebook, and handed it to Malone.

"This is what I called you about."

"What the hell is this?" He stilled.

"It's a book Kevin Blackstone kept with notes on his neighbors and other people he knew. I'm in there. My cousin is in there."

"And you have it, why?" he bit out.

"I accidently took it when I retrieved my grandmother's brooch. And I've been trying to give it to you ever since."

"Apparently not trying very hard." He'd begun to pace. Not a good sign. "I've questioned you how many times since then?"

I didn't think he really wanted an answer so I kept quiet.

"Dammit, Caro, you took evidence from a crime scene."

"It wasn't a crime scene —"

"Stop. Don't even go there. It was a crime scene whether or not the tape was up."

I had no defense. He was right. I shouldn't have gone to Kevin's to get the brooch. I'd been flustered and accidently taken the notebook, and I should have told him about it when he'd questioned me about having been at Kevin's.

"Anything else you've neglected to tell me?" His earlier friendliness was totally gone.

I can't carry a tune to save my life, I hate brussel sprouts, sometimes I snore. I didn't think he meant any of those things.

"No."

Malone turned on his heel, walked to his car, got in, slammed the door, and drove away.

He hadn't given me time to tell him, but I didn't think he'd be happy about the fact I had a copy, and was still intent on figuring out Kevin's notes myself.

CHAPTER FOURTEEN

After I left Shar's I felt like I needed to be hosed down to wash off the cuteness. Seriously to each her own decorating, but someone should have worked with the girl. It wouldn't have hurt to scrub off some of Malone's hostility, either.

My guilt over not telling him about the book sooner didn't allow me to berate him too much for being aggravated. Still, if he threw a hissy fit with every innocent bystander who held back, he wasn't going to get very far in Ruby Point. People have secrets. Secrets they may not want to share. Didn't mean they'd killed anyone. The guy could use a lesson or three on how to encourage cooperation. If Malone treated everyone like he did me, no wonder the police weren't any closer to solving Kevin's murder.

My hand was a little sore but I didn't think it needed to be looked at. If Detective

Judd Malone was tough enough to take it, then, what the heck, so was I.

Why couldn't such a handsome devil have a decent attitude, or at least the decency to stay out of my way?

I continued on to my next house call, which was a new Ruby Point client, a blended family having difficulties. The people family part of the equation had blended very well. The kids had accepted their new siblings just fine, but the two dogs from the individual families were having a problem getting along.

I found the house easily, a bright cottage type, surrounded by flowers and palm trees like the others. The husband was the one who had called me, but I'd asked if it was possible for them both to be at home during our first session. I needed to get a feel for the human dynamics before I could make an assessment of any kind.

The dogs were both Chow Chows, Fidel and Flossie, and it was plain they did not care for each other at all. Like naughty kids, as soon as the dogs greeted me, they began to vie for attention. In a short time they were nosing each other away, shoving their bodies in front of one another, and showing other signs of aggression.

Sumner Garst and his new wife, Ginny,

had met at a "dog and drinks" social event. Both were Chow lovers. It had seemed to be a match made in doggie heaven. But as far as Fidel and Flossie were concerned the honeymoon was over. The key to getting them to get along was going to be co-operation and consistency.

I'd worked with Sumner and Ginny on some simple techniques for their daily walks and the dogs had reluctantly tolerated being together. The family members would have to be firm. Chow Chows are great dogs but they're an independent breed and not very sharing with their possessions. Nor their people.

We were practicing out in front of the house so that the distractions would be the same as they were on their daily walks. We'd just completed a circuit of walking the dogs together when two police cars sped by.

Now two police cars in downtown LA would hardly cause you to drop your latte. Two police cars in downtown Laguna Beach is a big event, and two police cars in the gated community of Ruby Point was down-right bizarro.

I stepped to the end of the driveway to see if I could tell where they were going. Down the street a bit, a man worked on the wine-red bougainvillea spilling out of the stone planters in the middle of the street. It wasn't the same guy Zeus had taken a bite out of the day Kevin was killed. This guy was older and stockier. I'd watched for the original landscaper, but I hadn't seen the guy since that day.

The cruisers had turned the curve so they were definitely headed toward Kevin's. I swung around and nearly plowed into Sumner and Ginny who'd followed me to the end of the driveway.

"Are you ready to try more distance?"

"Of course." I could tell from their expressions they were curious about where the police cars were headed. Fidel and Flossie may have been curious, too, but it was hard to tell under the profusion of fur. The five of us moved in the direction the cars had gone. The dogs were doing great. I'm sometimes surprised at how quickly the techniques make a difference.

Once we rounded the corner, I could see the police weren't at Kevin's. They were parked in Diana Knight's drive. And not only that, there were several officers with shovels digging up her flower beds.

We continued down the walkway, and as we got closer I could see a crowd had gathered. Diana was out front with Barbary, her latest foster dog. He was a basset hound puppy from the ARL. The poor dog had lost his eye, probably in a fight. He was the only ill-tempered basset hound I'd ever met. Most hounds are pretty docile and very loyal, but I suspected Barbary had been abused. The little guy was not likely to be adopted and his days had been numbered, so Diana had taken him in. No big surprise there, huh? He stood like a sentry by her side.

As I moved toward Diana, I noticed Detective Judd Malone standing to one side watching the excavation. Great.

"Detective." I approached him.

"Ms. Lamont." His unsmiling face said he wasn't open to pleasantries.

"What's going on?" I hoped the quiver in my voice wasn't as obvious to him as it was to me.

He stood immobile, feet planted apart, not looking at me. "Following up on a tip."

"A tip about what?"

Malone finally looked my way. His laser blue gaze pinned me. "Lots of curiosity for a pet psychic."

Now that was just a low blow. I could feel my face get hot and I reined in my temper. If I hadn't thought he'd arrest me, I'd have been tempted to bop him upside the head.

"Not a psychic," I corrected, although I

170

knew he knew better. "A *psychologist.*"

Suddenly one of the officers who'd been digging motioned Malone over. He slipped on some gloves, picked up whatever had been unearthed, and dropped it in a paper bag. He said something I couldn't hear. All the others stopped and began to pack their gear.

In a very short time, the police cars were gone and the crowd dispersed, Detective Malone along with them.

I let Sumner and Ginny know I'd catch up with them later and approached Diana who stood on her front steps, holding what must have been a search warrant and shaking her head.

She motioned me inside and we made our way through the assorted pets to her kitchen. Diana picked up Mr. Wiggles, tucked him in the crook of her arm, and poured us each a glass of sweet tea.

"What do you think it was they dug out of your flower beds?" I pulled out a chair and sat, still baffled at the swarm of police who'd swooped in, excavated Diana's landscaping, and then, apparently having found what they were looking for, left without a word. They didn't even clean up after themselves.

"I don't know what it was, but the City Council will be getting a bill from me to

replace my American Beauty rose bush."
She set the glasses on the table and joined
me. "I've been trying for three years to get
that thing to grow and now it's gone. *Pffft!*
Just like that." She flicked her hand.

Diana seemed more concerned about her
roses than the anonymous phone call that
had sent the police to dig up her flower
beds.

"I'm sure it will end up the tip was nothing more than a hoax," I reassured her.
"They can't really think you had anything
to do with Kevin's death."

"Well, they surely can't think it was me
anyway, because I told them I was with you
at the time."

"You what?"

Holy crappola.

In clearing myself by providing the Whole
Foods receipt to Detective Malone, I'd
proved I wasn't in Ruby Point at the time
of the murder.

I'd also unknowingly blown Diana's alibi.

"Diana, hon, we weren't together." I
couldn't believe she'd outright lied to the
police.

"I know." She continued to absent-
mindedly pat Mr. Wiggles.

"Here's the problem, sugar. Detective
Malone came asking about exactly where

172

I'd been because I was supposedly the last one to see Kevin alive and I provided him with my receipt from the grocery store as proof."

"Proof of what?"

"Of where I was and at what time."

"Guess that blows my alibi then, huh?" She didn't seem terribly upset by the revelation.

"It does." I hoped she realized Malone was not going to take kindly to her playing loose with the truth. "Why would you lie about where you were, Di?"

"None of their business where I was." She set Mr. Wiggles on the floor, gave him a final pat, and began picking up the kitchen.

She was right. None of their business. I couldn't argue with the concept. "It will look bad that you lied, hon," I said gently. "You want to talk about it?"

"Can't say that I do." Diana slid another dish in the dishwasher. "Thanks for your concern, though."

Okay, fair enough. She didn't want to discuss where she'd been. I was sure she had good reason not to share her whereabouts with the police. I hoped she knew what she was doing, because there was a killer on the loose.

CHAPTER FIFTEEN

They had arrested Diana. Melinda called me. Mel and her friend Darby had heard it at the Koffee Klatch. It was understood that we still weren't speaking, but bless her heart, she didn't want me to hear it on the news.

I couldn't understand why Diana hadn't called me herself.

She knew I would call her attorney or bring her lipstick, or whatever a best friend was supposed to do in these circumstances.

I had one appointment scheduled for this morning but it was Fluffy, who I could easily reschedule. Mona Michaels would be offended but then Mona was always offended. This would just give her an actual focus.

I looked up the number for the Laguna Beach Police Department and dialed. The woman who answered the phone was matter-of-fact but not terribly helpful. Apparently, Diana was being "processed."

I wasn't sure what that meant, but it couldn't be good. It sounded kind of like something you did to meat to turn it into sausage. I was pretty sure real life was nothing like the crime shows on TV, but if they were close at all it probably had something to do with determining her bail.

I just didn't know. But I knew somebody who would know. I fished Detective Judd Malone's card out of my bag.

I dialed the number but got voicemail. Again. He was probably screening my calls. I decided time was a-wasting while I was trying to figure things out, and I'd just go to the police station.

It was in a row of brick buildings not far from my office. City Hall, Police Station, Fire Station, conveniently located next to each other all in a row. They weren't huge buildings, but then, as a rule, Laguna Beach had a very small amount of crime. As a rule.

There was an information desk visible from the lobby and I approached it. The two uniformed ladies seated there glanced up. One looked like Arnold Schwarzenegger with boobs and the other a bit like Gidget. With a gun.

"Can you tell me where Diana Knight has been taken and if I can see her?" I asked.

"She's being processed." The expression

on Gidget's face told me she knew I'd been the caller she'd talked to a few minutes ago.

"What exactly does that mean?"

They glanced at each other and, I don't know if they both rolled their eyes, but it sure as shootin' looked like it from my angle.

"It means they're processin' her." The female body-builder stood to full height and I had to look up a bit, but I'm not easily intimidated.

"Well, that's just it, isn't it, hon? I've not had the opportunity to be a guest of your fine facility and so I don't know what that means." I smiled brightly.

Gidget and Arnold did not.

We were at a standoff, but tenacious is my middle name.

"Is Diana here?"

"Yes." Arnold set her mouth. Missy, Mel's bulldog, had a similar underbite, but the bulldog had a pleasanter temperament.

"When she's 'processed' she'll have her bail set, right? How long does that usually take?" I tried to hang on to my temper.

"We don't usually process murder raps here. They're usually referred to Orange County," Gidget said over her shoulder.

Yeah, right. Murder raps, usually. This was Laguna Beach. We had drunk drivers and disturbing the peace. Perhaps public intox

176

and the occasional break-in. I'd been in town for more than four years and hadn't heard of even one murder.

Until Kevin.

And there was about to be another one if they didn't tell me soon where Diana was.

I heard the door open behind me, but didn't turn to look. I didn't want to break eye contact and give the uncooperative clerks a chance to walk away from me.

Finally the noise behind me got so loud I had to look over my shoulder.

What the heck?

There were at least thirty reporters and photographers crowded into the small lobby. They were intermittently checking their cameras, shouting out questions, and elbowing each other.

I moved aside to let Arnold and Gidget deal with them. While the two were busy with the swarm, I slipped down a hallway beside the desk.

As I made my way deeper into the department, the noise subsided. I didn't know how to get to the jail part of the building and wasn't sure if I was even heading in the right direction, but clearly I wasn't going to get any assistance from those two. I figured if anyone stopped me I'd claim I was there for my Detective-Malone-ordered fingerprinting.

I came to another hall where uniformed officers moved along with purpose, but I'd learned my lesson about asking questions. I kept going. Further down was a door with a sign above it that said *Chief of Police.*

That was it. I'd get some answers there or I'd . . . I'd . . . well, tarnation, I didn't know exactly what I'd do, but I'd do something.

As I started toward the office, I noted an open doorway on my left.

Diana sat in the room with a desk and two chairs. I didn't think I'd ever seen her sit so still. This was a lady who was always in motion.

My heart plunged to the tips of my toes.

I loved Diana like she was my own grandmother. Granted she was nothing like my no-nonsense Grandma Tillie had been. While Grandma Tillie had enjoyed the fruits of a successful life there was no fluff to her at all. Diana had lived the Hollywood life with glamorous parties, handsome leading men and all kinds of glitz.

Grandma Tillie would've called it nonsense.

Even arrested, Diana was perky in pink, her silver hair styled. Diamonds flashed on her folded manicured hands.

Grandma Tillie would've called it showy.

Still, in some essential ways the two would have had a lot in common. They would have gotten each other. On the surface they were both tough cookies, but at their core, where it concerned the things they believed in, they were all heart.

There didn't seem to be anyone paying attention so I slipped inside the room.

"Oh, my gosh, Diana, I got here as soon as I could," I said. "The lobby is full of reporters."

"How many are there?"

"I don't know, probably twenty or so." It seemed to me the number of the varmints was irrelevant.

"Any big news people? Anderson Cooper? He's awfully cute." She sighed and smoothed the leg of her white chinos.

"I couldn't tell. I didn't recognize anyone." I moved forward and gave her a hug. "Are you doing alright? Mel said they'd arrested you. Have they actually charged you?"

"Mostly I've just been sitting here waiting."

"I can't imagine how all those reporters found out so quickly." I sat across from Diana in the hard grey chair, hoping I was out of view of the doorway.

"I know how, Caro dear." Diana smiled a

conspiratorial smile. "I called them."

"You what?" I nearly fell off my chair.

"You know what they say. There's no such thing as bad press."

I had to say from experience that I heartily disagreed with that adage, but suddenly the lobby full of reporters made sense.

"Don't worry, as soon as they set bail, we'll get you out of here." I reached across the desk and patted her hand.

She took my hand in hers. "Caro, honey, I'm not going anywhere."

"What?"

"I figure we can get a little extra media attention for the Fur Ball. Good idea, yes?"

Good idea, no.

What would be a good idea was for Diana to explain where she'd been instead of with me. It would be a good idea for the police to do whatever they needed to do in order to get her "processed" and released.

It would be a good idea for me to find Malone.

CHAPTER SIXTEEN

The next day Diana's arrest was the headline story in the *Los Angeles Times,* got a mention on CNN, and was the lead story on "Inside Scoop" the television version of tabloid reporting.

America's Sweetheart Charged in Homicide
Hollywood's Girl-Next-Door Arrested in Death of Next-Door-Neighbor
Silver Screen Star in the Slammer

And then because they couldn't resist: *Don't Tase Me, Di!*

Those were the main headlines. Along with some full-color pictures of Diana from the past and the present. Then below the fold was a replica of the Fur Ball poster — date, time, and other details were even legible. Maybe Diana's idea for free media exposure had worked.

The only problem was this wasn't a publicity stunt, at least not to the arresting officers. They were about to book her with real murder and she was locked up in a real jail cell.

Diana wouldn't let me get her out, but I could work on getting some answers. If I could point the police in the direction of the real killer they'd have to let Diana go.

First things first. I called Malone. I wanted see if he'd found out anything about the landscape guy and if he was questioning those who were mentioned in Kevin's notebook.

Dang. I got his voicemail. I left a message at the beep, though I didn't think he was going to hurry up and call me back.

I didn't have any appointments scheduled for that morning so I decided it was back to Ollie's. I had questions about what he'd seen, as well as the missing page in the book.

I could take his basket back to him. Maybe he had some more of those cookies on hand. My mouth watered at the thought.

In fact, speaking of cookies, I could return the favor. In a way.

I had a recipe I used for dog cookies. It was a healthy way to provide a treat when I was working with canines who needed encouragement. I called them — PAWS Good Dog Cookies.

Ollie had plenty of dogs to treat, so I'd

bet he'd appreciate some for his furry friends. I packed a dozen or so in a box, set them in the basket, and loaded it into my car.

The day was overcast and damp. The forecast predicted a drizzle all day so we'd get a good soaking. Thankfully not the torrents we'd had with the storms last year that had caused so many mudslides.

The security guard at the gate peered out to see who it was, but then recognized me and waved me in. I parked in the drive this time and rang the doorbell. It pealed out "God Save the Queen."

"Hello there, lovely lady. What brings you back to my lair?"

I think he was trying hard to carry off the Mr. Dangerous routine but now that I had a picture of him as a cookie-baker in my head, the bad-boy persona was ruined.

"I wanted to thank you for the cookies and the return of the items I dropped." I paused. "I also wanted to ask some questions."

"I thought you might, luv." Ollie wiped his face with one beringed hand. "I thought you might. Come on in, then."

He held open the door and motioned me inside.

The living room was as I remembered,

opulent with rich dark colors and heavy antique furniture. Ollie appeared to be dressed in either the same clothes as the last time I'd seen him, or an exact replica.

His eyes were covered by sunglasses and his long black hair was loose today, not in a ponytail. I now recognized the quintessential signature look. Old Eighties rocker.

"Thanks for seeing me." I carried the basket of dog cookies in and placed it on his heavy Baroque-style coffee table.

Elvis galloped to meet me.

"Hi there, fella." I sat down and stroked his pitch-black fur. Diana was right. The animals were well cared for. Elvis' coat was healthy and silky, as if it had recently been brushed. "You are one handsome fella."

"Thanks, duck." Ollie snickered at his own joke. "I've been told such, but not lately."

"You heard they arrested Diana?"

"No, luv, I'd not heard."

"Yesterday afternoon." My voice shook a little. "She's still in jail."

"Bollocks." The guy paced and turned in circles, muttering to himself. I wondered about his stability.

"Are you okay?"

"Yeah, yeah. I'm okay. I'm just utterly gobsmacked, luv."

I very much appreciated the word. Gob-smacked. I was feeling gobsmacked myself.

"I'm trying to help her but she won't let me post bail."

"Stubborn old girl, she is." He dropped into the nearest chair and then no sooner had his bum hit the seat than he stood again and resumed pacing and circling. "Bollocks."

"Ollie, can we talk about the day Kevin was killed?"

"Alright then, what do you want to know?" Ollie sat and Elvis parked himself right up against his master's legs as if sensing his agitation.

"Did you see anything? Anything at all? This is very important."

"Alright."

"There was a landscaping worker that Kevin and I talked to. Did you happen to see him?"

Probably not, but it was worth asking.

"No, duck, I was having me a kip in front of the telly."

I must have looked confused.

"A sleep. A nap, luv," he explained.

"Ah."

"I woke up and I was out back having a look about. Takin' some fresh air."

"About what time was that?" I asked him.

"No idea." He shrugged. "I saw you come. So . . . before. No, it was after you'd gone. You know it's all a blur to me, luv." He shook his head as if to clear the cobwebs.

"Take your time."

"The yoga lady goes there most every day, and she was there after you left."

"Mandy?" It was a good thing I was sitting down.

"Yeah, yeah, the workout wench."

"You're sure?" One of the other dogs was awake now and came to check me out. She was well-groomed Sheltie and I slipped her a treat.

"Absolutely sure." He absently stroked Elvis' head. "Mostly I notice because whenever she goes there, Blackstone puts his dogs out back. Doesn't do that with any other visitors. But always when the workout woman is there."

"He shut his dogs outside this time when she was there?"

"Hmmm." He seemed to be in deep thought. "I did yoga once. Kind of liked it. Do ya think I should try it again? Don't know I'd want to work with her though. Not a very calm sense about that one."

"Ollie, did you tell the police you'd seen Mandy at Kevin's house?"

"They didn't ask. The coppers and I aren't

on very good terms," he mumbled.

I suddenly noticed Ollie was snacking on the dog cookies.

"Those are —" I started to explain they were for the dogs but then there wasn't much in them other than shortening, corn-meal, cheese and flavorings. Nothing that would hurt a human. I left it alone.

"What about the next day?" I sat back. "The day after Kevin was killed. The day we met."

"You." He tapped his foot. "Just you. That's all, luv."

"Not someone after I left?" I wondered if he'd noticed the police car.

"Oh, the yoga lady took the yellow tape down the police had put up."

Well, that explained why no crime scene tape. Mandy'd probably thought it was an eyesore. "Anyone else?"

"No, 'fraid not. These are good." He held up a cookie, took a bite, and then picked up another and offered it to Elvis.

Okay, so the guy was a little off kilter. Ollie might not be a very reliable witness, but I believed him when he said he'd seen Mandy after I'd left.

Mandy, who had claimed to not know Kevin very well at all. According to Ollie she was a regular visitor at Kevin's, which matched completely with the rumor Walt had heard about Mandy and Kevin.

I had one more topic to cover before I left. "Ollie, the little book."

"Yeah." He moved around the room, passing out cookies to the rest of the dogs.

"Did you look through it?"

"Yeah." He continued his cookie distribution without looking up.

"So you saw the entry about yourself?"

"Right." He'd served everyone and dropped into the chair next to me. "And you and your cousin."

"I assume the notes about you made sense to you, just as the ones about my cousin and me were pretty easy for me to decipher."

He nodded.

"Any insight on the others?" I figured having lived in the community for much longer than I had, he probably had more background on some of the people mentioned.

"Not so much. Gossipy, tabloid-like stuff that."

"I agree. But do you think there might be anything in Kevin's notes that could've been worth killing to keep secret?"

"Dunno. That's why I thought you should have it."

"Thanks for your trust, but I've given it to the police. Maybe it will get them to look for the real killer. I hope it will."

"Your call, luv." He didn't seem at all worried about the idea the notes on him would become police evidence.

"One more thing." I had to ask. "There was a page missing.'

He stilled. "Right."

"Any idea whose name was on the missing page?"

"No idea." He looked me straight in the eye.

"Right." I got the message. Leave it alone. But I couldn't leave it alone. "Whose page was it, Ollie?"

He looked at the floor, rubbed his neck and raised his gaze to mine.

All at once, I realized who'd been missing from the Ruby Point residents listed in the book. "It was Diana, wasn't it?"

He nodded.

Oh, man. If I'd figured out Diana's entry was missing, I was pretty darn sure Malone had figured it out, too.

The big galoot had tried to help and only made things worse for Diana.

When I left, I promised to come by again and bring some more of the dog cookies. I'd leave Detective Malone another message, then I would pay Ms. Beenerman a visit.

I might lose a client out of the deal but I didn't give a rip. Truth was, I did the pet therapy gig not because I cared about the business, but because I cared about the animals. And I cared about Diana. I couldn't let her be accused of a crime I knew she hadn't committed.

CHAPTER SEVENTEEN

I didn't know who killed Kevin, but I did
know too many people were keeping secrets,
and those secrets could be preventing the
police from finding the real killer. Those
secrets were keeping Diana in jail.

I checked my phone. Still no message
from Detective Malone. I wished he'd call
me back, and I debated running down to
the Police Department to talk to him. But I
figured I had time before my next appointment to see Mandy or try to find Malone. I
opted for Mandy.

Mandy's Place was in what passes for
downtown in Laguna Beach. The two-story
structure had shops on the bottom floor and
then the bright airy yoga studio on the top
level.

Whether you were a male or female, the
first thing you noticed about Mandy Beenerman was her boo— ah . . . body. Probably
you noticed for different reasons depending

on your gender, but you'd have to say the woman had maximized her assets.

Her blonde-streaked hair was pulled back in a ponytail and her hot-pink workout spandex hugged curves perfected by her signature Mandy's Hot Yoga Burn. And her plastic surgeon.

I was happy to note she and I were alone in the studio.

"Hi, Caro," Mandy chirped. She had on her business face and her tone was neutral. But, like a dog who isn't sure what you're doing on her turf, I could sense the wariness in her stance.

"Hey, Mandy." Though considered slim and fit in most circles, I suddenly felt awkward and huge. Mandy had that effect on most of us. It was a Barbie doll ideal, impossible to achieve, but that was what kept customers coming back.

"I stopped by because I have a few questions about your relationship with Kevin Blackstone."

"Relationship?" she squeaked. "Kevin and I didn't have a relationship."

"That's not what I hear."

"Well, then, you have a hearing problem."

Interesting. We'd gone from cheerful business tenor to I'm-going-to-yank-your-hair-out-mean-girl pitch in a matter of seconds.

192

"You know I'm not the enemy, sugar." I kept my voice even and my stance open. I should have had this conversation in a more relaxed setting, but I hadn't realized she'd nip at me right away. "I don't believe you killed Kevin. I think you cared for him a lot but I'm afraid the police wouldn't see it that way if they knew you were at Kevin's right before he died."

"How would they know?"

Bingo. She hadn't said she wasn't there.

"Well, for instance, if someone saw you go into Kevin's house." I watched her closely for a reaction. She hadn't moved but she looked ready to bolt.

"No one saw me."

"Really? You're sure about that?"

"I wasn't there." She said it with a great deal of firmness, but she'd developed a tick in her right eye.

"You were there right after I left."

"Hypothetically, if I had been at Kevin's that wouldn't prove anything."

"Drop the act, Mandy. There's nothing hypothetical about Kevin's murder. He's really and truly dead."

"Oh, my God." Her face suddenly crumbled. "I know he is."

I abruptly felt bad for making her freak out, but then wondered at my own sanity if

193

it was misplaced sympathy for a murderer.

"So, why'd you do it, Mandy?"

"I didn't, Caro, you've got to believe me."
Now huge tears streamed down Mandy's
perfectly tanned face. "I liked Kevin. I
really, really liked the guy."

"Yeah, that's what I've heard."

Her turquoise orbs widened, she blinked
and the tears suddenly stopped. "What've
you heard?"

"Just that you and Kevin were a lot friendlier than most people thought."

"You think Kevin and I were having an
affair?" she asked.

"That's what I've been told."

"You can't tell anyone that, Caro. If you
do, I'll be ruined."

I didn't really think she would. I'm sure it
would come as no surprise to y'all, but
infidelity is not unheard of in southern
California. And if being faithful to one's
spouse was a criteria for doing business
there were going to be several empty store-
fronts.

"Here's the deal. I was at Kevin's right
after you were there, but he was fine when I
left him. Perfectly fine."

"Mandy, I'm going to have to tell the
homicide detective."

"Can you at least give me some time? I

need to talk to Andy."

I hesitated. It seemed fair enough that she should have the opportunity to tell her husband if she was owning up to being at Kevin's and to the affair. I sure wished my unfaithful spouse had had the cajones to tell me to my face.

Instead I'd had to learn the truth from a process server who'd slapped a paper in my hand, a paper notifying me of charges being filed against the therapy practice because the client Geoffrey had been sleeping with had decided to take legal action when her pro-quarterback husband had discovered the two of them together.

I refocused on Mandy. She stood staring at me. My trip down marital memory lane must have been longer than I thought.

"You've got one day. One day, and then I'm talking to the homicide detective in charge of the case."

I hoped I was doing the right thing. Phrases like "withholding evidence" and "obstruction of justice" kept flitting through my mind.

"Thanks, Caro."

I turned on my heel and walked out of the studio. I hoped Mandy held up her part of the bargain. I didn't look forward to having to play the tattle-tale role, but I would if she didn't come clean.

CHAPTER EIGHTEEN

I stopped by to check in on Diana, and then went by her house to assist Bella with the pet menagerie. Bella could take care of the feeding and watering, but getting them all the necessary exercise was more than one woman could handle. Especially one very nice lady who was also keeping the household in order and fielding calls from reporters.

"*Hola,* Caro." She appeared a bit harried when she answered the door.

"Hi, Bella." I gave her a hug. "How are you holding up?"

"No so bad." She picked up Mr. Wiggles who had followed her to the door and motioned for me to come in. "I wish Missus Diana would come home. It's no good for her to be in that place."

"I know. I've done my best. We've all done our best to try to get her out. But she's having none of it. She's staying put." I stepped inside.

"I know you have tried." She sighed.

"How are the kids doing?" I indicated the collection of pets who had followed Mr. Wiggles.

"They are well, but a little *agitado,* um, stir crazy, you know."

"I think I can help with the stir crazy problem." I could tell she was overwhelmed.

The dogs were used to frequent walks and romps at the dog park. I believed it was part of what kept Diana so fit. Her animals were never neglected in the exercise department.

"If you wouldn't mind getting me their leashes, I'll take Barbary and Mr. Wiggles for a walk. I refuse to walk the goat, but I think he's probably okay."

Bella shook her head and walked off. I knew the head shake didn't mean she was opposed to my walking the pair; it was a comment on the craziness of the Diana Knight household ruled by pets.

She returned with the leashes, and I hooked up the two pooches.

"Come on, Barbary." The basset hound's temperament had improved in his time with Diana, but he still eyed the little puggle as if he hadn't made a final decision on whether Mr. Wiggles was friend or foe.

Once I had them ready to go, I grabbed

some "mutt mitts" from the container Diana kept in the entryway. Ruby Point, as well as the rest of the community, was pretty serious about doggie clean-up.

We walked the length of the driveway with a few stops to sniff and mark. The territory must have seemed familiar because Barbary and Mr. Wiggles were soon ready to move on. Turning right onto the sidewalk, we headed west toward Ollie's and Kevin's end of the street.

Just past Kevin's I could see a guy working on the planter where Kevin and I had talked to the gardener on the day he was killed. My heart stopped in its tracks, and I must have also stopped because the two dogs were looking at me like, "what are we doing?"

Could it be the same guy? He was the right height and build.

I slowly walked toward him, a little afraid that he would bolt if he recognized me. He had to know that he also was one of the last people to see Kevin Blackstone alive, and though I'd told Detective Malone about him, he had never come forward.

"Sir?" The dogs and I were closer now, and I could see he was replacing the flowering plants in the planter. He didn't look up.

"Hello." I tried again louder and this time

got his attention.

"Miss?" He jerked his head up in surprise. Apparently he'd been deep in thought.

It wasn't the same guy.

Darn.

Same size, same build, even the same approximate age, but with a pleasant face, friendly and open, unlike the surly character Kevin and I had encountered.

Still, maybe he could help me find the mystery gardener.

"Hi, I'm Caro Lamont." I held out my hand wishing I had a business card with me. "I'm a pet therapist, and I had an incident here about a week ago with dogs belonging to one of my clients."

"Okay." He nodded but I got the what-does-this-have-to-do-with-me point.

"One of the dogs actually nipped a horti-culturist who was working right here." I indicated the planter.

"Not these dogs?" He reached down to pet Barbary, and the temperamental basset hound who tolerated few people actually inched closer.

This guy, unlike the surly one, clearly was a dog person.

"No, not these guys. It was a German Shepherd dog. He's usually pretty friendly, but this man swung a shovel at the dogs and

Tommy Boy just reacted."

"Idiot. The guy, I mean."

My sentiments exactly.

"What's your name?"

"Jake."

Jake and I were of the same mind about the other man's lack of sense.

"Jake, are you employed by Ruby Point or another company who provides the horticulture services?"

"Oh, we work for Green House. They handle quite a bit of the landscaping in the gated communities around here."

"Do you know the other workers pretty well? If I described the guy do you think you might be able to help me identify him?"

"Sorry, no, I just started three weeks ago. I've been in training for two weeks, and then this is my first week on the job. I know hardly anybody."

Man. I knew it had been a long shot, but I'd hoped there was a chance he could put me in contact with the man who Kevin and I had talked to. That man had to have seen something. He'd been working within view of Kevin's house.

"Sorry," Jake said again.

I must have looked as crestfallen as I felt. "It's okay."

"You could talk to our supervisor, Leland.

He's been on the job for years, and he's the one that gives us assignments. He might remember who was assigned to this area. You know, if you can give him a date and time."

I could for sure give him a date and time. "That would be wonderful. How do I get in touch with him?"

He gave me the contact information, and I headed back down the walkway with the dogs. I had two suspects to present to Malone. If he'd listen. One was Mandy, a very strong yoga instructor who didn't want her affair with Kevin exposed. And the other was a landscaper who may have been upset with Kevin over a dog bite.

Both were a little weak, but I thought each one had potential. Either made more sense than thinking a silver-haired, former Hollywood starlet had tased Kevin.

CHAPTER NINETEEN

I called Green House first thing the next morning and left a message for Leland. They said he was out in the field and they would have him call me back.

Next I picked up Kevin's dogs at the ARL for our dog park outing. Zeus and Tommy Boy were happy to spend some outside time, and I was happy to see they were doing so well.

It looked to be a blue-sky morning so I'd packed on the sunscreen and plopped a hat on my head. There's a little shade at the Laguna Beach Dog Park, but not much, and I liked to play with the dogs anyway. Sitting under a tree wasn't the idea.

Zeus and Tommy Boy knew where we were, but were too well-behaved to attempt a bolt. We went down the walkway and across the bridge, and through the first gate. I carefully closed it before opening the second gate. Once through, I grabbed a couple of doggie doo bags, entered the big dog area and then turned the guys loose to run. They took off toward the furthest corner of the park and then circled back.

I stood waiting for them to return, already glad for the hat. They raced like two human brothers in a foot race on the playground, first one in the lead and then the other.

The hills rose in front of me creating a barrier on the one side. The other sides were blocked by high chain link fences. It was the perfect spot for a dog park, outside the main part of the city, with a big grassy area and lots of room to run. The place closed once a week for maintenance, and it showed.

"Hello, Caro, isn't it?"

It was the guy I'd run into on the beach. Well, I guess technically he (or rather his dog) had run into me.

What was his name? Mac.

No, wait, that'd been the dog's name.

Sam. That was it.

Sam . . . something Greek or Italian sounding. Gallanos. My brain finally retrieved his last name. Probably Greek, I guessed. Today he was in jeans and a white cotton piqué Ralph Lauren polo. The white showed to advantage against his dark skin. He looked good.

Mac raced to join Zeus and Tommy Boy's

playground fun. He looked good too.

"Yours?" Sam indicated the two Shepherds. "Where's your other guy?"

"He's at home."

"Ah, stepping out on him are you?"

"These are Kevin Blackstone's dogs. They're being kept at the shelter, and I brought them to give them some exercise."

"Oh, Kevin Blackstone. That's the guy who was killed, right?"

"Yes, they're holding his dogs until they hear from his family."

"Strange business that."

We talked a little bit more, and then he called to the Collie. Mac was well-behaved at the dog park. It was apparently just the beach where he got over-excited.

I knelt to scratch Mac's handsome head, and gave him a hug. I was definitely smitten. With the Collie, of course. His intelligent brown eyes met mine in understanding, and in a moment all was right with the world. He leaned into me and nuzzled my arm for another hug. We were buds. I complied, and he lifted his head to thank me. I gave him a final squeeze, and reluctantly got to my feet.

Zeus and Tommy Boy joined us. They were two happy dogs, their tongues hanging out, and their tails wagging. I took them to the dog fountain for a quick drink of water before we headed out of the park.

"Nice to see you again," I called to Mac and Sam.

As I got the dogs settled back in the car, my cell phone rang and I pushed the button to answer.

"Ms. Lamont?"

The voice was vaguely familiar. "Yes?"

"It's J.T., Kevin's brother. I wondered if you'd consider having lunch with me. I'd like to talk about Kevin."

Heck, it wasn't like I was booked, and I could certainly spare an hour or two for a grieving family member. It had to be difficult no matter the circumstances. If anything, it was even worse when it was so sudden and senseless.

Besides, J.T. must know things about Kevin the rest of us didn't. Maybe there were insights he could give that would help me figure out who had killed Kevin. So I accepted and we agreed to meet in about an hour. He asked me to pick a restaurant and I suggested Mozambique, one of my favorites.

I dropped Zeus and Tommy Boy off at the ARL and had a quick chat with Don about the dogs. On my way home, I tried Detective Malone again. I still hadn't heard back from him, and I not only wanted to try out my two theories on him, now I also wanted to see if I could find out what he knew about Kevin's brother. I left *another* message.

Mozambique was already busy when I got there. I stopped just inside the entry to let my eyes adjust and to enjoy the delicious smells. I hadn't thought I was hungry, but the blend of grilling and exotic spices had my tummy rumbling.

I'd changed because my clothes were muddy from my time at the dog park. I wore black jeans with a bright red tunic I'd bought at the Farmer's Market a couple of Saturdays ago. It probably clashed with my hair, but I didn't care. I loved the unique design and the comfort of the fit.

Zeus and Tommy Boy were doing well, all things considered, but according to Don they couldn't stay at the shelter for much longer. I hoped Kevin's brother was willing to take them or, if not, that he'd be willing to release them to a German Shepherd rescue project.

Actually I was rooting for J.T. because I'd hoped the dogs could stay together. The likelihood of the rescue group being able to do that would be slim. It wasn't impossible, but it made placing them more difficult.

I gave my name and the hostess escorted me to a table in the back dining area. Kevin's brother didn't look at all like him. Where Kevin had been tall and bulky, J.T. was short and geeky. Kevin had always reminded me of a football linebacker. His brother seemed more of a debate team sort of guy. It wasn't unheard of for brothers to be radically different, but I couldn't see a single bit of Kevin in J.T. Just first impressions mind you, but I find that often gives you an insight you don't get if you think too much about it.

After J.T.'s phone call the other day, I'd wondered how he'd known to contact me. I knew how he'd gotten my number. He'd called the PAWS number to reach me. That number was prominently displayed on the door, on my flyers, and on my website. Or all he had to do was ask around.

But how had he known I was the last person to see Kevin? Or at least the last one the police knew about. If I could get Detective Malone to call me back I would correct that error.

As for why J.T. wanted to talk to me — well, that just wasn't clear.

As I approached the table, J.T. rose and held out his hand, "Carolina Lamont?"

"Caro, please." I shook his hand, again struck by the disparity between the two brothers. Kevin's hands had been big and meaty. J.T.'s were small and smooth.

Maybe Kevin and J.T. had different fathers. My brother and I didn't look much alike either, and that was the case with us. We both had Mama Kat's heart-shaped birthmark on our backsides, though. That was a family trait we didn't generally share in public. So unless I mooned you, you'd never know.

"And you must be Kevin's brother." I moved to sit down. "Please accept my condolences."

He waited until I was seated. "I'm guessing Kevin never talked about me?"

"No, I'm sorry, he didn't." I wasn't going to pretend otherwise.

"That's understandable. We'd kind of gone our separate ways the past few years."

"Where are you from?" I sipped from the glass of water the waiter had placed in front of me.

"San Francisco." He signaled the waiter. "What would you like to drink?"

I ordered an iced tea. The dining room was packed but the hostess had placed us in a quiet corner so it was a little easier to converse.

He picked up the menu. "What's good here?"

I'm a Texas girl through and through and so normally a nice grilled steak is right up my alley, but not at Mozambique. I didn't need to look at the menu. As always, I'd come for the Peri-Peri prawns and sweet potato fries.

Across the room, I spotted Sam.

Man, seemed he was everywhere I was lately.

He'd cleaned up too, and was with a big group of people, all of whom looked like they'd just stepped from the pages of *Town and Country*. He smiled and waved.

I waved back, and then turned my attention back to J.T. and the server who was waiting to take our order. When the server left, I focused my attention on Kevin's brother.

"How are you doing? Do you have other family in the area?"

"I'm doing alright." His eyes roamed the room. It was a little rude, but I could understand why. Mozambique is beautiful with its elegant African décor. "I've only been to Kevin's house once since I got here. I believe the police will be done with the property tomorrow. Then I'll be able to go in and begin sorting through Kevin's belongings."

"That must be hard."

"Yes." He sipped his wine. "The reason I wanted to talk with you was two-fold. I understand you may have been the last person to see Kevin alive."

"Well, except for whoever killed him," I reminded him.

He looked a little shocked at my frankness.

"I'm sorry to be so blunt, but that's the truth. Someone was there after I left. Someone who either meant to kill your brother, or at the very least scare him. And it wasn't Diana Knight. The police should be looking for whoever that was," I added for good measure.

"Uh-huh." Kevin's brother watched my face intently almost like he was reading my lips.

The server arrived with our food and J.T. leaned back to allow her to place the plates on the table. He waited until she'd gone and then cut into his lamb and took a bite.

"Ms. Lamont. Uh, Caro. This may be uncomfortable for you, but I was wondering if you could fill me in on the details of why you were at Kevin's and what happened."

The Peri-Peri prawns were as tasty as ever.

As we ate, I told him about the dogs and my house call to Kevin's. I tried to include as many details about Kevin as I could recall. I detailed the time I was there, what we'd done, and the confrontational interaction with the horticulture worker.

"You know, J.T., I think he may have some information about Kevin's death. Perhaps he may even be involved, but I don't want to jump to any conclusions. If we could locate him at least the police would have a chance to talk to him about what he may have noticed."

"I see."

I waited for him to ask about the dogs but he didn't. I guessed his lack of interest might mean he wasn't much of a dog person.

"I wondered about Kevin's dogs. Were you planning on taking them?"

"I hadn't really thought about it."

"Do you have pets?" I was of the opinion even if you weren't a pet person you could always be converted. Kevin had taken to pet ownership like a fish to the ocean.

"No, I don't. I travel a lot."

Okay, there was not a trace of wistfulness in his tone. Could be J.T. wasn't a candidate for conversion to responsible pet owner. Absentee pet parents are not a good thing.

I sighed. I'd really been hoping for an easy transition for Zeus and Tommy Boy.

Kevin's brother leaned forward in his chair. "Another thing, at any time did Kevin give you anything to keep for him?"

Uh-oh. Like a little black book? That he didn't exactly give me. And that I didn't think should be in anyone's hands for fear of the information it contained being used to hurt people. Just exactly why would J.T. want that book? Shoot. It didn't seem likely it would be for a good reason, which made me glad I'd given it to the police. I could answer honestly without giving anything away, so I did.

"No."

"Maybe something he just wanted you to hang onto."

"I'm afraid not."

"Was there anyone else Kevin was close to who he might have asked to keep something for him?"

The more he pushed the more uncomfortable I felt. I couldn't imagine why Kevin would have asked someone else to keep anything for him. Except the book. But then a week ago I hadn't imagined that Kevin kept a book with dirt on everyone he knew.

Maybe I was over-reacting. Kevin could have had a treasured family heirloom that

J.T. had a special attachment to.

"What is it you're looking for? Maybe if I knew I could be more helpful."

"Oh, nothing specific."

Hmm. If he'd been looking for the family Bible or their grandfather's pocket watch, I didn't think he'd be so cautious. It sounded like he might not know what it was he was looking for, and that didn't seem quite right.

As if sensing he'd said too much, J.T. backed off.

We sat in silence for a couple of minutes. I wondered if I could excuse myself to go to the restroom and climb out the window. I wasn't quick enough. Our server appeared and asked if we needed anything else. We both shook our heads.

She offered the dessert menu. Again we shook our heads.

J.T. waited until she was gone before continuing, and I appreciated his discretion. "I understand you're friends with the woman they've charged with my brother's murder."

"I am." I took a sip of tea. "But Diana didn't kill Kevin."

"She didn't? How can you be sure? She had confrontations with him before. Do you think she meant to scare him?"

"I don't think so." Glad to be away from

the topic of missing items, I explained to him what Diana was like.

"Clearly you're fond of her." J.T. smiled for the first time and it warmed his face. "I have to say you've convinced me of her innocence. But the police tell me they have evidence she had purchased a Taser."

"What? Why would Diana have a Taser?"

"I don't know. I guess the police will have to sort that out."

I didn't have huge faith in that happening. When the bill came, Kevin's brother insisted on picking up the check, which was decent, especially for someone who'd freaked me out. On the one hand, J.T. seemed pleasant and fairly harmless. But then he'd been so insistent and unwilling to say what he was looking for. It didn't add up. Polite to the last, I thanked him for lunch, offered my condolences again, and took off.

I should have gone straight to the police with my concerns, but I could hear Malone berating me for thinking there was anything suspicious about Kevin's innocuous, grieving brother. I had a solid afternoon of appointments booked, and I'd done my duty when I gave Malone the book. It seemed like I might have better luck finding Kevin's killer if I avoided him for a few more hours.

I'd have more time the next day, anyway. I

had only a few pet house calls, a number of errands, and then Grey Donovan was having a show at his art gallery in the evening. It was a community event with a lot of people in attendance so it might be the perfect time to see what the buzz was about Kevin and the investigation. It would also be a chance to find out if anyone else had been contacted by Kevin's brother. It wouldn't hurt to find out more about him. Also, sometimes when people are relaxing and not really thinking about it, they let slip some of their secrets.

CHAPTER TWENTY

The ACT Gallery was packed with people and their pets. It was a veritable zoo of diamonds, furs and designer togs. The diamonds were on the people, the fur on the pets, the Prada and Chanel on both.

In Laguna Beach, it was just a given.

I caught Grey Donovan's attention across the packed room and waved.

Normally I loved Grey's gallery events, but then I always looked forward to dishing with Diana on who was there and who was wearing which designer. Who was a hit and who was a miss. Diana could pair sweet and snarky in such an adorable way. Tonight I couldn't stop thinking about her sitting alone in a jail cell.

Although come to think about it, Diana was hardly ever alone. In addition to me (and the press), she had tons of other visitors. Dino brought her fresh Italian cuisine. Bella brought her books to read. She'd even won over the two hard-ass desk clerks who frequently snuck in special things like caramel macchiatos, Diana's favorite coffee drink, and fresh avocadoes, which I knew Diana was not eating but using on her face. She swore an avocado mask was the best facial in the world. And here I'd been thinking avocados were good for you, but you had to eat them to get the benefits.

Who was I to say? The lady appeared ageless.

Tonight's event was well attended. I mentally catalogued who was with whom, who was no longer with whom, and who was wearing what, to report to Diana tomorrow.

I noted Mandy Beenerman in a striking black and white spandex number that showed her enviable yoga body to advantage.

Her husband sported an attractive ocean blue Christian Dior shirt and entirely inappropriate Michael Kors bermudas.

Don't get me wrong, there's nothing wrong with Michael Kors. But shorts, even four-hundred dollar ones, at an invitation-only art function? Questionable. In Texas we may wear boots to a high-falutin' society feed but at least they're our dress boots.

Teri Essman, the mayor, was talking with

Deke Ostrem, a local developer. Her Honor the Mayor's pantsuit for the evening was a very attractive black Donna Karan.

The developer sported Pucci, Gucci, and his ever present accessory, silicone-enhanced-super-model arm candy. His ex-wife, a few feet away, was dressed to impress (or something) in a siren-red blouse (perhaps Dior, perhaps not — Diana would know), an unfortunate leather mini-skirt, and a post-divorce plastic surgery fiasco that caused her to look perpetually surprised.

I spotted Davis Pinter and the charming Huntley observing the chaos from a vantage point in the corner of one of the raised viewing areas. Davis was, as always, dignified in a conservative Burberry suit and Huntley was properly attired in his own creation, Cavalier King Charles fur. They were both on my best-dressed list and both adorable.

Mona Michaels was front and center. No surprise there. Fluffy, her afghan hound, was by her side. Both pointed noses were in the air, and they wore matching Hermes scarves. And matching diamond collars.

Get real. I shook my head.

It was awesome for Grey to have such a big turnout, but in truth, it was difficult to see the artwork for all the people. This was Grey's "Spring Abstractions" event and he was featuring several up-and-coming abstract artists. I was particularly interested in Katzumi, a young Turkish artist. I might have to come back another time to actually get a decent look at his art.

"Caro —" Dino Riccio hailed me from near the hors d'oeuvres table. The way his gaze roved from the table to the crowd, I guessed his restaurant was catering the affair. I made my way to his side through the throng of people.

"How are you?" I leaned in to kiss his cheek and snag a crab cake while I was at it.

"Worried about our Diana, Caro *miniera*. I am very worried about our Diana." Dino sighed. He caught a passing waiter and handed me a glass of champagne.

I took a sip and glanced back at the chattering crowd. "You know she'll hate missing this. If I thought I could get away with it, I'd snap a picture with my phone. But Grey's pretty persnickety about any photos at all."

I understood his reasoning. The same folks with no fashion sense also often had no common sense, and suddenly, pictures of artwork popped up all over the Internet with no credit to the artist. He did allow the press but even they had to sign some agreement he'd had drawn up.

Across the room the door opened and Sam Gallanos stepped through.

First the dog park, then Mozambique, now here. I didn't cotton much to pretty boys but, as Diana would say, this guy was easy on the eyes. There was no harm in looking.

On his arm was a striking older woman in vintage Balenciaga that would have looked stuffy and ridiculous on someone younger. On her it looked rich and classy.

Diminutive in stature. Dark hair, dark eyes like his, flawless complexion. Her small hand was tucked into the crook of Sam's arm, his larger hand laid on top. He smiled down at her affectionately and nodded to Grey, who was near the entry.

Samuel Gallanos was truly a gorgeous guy but not in an over-groomed, over-tanned, over-the-top sort of way. The tan didn't look tanning bed induced. It was likely from his time on the beach or his penchant for tennis. I guessed tennis from his dog's name.

I recognized the custom-tailoring in his untucked Egyptian cotton shirt, and I was sure his closet was full of clones of the dark Armani slacks he wore. But the accompanying gold jewelry so often sported by the Mc-Billionaires around town was missing.

Thank God.

It was hard to put my finger on exactly what it was, but he stood out in the gallery crowd like a best of breed at the dog park. His sex appeal reached across the room and shook my female hormones awake in a way I'd hadn't felt in a very long time. To tell you the honest truth, I'd rather suspected that part of me had died.

"Your tongue's hanging out, Caro."

I recognized Grey's voice without turning around. "Is not."

I shifted my drink and offered my cheek for a kiss. "Where's Mel?"

"On a buying trip to New York." He smelled like a combination of fine wine and the outdoors, and his rough chin brushed against my hair as he leaned toward me. "I'll be sure to tell Mel you asked about her."

"You do that, sugar." I patted his arm, feeling the surprising strength beneath the suit coat. I always had the sense there was more than meets the eye with Grey. Something just under the surface.

Grey did nothing for me in the lust department, but I loved him like a brother, and had hoped to add him to the Montgomery extended family.

Of course, that depended on Melinda. The

girl was an idiot to mess up her engagement to this hunk. I wasn't even sure what the exact problem had been. Let me assure you, though, my insufficient information was not for any lack of trying to stick my nose in their business.

Mel wasn't talking to any of our family about what had happened and Grey was far too discreet.

"How's my darlin' Cobie?" Cobalt was Grey's Weimaraner and probably the smartest dog in the whole wide world. He didn't do brain surgery, but I'm sure he could've if he wanted to.

"He's great." Grey smiled the proud papa smile of those of us who don't have children but instead have fur-kids. "I took him with me on my last trip and he loved it."

"I'll bet he did."

"Have you met Sam and his grandmother?" Grey nodded in their direction. By this time they'd moved from the doorway into the main viewing room.

"I've met Sam. I ran into him on the beach. Literally." I watched as Mr. I'm-Too-Sexy-for-This-Room stood smiling down at the elderly woman by his side. He seemed oblivious to the females who were drawn in his direction like they'd just spotted a shoe sale at Neiman Marcus. "What do you know about him?"

I watched as single women, and a few married ones, were caught in his undertow.

"Quite a lot actually." Grey's eyes lit with impish amusement. "But it's always best you learn those things on your own."

"Brat." I smiled when I said it.

"I've got to mingle." He glanced around the room and then stopped. "I've not been to see Diana. Please tell her hello for me, and, Caro, I know you've been asking questions. I know asking you to stop would be a lost cause, but promise me you'll be careful."

"Always." I waved him on. "Go. Schmooze."

I'd had enough of the crowd, but I really wanted to use this opportunity to hear the gossip. I wanted to know if there was anyone who'd seen the Ruby Point gardener I was beginning to think was a figment of my imagination. I wanted to know if anyone was overly happy about Diana staying in jail. I wanted to know who was most uncomfortable with my snooping, and who knew anything about Kevin's brother.

I made my way around the room. I sipped champagne. I talked art and dogs. I commiserated about the awful parking that was sure to come with warm weather and tourist season.

I promised to help on a volunteer crew with the Trash Bash beach clean-up. All the usual chatter. Many people who knew Diana and I were friends asked about her, and I watched their reaction as I explained she was refusing bail.

Nothing suspicious. Concern for the most part. Astonishment she'd stay in jail. A bit of amusement at her publicity stunt. The lady was known for being a little eccentric.

My feet were killing me. I slipped off one of my Christian Louboutin pumps and wiggled my toes to get a bit of circulation back. I loved the shoes, adored the heels, but there was no sitting at these affairs, and I was ready to be done.

I felt his warmth before the whisper of his breath on the back on my neck. "Difficult to see the art with so many people, isn't it?"

I turned into Samuel Gallanos, who was standing so close I couldn't imagine how I'd not heard him approach. I guessed he'd qualify as the strong but silent type.

"It is." I slipped my shoe back on and stood at full height. Unlike Detective Malone, Sam didn't tower over me. With the Louboutin heels, he was only a bit taller. But like Malone, he conjured an awareness, a heat.

What a dang inconvenient time for my female hormones to decide they weren't dead. And with two men in the span of a week. Go figure that.

"Do you have a favorite?" He inclined his head toward the artwork.

"I'm partial to Katzumi."

"Ahh, the Turk, a good choice. A sense of passion behind the facade."

He smiled and I suddenly felt as if we were talking about more than paintings.

"Your grandmother is beautiful."

"She is," he agreed. "In all ways."

I got the concept. Grandma Tillie had been beautiful in all ways, too.

"I came over here with the lame idea of asking you to dinner to make up for my dog's bad manners." He flashed a self-deprecating smile. "But on the way over, I decided you are a woman who values honesty above all things. So, I'll simply confess that I'm intrigued by you and I want in the worst way to take you to dinner and get to know you better."

It was flattering to be the target of the most eligible guy in the room. It was smart he'd abandoned a line that was an easy no. It was refreshing he hadn't thought I was an easy yes.

Still, I didn't think dinner with Sam Gallanos was a good idea. I had a murder to solve, a friend to get out of jail, and a mother to divert.

I didn't need a distraction right now. Albeit a charming and handsome one. If he was still around after the universe was back in alignment, I might think about it.

He took the "no" graciously. But I had the sense he wasn't giving up.

In all seriousness, I wasn't sure I wanted him to.

I admire gumption and grit and, in spite of his fancy polish, I believed Sam Gallanos had those qualities in spades. I went home that night with a little more to think about than Kevin Blackstone's death and getting Diana's name cleared.

CHAPTER TWENTY-ONE

Diana had turned the Laguna Beach jail into a five-star hotel. I went to visit her first thing the next morning. The guard escorted me to the holding area where Diana had added a rug and fresh flowers.

"Hello, hon." I kissed Diana on the cheek. "How are you today?"

"Good, Caro. And you?"

"I'm fine." I handed her a bag of goodies. "You missed one heck of a gallery event last night at Grey's."

"I did?" Diana rummaged in the bag I'd brought. "Shoot. I would've enjoyed seeing the sights."

She looked up at me with interest. "What did you wear?"

"A Stella McCartney botanical print. You know, the sort of tropical one I bought the last time we went shopping up north."

"Ah, I remember. All those vibrant colors. Beautiful with your coloring, Caro. I wish I had your gorgeous red hair and flawless complexion. And your height and carriage." She grinned her signature impish grin. "If you weren't so doggone nice, I'd be so green with envy I couldn't stand to be around you."

"Oh, quit."

"Now tell me what everyone else wore and who was with who." Diana settled back in her chair.

I filled her in on the particulars of who'd been in attendance and what they'd worn. We had a laugh over Mona and Fluffy and their matching collars. I left out the part about Sam Gallanos and his dinner invitation. And my refusal. I didn't need Diana giving me a hard time about my lack of a social life, too.

Finally, I brought out my folder of Fur Ball details and Diana and I pored over what was left to be done. Ticket sales were going well but weren't at the level where we'd wanted them. We needed a few more people to buy full tables for the ball.

Once we'd finished I had one more item on my agenda.

"Diana, I had dinner with Kevin's brother."

"You did?" She looked up from the Fur Ball notes. "I didn't even know he had a brother."

"Seems none of us did." I reached across and took her hand. "Diana, he mentioned the police told him you had purchased a Taser."

"That's right."

She said it so matter-of-factly I wasn't sure I'd heard her right.

"Why would you need a Taser?"

"Caro, I'm a woman alone. I don't have staff who stay in the house." She sat up and smoothed her jacket. "I'm not sure I could actually shoot a burglar, but I figured I could shock one."

"Was there some reason you were afraid?"

"Not afraid, my dear. Just prepared."

"Is that what the police dug up in your garden?"

"I didn't bury my Taser. That would be silly. It wouldn't do me much good buried in my roses now would it?"

"Well, what did they dig up then?"

"They said they got a phone call that the murder weapon was buried in my roses. And sure enough it was. But it wasn't my Taser. I showed them I still have mine."

There was a commotion at the door, and then an older gentleman was ushered in by Lorraine (the one I'd originally labeled Gidget). This guy didn't look like the usual reporter so I wondered what Diana was up to now.

"Good afternoon, Diana, my dear." He took her hand and kissed it.

Gosh, a polite one, too.

"Thank you for stopping by, Paul." Diana said it like she was holding court in some elegant drawing room. "Paul, this is my good friend, Carolina Montgomery Lamont. Caro, this is Paul Kantor. He's my attorney."

"Of the Texas Montgomerys?" He reached out to shake my hand.

"Yes, the Texas ones." I shook his hand and tried not to hurt him.

Oh, my Lord. This was her defense attorney? No wonder she was still sitting in jail. He seemed like a very nice man, and he certainly had extremely elegant manners, but I'm not sure he'd ever been in a jail cell before.

He looked around as if taking it all in.

"I'll excuse myself so you two can talk strategy." I gathered my papers. "You're getting her out of here, aren't you?"

"I'd certainly like to do so, my dear. But our lovely Diana is insistent on staying put."

"Paul says they'll probably reduce the charge from murder to manslaughter." The terms rolled off her tongue like a she was detailing her grocery list, not talking about charges that could have her spending the rest of her life in prison.

I looked at Paul, who seemed smitten with Diana, and wondered at her understanding of what I'm sure he'd painstakingly explained. "Then bail can be set?"

The attorney nodded and started to explain, "Then —"

But Diana interrupted. "Then I'll have to plead guilty or not-guilty and they'll set bail. But I don't have to pay it, just because I can. I can *not* pay it and stay here."

I'd always felt Diana's mind was as sharp as they come. But maybe we were dealing with the sudden onset of confusion brought on by all of this stress.

"You have to be out in time for the Fur Ball," I told her, my tone firm. "You can't miss it."

"Well, I certainly hope to be there, Carolina, sweetie, but I can't promise." She smiled an unconcerned smile. "You're doing fine. And you know, I think I'm doing more good for the cause here."

Great. She thought she was Joan of Arc and the dogs and cats were the French. I still couldn't believe her flawed thinking in using the murder charges like a publicity stunt. I couldn't argue with the results, however. The ticket sales were booming and donations to P.U.P. (Protecting Unwanted Pets) had come in from all over the country. We even had a substantial donation come in from a lady in Australia who'd seen the story and was moved to contribute.

Diana turned back to her attorney. "Now, Paul, I've been contacted by the national pet rescue group to serve as their spokeswoman, but I'd like you to look through the contract first before I send it on to my agent."

For Pete's sake, the woman was a sharp cookie when it came to business, but a nut when it came to taking care of herself.

I had to get her a different lawyer. A criminal lawyer. And I had to get her out of jail.

I had to — or the police had to — find the real killer so Diana could go home.

The day was filled with appointments with clients. I'd rescheduled Mona Michaels and her star dog, Fluffy, from the day Diana'd been arrested. Fluffy had her own bedroom, her own refrigerator, and her own daytime Emmy. As I'd figured, Mona was *extremely* offended I had inconvenienced her for something as trivial as Diana being arrested for murder. Unlike my other stops, she didn't even want to know the horrid details.

If it didn't involve her, Mona simply wasn't interested.

I asked about Cliff and was rewarded with the information they were divorced and shared custody of Fluffy. It didn't help me with what the notation "ck inv" had meant in Kevin's book. As far as suspects go, I would love a reason to think it was Mona, but none came to light. Mona could kill your social status with one phone call, but as far as killing Kevin, she just didn't seem to have a motive.

My last house call of the day was in Ruby Point checking in with Sumner and Ginny and their Chow Chows. They'd been conscientious with their exercises and seemed to be doing well. Since I was in the vicinity, I stopped in again and checked on Diana's menagerie. No worries there. Bella was doing a great job.

As I pulled out from Diana's drive, I noticed a car turn into Kevin's. I slowed as I approached. A silver Jaguar sedan was parked next to the front hedge. The door swung open and J.T. got out.

I pulled into the driveway. J.T. approached my car.

I opened the door and stepped out. "Hi, how are you doing?"

"I'm doing fine. How about you?" His

expression was concerned.

"I've got a lead on the landscaper I told you about. The one Kevin and I had the encounter with the day he died." I didn't know if Malone had talked to him about Kevin's book, and it didn't seem appropriate for me to bring it up if he hadn't.

"Thank you for continuing to try to find my brother's killer. I know Kevin thought a lot of you."

"Did you find the item you were looking for?"

"What item?" His voice was a little sharp.

"The one you asked me about. You know, you asked if Kevin had given me something to keep."

"Oh, that." He glanced around. "No, I'm still looking. If anyone mentions something Kevin left with them as you're investigating, you'll let me know, right?"

"Sure . . ." I waited for him to go on, but he didn't. "It would help if I knew what the 'something' might be."

"Hard to say." He smiled. "But let me know if you hear anything."

He turned from the car. "See you later, Caro."

"Bye." I climbed in, put my car in gear, and backed out. As I turned toward home, I glanced at my cell phone. I'd missed a call from Detective Malone.

Great. This was no time for phone tag.

I found J.T.'s lack of transparency about what the heck he was looking for pretty irritating. I know, I know. I shouldn't be too critical when it comes to being irrational about a family inheritance. But seriously. At least Mel and I knew what it was we were fighting over.

Was this missing item so valuable that J.T. thought whoever had it might claim ownership? Or claim a finder's fee? It was impossible to help him if I didn't even know what it was that was missing. Seriously, his thinking was strange.

As soon as I got home, I called Walt. He gave me the names of a few criminal attorneys. It was after office hours so I got voicemail or answering services. I left messages asking them to call me.

Next, I called the jail and asked to talk to Diana. Gidget told me she was in the middle of a phone call with CNN. I hoped she'd held out for Anderson Cooper. Gidget promised to pass on my message about potential attorneys, and also let me know Diana was running low on avocados.

CHAPTER TWENTY-TWO

The next morning the headline in the Orange County Coastline Pilot, proclaimed: "I'm Innocent! Says Diana Knight — Just Like the Innocent Animals Who Are Put to Death Every Day." There was a good picture of Diana and a great picture of Mr. Wiggles. How she'd smuggled him in for the photo shoot, I could only guess.

I knew she missed him and her other fur kids. The article went on to talk about the need for spaying and neutering dogs and cats, and the overcrowding in animal shelters. Diana knew all the numbers by heart. This was her passion, and she'd found a very public soapbox.

A national soapbox.

A soapbox she wasn't about to give up willingly. I was afraid even if the police found out who really killed Kevin Blackstone, Diana might insist on staying in jail.

I left without breakfast, my newspaper

tucked in my bag. I'd stop and pick up a coffee on the way to the office.

My cell phone rang while I was in line at the Koffee Klatch. I saw from the number it was Mama and thought about letting it go to voicemail. But I am a grown woman, and I ought to be able to deal with talking to my own mother. (That was the lecture going on in my head.)

I hit the button and took the call. "Hello, Mama."

Verdi, the burgundy-haired, multiply-pierced barista behind the counter, mouthed, "Your usual?"

I nodded ascent, glad Verdi was so sharp. She always seemed to remember what all of us regulars ordered.

"Well, of course, I'm up. It's nine o'clock in the morning here."

Which meant it was nearly lunchtime in Texas. Kat Lamont was good with numbers whenever she was figuring a discount at Neiman Marcus, the tip for her hair stylist, or a donation to her favorite charity, but she refused to keep straight the two-hour time difference between California and Texas.

"I'm on my way to the office."

Mama Kat had made it absolutely clear she was not ready to acknowledge my pet

238

therapy practice was a business by any stretch of the imagination. I might have been insulted, but she'd never really acknowledged that my family counseling practice was a business either. They were all things I was just doing for a while, until I saw the light and decided to take on all her charity work.

Don't get me wrong. The woman does good. And she's good at it. But it's not my calling.

I handed some cash to Verdi, dropped a dollar in the tip jar, and took my hazelnut latte.

I whispered, "thank you" to the girl as she handed over my change.

"No, Mama. I haven't been on a date lately." I dropped the coins in my bag and closed it.

Suddenly I noticed the silence.

I looked around at a newly quiet Koffee Klatch. Many of the patrons smiled in amusement at my chagrin and then looked down, inordinately interested in their coffees and pastries.

Great, now everyone in the place knew my social life was on the downhill slide. It was a small shop where no conversation was ever private unless you took it out to the sidewalk. Still, I hadn't meant to broadcast my dateless status.

I ducked out the door and headed back to the office, phone to my ear, responding every once in a while to Mama's litany of gossip about Dallas society with an "uh-huh."

"I have a date for you."

"What?" That one got my attention. "A date?"

"Oh, sweetheart, you are going to thank me for this." She took a big deep breath, which I knew meant she was lying through her teeth. "He's an attorney in Long Beach. With one of those investment banks, I'm afraid I can't remember which one. Anyway, I gave him your phone number."

"Mama —" My voice should have warned her. "I'd appreciate it if you'd just butt out of my love life."

"Carolina, honey, you don't have a love life for me to butt in or butt out of."

"Still, that's my business."

"Don't be mad. It's like your grandmother used to say, you sit on the shelf too long and you sour. It's time to get out and live, girl."

"That's what I'm doing, Mama, but I've got to do it on my own."

By the time I got to the office and off the phone I was madder than a wet hen.

I don't know whether I was angrier about her meddling in my love life, or the fact that she was right, and I truly didn't have one. I could have a love life if I wanted to. Hadn't Sam asked me out just last night? Yes, he had. That I was focused on getting my best friend out of jail instead of the state of my social life was to my credit.

Later that morning, Samuel Gallanos called my office and asked me to lunch. And in a weak moment I accepted. My "take that, Mama!" rationale might not have been to my credit.

I reasoned I'd turned him down on the dinner and so Mr. Persistence opted for lunch. Lunch seemed safer. Less intimate. Still, if it hadn't been on the heels of that stupid phone conversation with my mother, I knew I would not have caved so easily.

Dating Sam Gallanos might prove to be a nice pastime but it would be a complete waste of time. If I was going to go to the trouble to actually go on a date, it should be with someone who was interested in a real honest-to-God relationship. I was thirty-one and a half and I loved my single life, but if I was going to bother with a date, it should be one with at least a snowball's chance in hell of leading to a future.

All the signs around Sam pointed to player.

The beautiful people, the expensive clothes, the carefree attitude. Based on what I'd seen, I didn't think he had a job, which meant he probably inherited money.

Major player.

Well, it was just lunch, and all of Mama's baiting on the phone had worn me down. As was often the case after talking with Mama Kat, I felt like I'd been pulled through a knothole sideways.

Once I'd accepted I had second (and third) thoughts about accepting a lunch invitation out of wanting to spite my mother, I offered to meet him at the restaurant of his choice. Naturally he insisted on picking me up.

That meant I had to get home in time to change and be ready. And then I needed to see what I could find out about J.T. Blackstone, track Malone down to find out what he was doing to catch the real killer, and get Diana a lawyer who knew his way around more than probate court. I shouldn't have said yes to Sam. Time was a wastin'.

Would you just listen to me? I hadn't even gone to lunch yet and I was already wishing it were over.

Maybe Mama was right, and I had become

antisocial.

Oh, well. It was too late to renege. At least Sam had a big plus in his corner — I loved his taste in dogs.

I got back home at ten to one, which didn't give me much time to dress. I decided I was not going to get all gussied up. I pulled on a long Ralph Lauren skirt, a bright turquoise off-the-shoulder top and threw the necessities in my new turquoise leather Lynne Curtin handbag. You know, the shaggy leather style. I know she's no longer the "it" local designer, but I loved the bag, loved her jewelry, and felt for her hard times.

I was hunting for shoes to go with the casual look when the doorbell rang.

You see, Detective Judd Malone. I do *have a working doorbell.* And Sam was man enough to use it.

Opening the door, I was again struck by his amazing good looks. There's handsome and then there's Handsome. Sam was the latter.

"For you." He handed me a bouquet of Texas bluebonnets.

I confess if his handsomeness had made me weak in the knees, the flowers nearly made me fall over.

I was touched. The Texas state flower is a

wildflower and not easy to acquire. I was awed and homesick all at once. The bluebonnets made me miss the ranch and long for Grandma Tillie. Oddly enough, they even made me miss Mel, my only local connection to home and my family.

There was a time when we'd first moved to Laguna that we'd get together for dinner or a movie night and talk about home and our crazy family.

I shook my head to shake off the sappiness I was feeling. I realized "His Handsomeness" was staring at me.

"I'm so sorry. Please come in." I stepped aside so he could enter, and I had the passing juvenile thought that if I could get a picture of this event, Mama would be extremely impressed and might leave me alone for a month or two.

No, strike that. Ms. All-My-Friends'-Daughters-Are-Married would be picking out china patterns for us.

"I'll put these in some water." I carried the bluebonnets into the kitchen and rummaged until I found a vase the right size.

The flowers were a nice gesture. An unexpected one. I suddenly hoped I was dressed appropriately for what he had planned. So much for wishing the date was over before it had begun.

"I wasn't sure . . ." I looked around and didn't see Sam. Then I heard a low *ruff.*

There he was on the floor playing with Dogbert and being very closely watched by my two guard cats. Thelma and Louise both moved in for a pet and a tummy rub.

Sam scratched each one behind the ears. Their favorite thing. Next to tuna, that is. He now had feline fur friends for life.

He shifted his attention back to Dog. His linen slacks no doubt picking up cat and dog hair and who knew what else from my floor. For cryin' out loud, I would've vacuumed if I'd known the man was going to roll around on my floor.

He looked up and saw me. "Ready?"

"I am." I picked up the sandals by the door and slipped them on. They'd have to do.

Though the flowers had been unexpected, the car in front of my house was exactly what I'd expected. A light blue Ferrari convertible was parked at the curb. It was the new California classic, reminiscent of the older models, a perfect metallic blue, and in the backseat was Mac, the Collie, tongue hanging out, goofy smile.

How did the guy do it? The perfect flowers, the perfect car, the perfect dog.

I almost just laid down in my driveway

and said, "Okay, sugar, go ahead and take me now."

He held the door, and I slid in and turned to take Mac by his dog cheeks and give him a nuzzle.

"Hi there, cutie. I didn't know you were joining us."

The big dog nuzzled back and panted his appreciation. Sam slid behind the wheel and started the car. The Ferrari purred to life. We shared a glance of appreciation as the car glided through my neighborhood and onto PCH.

The Laguna Montage is elegance at its best, and the valet didn't bat an eye at my casual attire or Sam's dog. Sam handed the uniformed guy the keys to the Ferrari while another opened my door and offered me a hand.

I climbed out of the car with a bit less grace than I'd hoped for, but no one blinked an eye.

Another staff member in the Montage uniform met us just inside the door and escorted us to the elevator.

"This way, Mr. Gallanos. Ma'am." He held the elevator door and started to join us but with the slightest motion of Sam's head he backed off.

"I hope you have a great lunch." He

stepped aside.

"Thanks, Thomas."

Okay, Sam, you surprised me with the blue-bonnets and your comfort in my very casual pet-friend household, but this restaurant pick was predictable.

I not only had been to the luxury destination many times, but it was also the place Mama always wanted to come when she was in town. She wanted to see and be seen. Everyone who was anyone would know about our lunch date before we'd been served dessert.

Hell's bells, someone was probably telling Mel right now. She'd have the Texas clan notified before supper time.

I guess the upside was that Mama would know I'd been on a date. I'd bet you dollars to donuts I'd be getting a phone call within twenty-four hours.

The elevator opened on the lower level so I assumed we were dining at Mosaics Bar and Grille. I knew the menu by heart and was already making my entrée selection in my head, when the maître d' spotted Sam and motioned to one of the other staff members.

A picnic basket and a beach bag were handed over, and we continued right through the restaurant area and down to

247

the beach walkway. We climbed down to the beach with Mac and me following Sam, who seemed to know where he was going. In short order we were on the sand. A minor rock formation to traverse, and we were in a more secluded part of the beach.

Sam opened the bag and pulled out a blanket that he settled on the sand. He anchored it with the picnic basket.

Alright, he'd surprised me again.

Opening the bag a second time, he unearthed a Frisbee, which got Mac's tail wagging like crazy. Sam handed it to me.

"Go on, you two." He smiled, reached in his pocket for sunglasses and leaned back on the blanket, lifting his face to the sun.

Mac and I didn't need much encouragement. Off we went.

The day was brilliant. Perfect So Cal weather.

This was why I lived here. How could I have forgotten?

Sam soon joined us in the Mac and Caro Frisbee Olympics and the three of us raced back and forth in the surf.

I coveted the guy's dog. I'd had a Border Collie growing up on the ranch, and if I had the room I'd add one to my brood without hesitation. I wanted one badly, but I just didn't think it was fair in the limited space I had.

I also coveted the man's exuberance. Sam was clearly a hold-nothing-back kind of guy. There was nothing careful or cautious about him. You didn't have to know him long to know he was an all-in sort of person.

When we'd completely worn ourselves out, we fell onto the sandy blanket, Mac's fur, Sam's pants, and the hem of my skirt all damp from the waves. We unpacked the food. Roast beef, bread, several cheeses, chilled wine. Special dog food for Mac.

We talked for hours. Sam Gallanos was truly a master listener. He prodded just enough. Not pushy but interested. We talked about my time growing up on a ranch. It had been clearly different from Sam's childhood. I shared my worry about Diana and my frustration with her lack of concern over her fate and her stubbornness in using the situation to campaign for animal rights.

Once I'd worn myself out with dumping all my troubles on his very broad shoulders, we sat in silence for a while. I enjoyed the pale cream of the sand, the heat of the sun, and the whoosh of the surf.

"This was exactly what I needed today." I held my wineglass in a toast to Sam. "How did you know?"

"Because it was exactly what we needed

too. Mac dog and I." He leaned over and touched my cheek with the side of his finger. "Life is to be lived, Caro *kopelia mou*."

I didn't know what the expression meant, but he had me at "dog."

It might be I'd been just a little hasty in dismissing Sam as an unwanted complication in my life.

Confession time. When I got home I should have savored the day. It had been perfection.

But remember this is me, Carolina Alexis Montgomery Lamont, and I did not trust perfection. So when I got home, instead of running a bubble bath and dreaming of what might be, I Googled Sam on the Internet.

Better to burst a bubble when it's a small one. That's my motto.

Here's what it said:

Sam was born Samuel David Gallanos in Greece. At the age of 9, Sam and his parents moved to California, United States. His parents divorced and his father returned to Greece. His mother, Daphne (Drakos) married Greek/American movie mogul Michael Skouras. The two were killed in a car accident when the boy was twelve. He was raised by his maternal grandparents, Dmitri and Dorothea Drakos of the Drakos olive oil fortune (Drakos International). They relocated to southern California with their daughter. Sam graduated from USC (University of Southern California) cum laude with a B.A. in Ancient Philosophy and Literatures.

My first thought was "Oh my God, how tragic," and my second thought was "Could the guy possibly have picked a more useless major?" But who was I to criticize? I had a doctorate in psychology and I was a pet therapist. The irony did not escape me.

After the bio I continued searching. I really hate when I'm proven right, but the guy was a major player. There were links and more links to pictures of him at every society event you could imagine. You wouldn't believe the women he dated. This guy was way out of my league.

Well, it was a good thing it was a league I wasn't interested in playing in. Not for more than a lunch date, at any rate. Not if I was going to figure out this whole mess about Kevin's death and get Diana out of jail.

CHAPTER TWENTY-THREE

Late that afternoon, I had an appointment with Leland at the Green House offices.

There was a light sprinkle of rain so I'd left the top up on the Mercedes. I pulled into the lot and parked, walked up the flower filled flagstone pathway, and into the office. Leland came out to meet me and then ushered me back to his office, which was a cubbyhole filled with paperwork and landscaping magazines.

"You said on the phone you had some questions about one of our employees?" He seemed a bit harried.

I explained the situation to him and described the worker. A phone call interrupted us. He gave some instructions to the person on the other end and then looked at me.

"Yeah, I know who you mean."

"You do?" Thank God. I'd begun to believe I'd imagined him.

"I hired the guy because he had good references and I was so short-handed." He shifted the Green House cap on his head. "Joe, my guy that usually did the Ruby Point flowers, who'd been my lead guy there for several years, was killed."

"He was killed?" I hadn't heard any reports about it. Another death involving Ruby Point. Why hadn't that been on the news? Surely the police had to know about it.

"Yeah, he'd been a good worker, but Joey had a drinking problem. I thought he had it whupped this time, but I guess not. Some hikers found him out in the state park. Poor guy'd been hit over the head and robbed. Probably drunk. Sad case."

Maybe. Maybe not. I leaned a little closer. "When was that?"

"Let me see, couple of weeks ago probably. He didn't show up to work so I figured he must have fallen off the wagon. I called his family, but they hadn't reported him missing or anything. I think they figured the same thing."

Holy moly. Two suspicious deaths inside of a month. What were the odds they were unrelated? "And the guy I described?"

"Yeah, Spike." Leland shifted paper from one place on his desk to another.

"His name was Spike?"

"Nah, his name was Hans Gruber, but I called him Spike 'cause it was easier to remember. Because of his hair."

Hans Gruber? Any doubt I had that Joe's death was just bad luck evaporated. "Not much of a movie-goer, Leland?"

"Huh? No, not much time."

I recognized the *Die Hard* bad guy reference immediately, but obviously Leland hadn't. It smacked of a quickly created phony identity. Spike, aka Hans, was looking more and more like the Ruby Point bad guy every second. "Sounds like a fake name to me."

"Really?" Leland scrubbed his hand over his face. "Gosh, normally I check references and all real good. But I didn't in this case. I just called one of the names he gave me. I was so short-handed and we're so durn busy. 'Scuse me." He took a question via the walkie-talkie strapped to his belt, then holstered it. "Don't matter now though, anyway."

"Why's that?"

"Well, the kid hasn't shown up in more than a week. I shoulda checked those references better." I could tell he was itching to get back outside.

A short, stocky woman wearing a green

apron stuck her head in the office. "Leland, the supplier for those planters you ordered is here. Where do you want them?"

"I'd better get back to work." Leland was already on the move. "Sorry I couldn't be more help."

"Do you have a contact number for Spike?" I asked quickly.

Leland paused in the door. "The cell phone number he gave us just rings and rings. Can't even leave a message."

I thanked him and left one of my cards with him. If he heard from Spike, he agreed to ask him to contact me.

After my chat with Leland I was pretty sure there had to be a link between Kevin's death and Spike, the landscape worker. I turned the car toward downtown and the office. I *really* needed to talk to Malone. I tried his cell again, and got his voicemail again. It irritated me to think he was still screening my calls. That was just plain irresponsible. I had solid information that he needed to know about. Here I was, doing my civic duty and trying to get him in the loop, and he was being nothing but difficult.

At the very least, he should be working to get Diana out of jail. He had to know she didn't kill Kevin. The case against her was extremely weak. I couldn't believe the police were holding her at all. Well, there was the fact she'd had a Taser, but still, if she'd fight it at all . . . well, you know all that.

I left a message this time with the information on what I'd found out about the landscaper. It was way too coincidental that the regular worker had died and this Hans Gruber/Spike guy had conveniently shown up. And if I could figure this out, so could Malone. Why weren't the police more on top of things?

Back at my office, once inside and settled at my desk, I pulled my photocopy of Kevin's book out of the inside pocket of my Coach bag and went over it again. There had to be clues there about what had happened. Though my money was still on Spike, there was the possibility Mandy or one of the others whose secrets Kevin had detailed had killed Kevin.

I knew my secret and Mel's. I'd figured out a few of the secrets in the book and the others couldn't be that difficult to figure out. I planned to go through the entries again and see if any of them looked worth killing over. I didn't have to confront people, but if I knew who had secrets to hide maybe I could do some digging and see what Walt, Ollie or others might know.

There were the two entries about Mel and about me. Then there was Walt's: *Walter Cambrian, aw pht, blgr, wdr, snp, LB 23yr, ho*

It was pretty straightforward.

There was Ollie's: *Oliver Hembry, rck lgnd, sep w-fam, Rhde, arrst 1998 HK, LB 10yr, ho*

He hadn't seemed too upset by whatever it was Kevin thought he'd had. But then he hadn't explained the references either. I guessed rock legend, separated from his wife and family, Laguna Beach ten years, and home owner. The other items I wasn't sure about but could probably find the same way I'd found the background on Sam.

Ollie was followed by Mandy: *Mandy Beenerman, yga ldy, frmr chldr, swt dn, LB 6yr, ho fcls*

Mandy's I could partially get. Yoga lady, former cheerleader, the "swt dn" notation must have something to do with the affair between her and Kevin, but I couldn't figure out the abbreviation. Or maybe she did have a substance abuse problem and it was some new hybrid drug. And, though I hadn't realized they were in any financial trouble, it was possible Andy and Mandy's home was in foreclosure.

The next page was Mona Michaels: *Mona Michaels, btch Fluffy, sep dh Cliff, ck inv, LB*

19 yr, rtr

Again, this was someone I knew fairly well. I now knew for sure she and Cliff were divorced. The final decree was recent, according to Mona, so maybe Kevin hadn't updated his notes. I had no idea what "ck inv" might be.

And then there was one I hadn't paid much attention to when I'd been through the pages before, Shar: *Sharmin Summers, schwartz, tvstr, frm neb, nt 17, LB 3yr, ho*

I had no problem guessing her given name might be Schwartz, and the next two entries could be television star and from Nebraska, but the next one meant nothing to me. Nt? Not much to go on.

I sighed, frustrated with Kevin's codes and still unclear on why he would have even made the notes. There were more, but I left them for the time being.

The last page in the book had a bunch of writing that I'd decided was Latin. I could recognize only a few words. I'd dealt with it a bit in my therapy practice and in clinical diagnosis. But all in all, Latin was not my forte.

Wait a doggone minute.

I realized I knew someone who could tell me what Kevin had written and what it meant.

I called Grey and got Sam Gallanos' phone number. I could tell Grey wanted to ask why, but I decided I'd leave him wondering. The less he knew, the less he had to deal with deciding whether to share with Mel.

I reached Sam immediately. He seemed pleased to hear from me so soon, and he said he would stop by the office.

I resisted the urge to primp. The guy could take me or leave me just like I was. After our lunch, I'd changed into my usual blue jeans, dog hair, and a Laguna Beach Dog Park t-shirt.

Okay, I'll admit I did comb my hair and freshen up my make-up.

And put on perfume.

I studied the copies I'd made of Kevin's pages. I went over all of it one more time, but nothing made any more sense than it had before. Kevin had had a ton of dirt on a lot of people, but so far as I knew, he hadn't done anything with the information. What on earth was he keeping it for?

I sat at my desk, my chin propped on my hands. It made no sense.

The intercom buzzed me out of my reverie. "Yes?"

"Samuel Gallanos to see you, Caro."

If I'd thought Paris had drooled over

Detective Judd Malone, she was just about panting over Sam. It was just after five, and I'll bet she was glad she hadn't bolted at five o'clock sharp.

I went out to the front desk to get him.

"So this is where you work?" He looked around the office.

"Not so much." I indicated the sitting area. "I mostly work with pets in their own homes. I just hide here."

"This is nice." He looked around the room. "You have impeccable taste, Caro. You do things just right."

"Thanks, Sam."

He had no idea what that pronouncement meant to me. I'd never done anything "just right" for the people who mattered most to me.

"Here are the notations I called you about." I handed him the copy of the back pages of Kevin's notebook. "I'm wondering if you would be able to help me with what the Latin says."

Sam settled into one of the chairs looking more comfortable than he should. He pulled a pair of horn-rimmed glasses from his shirt pocket and put them on.

I sat quietly across from him and watched while he looked through the notes.

Man, what is it with guys and glasses?

Definitely increases the sex appeal. Not that Sam wasn't already at the top of the hot meter.

"I don't know, Caro." He slid the glasses down on his nose and looked over them at me. "The entries are odd. They don't make any real sense."

"They're just nonsense?"

"No, the sentences make sense. But they don't seem to fit together. This . . ." He pointed at the words on the page. "*Fallaces sunt rerum species.* It means things aren't as they seem. Or, literally, 'the appearances of things are deceptive.' "

"Well, I can sure as heck agree with that."

"But here's the thing. All of this is just a series of sayings or adages. Albeit, sort of obscure ones. Some from commonly read texts."

"Like what?"

"Like this one, *causa latet, vis est notissima* from Ovid. It means the cause is hidden but the result is well-known."

"Why would someone write all those out?"
What the heck? How would Kevin even know all of those?

"Hard to tell."

"They're just random? They don't go together in any way?"

"No, not really. Look, here you've got

bonitas non est pessimis esse meliorem." He moved across the room and sat on the arm of my chair. "Which translates to 'It is not goodness to be better than the worst.' And then right after it, *canis canem edit* meaning 'dog eats dog.' "

"Dog eat dog?" I understood the concept, but I wasn't any closer to understanding why Kevin Blackstone would write out a bunch of Latin phrases.

He put the glasses back on. "And here, *de omnibus dubitandum* meaning 'be suspicious of everything, doubt everything.' Followed by ZTB in ZTB, which means nothing at all to me. And then, *alea iacta est.* 'The die has been cast.' "

"Dang."

Sam stood and handed the pages back to me. "Whoever wrote this must have had some purpose in writing it all down."

I took the pages and laid them on my desk. "Is this about the man who was killed?" He tucked the glasses back in his shirt pocket.

I didn't answer for a full minute. It was police business but it seemed I was working harder on a solution than they were. I made a split-second decision. My best friend was in jail and I needed a friend right now. Besides I hadn't told Malone I'd kept a

262

copy and I'd feel safer if someone knew.

"There was a notebook."

"What was in it?"

"Personal details about people Kevin had written down. Things about their lives they might not want others to know about." I sat down at my desk. "I've turned the notebook over to the police but I kept a copy of the pages."

"You're not going to show me those are you?"

"I'm not. Not that I don't trust you, Sam, but I don't think people's personal information needs to be shared unless they choose to do it themselves."

"A woman of integrity. I admire that."

"Don't admire too much, Sam. I'm full of faults."

"Aren't we all?" The corner of his mouth lifted in a wry smile.

"Thanks for trying anyway. I appreciate it."

"If you'll make another copy of this," he indicated the page of Latin, "I'd be happy to write the meanings out for you."

"I may take you up on that offer. Thanks for coming by so quickly."

"One more thing, Caro." He stopped in the doorway. "I know you're worried about your friend, Diana."

"I am. I stopped in yesterday and her attorney came by. He must be ninety if he's a day."

"That's good she's talking to an attorney. Yes?"

"Yes, but I have my doubts. Not that he's not sharp and all, but I think he's a family attorney. He's handled her will and stuff like that. I don't think he's ever tried a criminal case."

"I would like to offer to help. I can get you the name of a good criminal attorney. She should not be sitting in jail while they are waiting for the next steps."

"I know, Sam. I've offered, but she won't do it. She wants to stay there."

He shook his head.

"I know, me too. She's making me crazy."

"If there's something I can do to help, just say the word."

I let Sam out and locked the door behind him since Paris had left. It had felt good to share Kevin's notes and my concerns with someone who didn't just blow me off and tell me to mind my own business.

Diana *was* my business. Now that Kevin was gone, Zeus's and Tommy Boy's welfare *was* my business. Something had upset those dogs and a lot of other dogs in Ruby Point. The more I thought about it, the more it seemed like there had to be a connection that I was missing between all those freaked out dogs, Hans/Spike, the missing horticulture worker, and Kevin's death. I wasn't going to just drop it until Kevin's dogs were placed in the best situation as we could find for them and Diana was out of jail.

I went back to the copies of Kevin's entries and my notes. Heck, I'd just start down the list and trudge through one by one until I hit pay dirt.

CHAPTER TWENTY-FOUR

After the bust on Kevin's Latin quotes, I'd gone through the names again and made note of those where I had appointments coming up. We'd just see what information I could glean while talking dog and kitty issues.

However, next on my list was someone who'd had a strange reaction to Kevin's death. Kendall, the dog groomer. I hadn't found a reference to him in Kevin's book, but the relationship and Kendall's reaction sure didn't sit quite right. So first thing the next morning, I headed to the Divine Dog Spa again.

"Full Service" the sign on the door said, and it was without a doubt a full-service salon. In addition to regular grooming, the spa offered pet facials, full-body massages, and special vitamin treatments for problem fur.

As always, it was a busy place. I waited as

a Labradoodle named Beau was booked for the "Works," which was not only the facial and the massage but also a "brightening treatment" and an oral hygiene regimen.

I waited until Beau was checked-in to approach the desk.

"Hello, Jade. Is Kendall in today?"

"He's in the back with a client." I loved that the canines weren't dogs or pets or anything so common. They were "clients."

"Do you know when he might be available? I'd like a word with him."

"I'll let him know you're here but it could be a while. He just got started with Cassie."

"I'll wait."

As I sat in the waiting room, I observed the spa.

Many pet parents dropped their pooches off and came back later to pick them up. I imagined they took advantage of the time to take care of some grooming needs of their own. Perhaps fit in a manicure or pedicure. Still others waited on site for the groomers to finish with their precious fur kids.

"Hello, Ms. Lamont." I'd been so preoccupied that I hadn't noticed Kendall gallop into the room.

He dropped into the chair next to mine. Today he was attired head to toe in giraffe patterned pants with a matching shirt. Do ya'll remember garanimals? Those paired tops and bottoms for kids where you match the animals? Well, that was the look that came to mind.

Anyway, whatever possessed the guy to think a giraffe print was appropriate attire I couldn't say. It was definitely a fashion statement. Maybe in his wacked out thinking he felt like it was his trademark look.

It was certainly memorable.

"Jade said you wanted to speak to me."

"Yes, about Kevin."

"What about Kevin?" His eyes darted around the room as if he didn't want the others to hear.

I decided to be straight up. "How did you know him?"

"We were friends."

"I don't think so."

"What, you don't think Kevin would be a friend to someone like me?" He was going for outraged but it didn't ring true. There was a slight shake in his voice telling me it was something else — uncertainty, maybe even fear.

"No, I don't think you and Kevin were friends." I turned to look him full in the face so I could gauge his reaction.

He'd frozen. His dark eyes widened.

"I think you had a secret, Kendall. Something Kevin knew and no one else did. Now that Kevin is gone you think your secret is safe, but it's not."

He still had not moved.

"Maybe it's even a big enough secret that you'd kill to keep it," I added for good measure.

"No, no, I would never." Kendall clamped his large hand over his mouth.

Potential sign of lying. Not "I did not," but "I would never."

"Kendall?" Jade motioned from across the room.

"I've got to get back to Cassie." Kendall stood, towering in his hoof-like shoes. "I . . . ah . . . I . . . we should talk."

"Name the time and place." I wasn't going to get anything else out of Kendall here.

"The Dirty Bird tonight at seven."

Oh, man. The Dirty Bird was the locals' equivalent of the Sandpiper Lounge.

"Really?" I wouldn't have thought Kendall a Sandpiper type.

"I don't get off until six. That's the soonest I can do."

He'd misunderstood my question. The time was fine. It was the location I'd questioned. Live music, lots of people, hard to hear.

Before I could suggest an alternative, he'd

hurried across the room to consult with Jade and get back to his appointment.

Fine. The Dirty Bird, it was.

I had some errands to take care of and then I'd meet him at the Sandpiper if that's what it took. I called the office to check my messages and headed back downtown. I had two more calls from new clients, a reminder about Dogbert's appointment at the vet, and a call from Zane at "Glitter" letting me know that Grandma Tillie's brooch was ready.

CHAPTER TWENTY-FIVE

In my experience, only blood relatives have the ability to make you completely lose your good sense. I pride myself on my good sense. Most everyone who knows me will attest to my rock solid sanity. Ex-husband excluded.

But when I found out Mel had picked up Grandma Tillie's brooch from "Glitter," taking full advantage of the fact that Grant was out of town on business, *using* Grant's young nephew who didn't know our history . . .

Well . . . I went a little nuts.

Mel had waltzed right into the store, in broad daylight, bigger than Dallas, and claimed to be my cousin. (Well, that part wasn't a lie, I guess. She was my cousin. But I tell you right now if you could disown cousins, I would do it today.)

She told that poor young man she was picking up the brooch on my behalf, paid for the repairs, and walked right out with it.

We must have missed each other by less than ten minutes. Gloria at the store had left me a message the repairs were done and I'd hot-footed it over to pick up my brooch.

Now it was in the hands of a jewel thief.

I drove through downtown like an Indy champion, squealing my tires, and double-parked in front of the Bow Wow Boutique. I walked in and directly through to the back room. Then I dumped Mel's black Alexander Wang bag upside down, spilling the contents onto her desk, not even caring that some of it rolled on the floor.

I picked the "Glitter" box out of the mess, turned on my heel, and walked right back out of the store.

Mel had been with a customer, and I know she didn't see me until she saw my backside headed out the door. By the time it dawned on her what I'd done, I was already in my car and pulling away.

A parking ticket flapped on my windshield as I put the car in drive.

Those crafty parking enforcement people are everywhere.

Melinda ran outside and motioned to one of the parking enforcement ladies who was just getting out of her little tiny hybrid "Parking Services" vehicle. Probably the same woman who'd just written me a forty-dollar ticket.

Mel gestured and pointed in my direction, but I was long gone.

Long gone, baby.

Like I said, it takes a blood relative to cause a person to act like a complete lunatic.

I decided to run by home and change. I'd wanted to put the brooch in a safe place anyway. No more carrying it around in my purse.

I'd bought one of those stand-alone safes and put it in my closet. I punched in the numbers I'd programmed, swung open the door, and placed the box inside.

There you go, Melinda Sue. Not so easy to get your sticky fingers on now, huh?

I looked through my closet for my True Religion jeans. I would already stand out at the Sandpiper, but I wanted to blend in with the crowd as much I could. At least until Kendall got there. I didn't think "blend-in" was in his vocabulary. I pulled on my jeans, donned a blue and white striped tank top, added some big gold hoop earrings, and I was ready to go.

After feeding Thelma and Louise, I took Dogbert for a short walk and then climbed back in the Mercedes and headed down-town.

Ah, the Sandpiper. The bar is a true dive for the local crowd, and I mean that in the fondest way. Nothing pretentious about the place.

"Hi, Mike." I paid my five-dollar cover charge at the sticker-plastered door and wondered if it was reggae night. I hadn't been to the local hole-in-the-wall for prob-ably a year but it hadn't changed. The smell of old wood, spilled beer and late night par-ties hit me as I walked in. It was the kind of place where everyone knew your name — at least by the end of the night, anyway.

The bartender studied me. I imagined what he saw was the prescribed Laguna Beach body whipped into shape by regular workouts. If he was really observant he might have noticed the expensive highlights, the designer jeans, and the years of beauty pageant posture that allowed me to cross the room without flinching at the stares.

Like a show dog's, the training was in-grained.

What I made sure he didn't see were the holes my divorce had put in my confidence. But you know what? Those had also made me stronger and wiser. I was no longer a greenhorn on the guy circuit.

I would not be fooled again.

I said hello to Chuck, the owner, ordered a drink, and sat down to wait for Kendall. The Sandpiper has to be the best people-watching spot in town. Kendall had said seven o'clock and it was ten minutes 'til. I wouldn't have long to wait.

By seven-thirty, I'd sipped at my drink for as long as I could. The place was beginning to fill up with after dinner drinkers and a young crowd of partiers. I'd been hit on twice by guys a good ten years younger than me. It was sort of flattering but it also sort of gave me the creeps. Guess I'd never make it as a cougar, huh?

I checked my watch again. I would give him fifteen more minutes and then I was out of there.

At eight o'clock I bailed. As I opened the door and stepped into the warm Laguna evening, my eyes adjusted from the darkness of the bar to the outside light. I'd parked my car across PCH and up a little ways on Brooks. There'd been few open spots. The fast food restaurant across the street was busy.

I inhaled in the dual smells of fried food and fresh sea air.

Gosh, I was getting to be an old fogey at thirty. I had a moment's pause when I noticed someone waiting in the shadows. I reached in my purse for my cell phone and my mace, just in case.

As the shadow stepped forward, I was surprised to see it was Detective Malone.

My heart went back to its regular rhythm. Sort of. I scrambled for something to say to cover my surprise. "Well, well. The elusive detective who can't return phone calls puts in an in-person appearance. To what do I owe the honor?"

Okay, maybe that came out snarkier than I intended. Malone had that effect on me.

"A regular hangout for you?" He ignored my question but looked me over from head to toe, as if the analysis might tell him what I was up to.

"I was meeting someone."

"Stood you up?" He was in black, as usual, which was part of the reason I hadn't spotted him at first.

"Hmm. Guess so." I didn't think I'd share who'd stood me up. I was pretty certain Malone wouldn't be happy to hear I'd scheduled a meeting with Kendall to talk about Kevin Blackstone.

He fell into step with me. "Let's take a walk."

"Official business, Detective?"

"No, I'm off-duty."

"Okay, where would you like to walk?"

"Doesn't matter."

We crossed PCH and walked north. The highway buzzed with evening traffic. Local workers done for the day, residents in fancy sedans and sports cars, teens driving the strip looking to see and be seen.

"Caro, I know you think you're helping Diana with all the questions you're asking, but what I really need is for you to leave this alone."

"Detective —" I began.

"Judd," he corrected. "I'm off-duty remember."

"Judd, you arrested my friend. My friend who wouldn't hurt anyone, who didn't kill Kevin Blackstone, and who is right now sitting in the LBPD jail."

"I know you're just trying to help, Caro. But please back off before you or someone else gets hurt." His tone seemed to hold genuine concern.

"I've found out some stuff," I said. "Stuff you should know about."

He sighed. "So what makes you think you know anything I don't?"

I'll admit, that gave me pause. For about half a second. "The fact that Diana's still in your jail."

"It's not technically mine."

"You know what I mean. Have you had a chance to look at Kevin's notebook?"

"That's police business."

"Fine. What about the dogs? And Spike, the Green House employee who was bitten by Kevin's dogs? The same guy who gave his real name as Hans Gruber."

Malone almost smiled, which made me think a little better of him. At least he knew his Bruce Willis movies.

"Did you know he's missing? And that another Green House worker was killed recently?"

"Would you believe me if I said yes?"

"I don't know," I said. "I'd like to. But with Diana still under arrest, I'm not buying it."

He laughed then, and I was annoyed to discover that he had a nice laugh.

"I was sure you wouldn't." There wasn't any ire in his words. "Seriously, Caro. Leave it alone. I don't want you to get hurt."

He was back to that quiet concern. Since I didn't know what else to say, I just walked. We continued our leisurely stroll past shops and restaurants. Gina's Pizza was packed. The outside stools were filled with people and pizza. The Italian spices assailed my nose and I realized I'd missed dinner. Malone touched my back as I stepped into

the crosswalk and I felt a shiver of awareness in my midsection.

Of course, it might have been hunger.

"Oh, and Caro . . ." His tone was still even
and friendly.

"Yes?" I glanced up at his face.

"We had a report of an attractive red-
headed shoplifter at the Bow Wow Boutique
this afternoon." He studied my face, clearly
looking for a reaction.

"Really? How awful." I fought back a self-
satisfied smile.

*Did that mean Malone thought I was attrac-
tive?*

We went another half-block.

"Was any merchandise stolen?" I hoped
my voice was full of innocence.

"Don't push it, Caro. I've about had
enough of you and your cousin and this
ridiculous battle over a family trophy." His
tone held warning.

I thought it best to leave that comment
alone. I have fabulous restraint at times.

"I might just lock you both up," he continued.

Oft times my restraint is short-lived. I
stopped in my tracks so he had to look at
me. "With Diana?"

He had the decency to look contrite. A
little.

Judd and I moved to the side to let a crowd of people pass and then turned back south toward Brooks where my car was parked.

The silence between us was as thick as the damp night air.

Judd Malone was a mystery. Quiet, a man of few words. Strong, intense, focused.

Good qualities in a detective. Good qualities in a man.

The wind picked up and rattled the palm trees. It looked like a storm was rolling in. I raised my face to the wind and let it toss my hair.

Malone caught my gaze and raised a brow in question.

"I love a good storm," I explained.

We looked at each other for a couple of beats, and then began moving again.

Almost under his breath he said, "I would have guessed that about you."

CHAPTER TWENTY-SIX

At first I thought it was the sheen of rain-drops on the pavement beside my car, and then I realized it was the glint of broken glass.

My driver's side window had been smashed.

"Any idea what they were after?" Malone abruptly morphed into total cop mode. He walked all the way around the car and peered in the broken window without touching anything. He pulled out his cell phone and called in the incident.

"You don't think it was just random vandalism?" A girl could hope.

"Probably not." He nodded toward the other cars parked along the same stretch. None of the others had been touched. "I'm not kidding when I tell you it's dangerous to keep poking around in this."

I took a deep breath and blew it out. "It could be someone thinks I still have Kevin's notebook. Or someone who thinks I have something that belonged to Kevin."

"Why do you think that?"

"Well. His brother was asking me if Kevin had given me anything to keep."

Malone shot me another irritated look. "When was this?"

"Yesterday."

"Why were you even talking to Kevin's brother?"

I explained about Kevin's dogs and how J.T. had wanted to know more about his brother's last hour. Malone glared at me the whole time.

"I think I convinced J.T. that Diana didn't kill Kevin," I finished.

Malone stuck his thumb between his eyes and squeezed his eyes shut like he was in pain.

Well, you know what they say. In for a penny, in for a pound. "Also, Detective, there are a couple of other things I think you should know."

Given the look on his face, I think at that juncture, Malone would've liked to just shoot me on the spot.

Thank goodness for me, his steely control prevailed.

I filled him in on my conversation with Kendall. And that it had been Kendall I was meeting at the Sandpiper. And what I suspected about Mandy and Kevin having an affair.

He was plenty mad by the time I was done confessing to all my "meddling."

I think that was the term Malone favored. Or it might have been "interfering." I believe I heard both.

Two uniformed officers arrived and took down the information they needed for a police report. They advised me that my insurance would need a copy of the report and instructed me how to obtain one.

Malone was no less angry by the time the LBPD squad car pulled away. Nevertheless, fine law enforcement professional that he was, he helped me brush enough of the shattered glass off my seat that I could drive home.

The wind continued to whip the bushes and trees as I drove through the streets to my neighborhood. Malone followed in his car.

I hit the garage door opener and pulled in. Malone stopped in front of the house. I flipped on the garage light and waved to let him know I was safely inside.

The storm finally broke as Malone pulled away.

■ ■ ■ ■

The next morning I woke up feeling like I hadn't slept a wink. I'd dreamt I was being chased by giraffes, roared at by a leather-wearing lion, and charmed by a brown-eyed fox who kept beckoning me into the woods. All this while trying to open a cage to release a beautiful Macaw.

No dream therapy was necessary to interpret my night terrors. My head. Yeah, it's a jungle in there.

Thank heavens, I didn't need to hurry to the office. I made some coffee and retrieved my phone messages while still in my pajamas.

One of the messages was from Leland, the overworked landscape manager I'd talked to yesterday. I hoped he had some new information about Spike.

I called him back and could hear a mower in the background so he must have been on-site somewhere.

"Just a minute, let me get where I can hear you."

"Okay," I answered, but I'm not sure he could even hear that.

"Hello? Are ya there?"

"Yes, I'm here." I stirred some cream into

284

my coffee.

"I wanted to call and tell you about the young guy you were asking me about."

"Have you heard from him?"

"Not exactly. Wait just a minute." I could hear him chew out one of his workers who was apparently trimming too close to a fountain and throwing grass clippings in the water.

"Hello?"

"Yes, I'm still here."

"Here's the deal. I got a call from the police, and the guy was killed in a hit and run accident up in Newport Beach."

"Really?" Whoa.

I was, to use Ollie's word, gobsmacked. "How did they know to contact you?"

"I guess my contact information on the back of a Green House card was the only thing he had in his pockets. Strange, huh?"

"Very." My mind buzzed with the possibilities. This couldn't be a coincidence. No way, no how.

"Well, that's all then. Got to get back to it. Just thought you'd want to know since you were lookin' for him."

"Thanks very much for calling me." I pushed the button to end the call.

Now what? It was possible my earlier theory had been right. The guy had been a hoodlum, and had taken the landscaping job hoping to gain access to the luxury homes in the gated communities served by Green House.

Maybe when his encounter with Kevin had gone badly, he'd taken off.

I suppose it was possible Spike getting run over was an accident, but with Malone's repeated warnings about me getting hurt, I doubted it.

I wondered if Malone knew Spike was dead. Just to make sure, I was going to call him. Not that I would gloat over being right about Spike as a strong suspect, but I needed to know if his death would get Diana freed. I dressed for the day in my Marine Room tank top and tan Michael Kors cargo shorts, then called Malone's number.

This daily call to Malone had become a regular thing. I might have to add Homicide to my speed dial.

I got his answering service. Again. So I called the police department, and Gidget told me Diana was still a guest.

That made me both annoyed and gobsmacked.

I'd dropped my car off to have the window fixed and they gave me a loaner. The new model Audi was fun to drive, but I missed my car. I stopped at the office for a few minutes, and then went by the animal shelter to check on Zeus and Tommy Boy and the depressed Labrador I'd examined a few days ago. One of the volunteers had found a great foster family who was willing to take her in. They were going to take her to the care center to visit her former owner.

There was also another dog who'd just come in that Don had called me about.

If a person can't take care of their pet, bringing them to the shelter is the best solution. But many people were either embarrassed or ashamed and just dropped them off out front without coming in, most times after hours.

That's not a good idea for a lot of reasons. The shelter's on a busy road for one thing, and the hills are full of non-domesticated wildlife for another.

Last night someone had dropped off a bad-tempered Maltese. A cute dog. It was hard to say if she'd been dropped off because she was a terror, or if the behavior Trixie, (the name they'd given her at the shelter) was exhibiting was because of fear and the instability of being abandoned.

That's what I was there to determine.

Because Trixie's aggression seemed to be

directed at people not other dogs, I recommended some sessions spent in social time with the other animals. Dogs truly are pack animals and sometimes it helps.

Still, you want to keep an eye on a small mean-tempered dog you've added to the mix. Much like a bully tossed onto a playground, a grumpy dog messes with everybody's feeling of safety.

After I'd spent a little time working with the Lab and checked in again on Trixie, I stopped by to see Zeus and Tommy Boy. They were in the exercise pen but were side-by-side as usual. They were brothers in arms, and again I really hoped they wouldn't be separated.

Don was busy supervising the cage-cleaning volunteers, but stopped to chat for a little while.

"How are they doing?" I asked.

"Really great." He smiled. I could tell he'd become attached to the pair.

"What a good boy." I patted Zeus's head and, using both hands, scratched his big furry neck. "Someone's going to be so lucky to have you for a friend.

"You, too, buddy." I'd turned to do the same neck massage for Tommy Boy when I noticed something sticky on my hand. "What the heck is that?"

I lifted my hand to look at it and realized the sticky substance was blood.

"Don, come here." I called him over. "Something's wrong with Zeus."

Tommy Boy came over and began licking the area on Zeus's neck where I'd encountered the blood.

I pushed him away and knelt on the floor to examine the wound. Sure enough, there was a section of his neck where the flesh was raw and exposed. The fur around it was wet with blood.

Don leaned in for a look. "What the heck?"

"My thoughts exactly." I reached over and pulled Tommy Boy to me so I could take look at his neck also.

"Well, would you look at this?" He had a matching wound, not as bad, but it posed a potential for infection. Zeus leaned in and tried to lick Tommy Boy's neck.

"Don't, hon, you'll make it worse." I redirected Zeus.

"Come here, boy." Don took hold of the dog's collar.

"Do you think someone could have hurt them, or something could have fallen on them?"

"I don't see how." Don shook his head.

"Me neither." I couldn't imagine what had

happened.

"We'll look around for any rough nails or torn sections of fence."

"In the meantime, we'd better have Dr. Daniel take a look at these. I'd hate to see something like this get infected."

"I agree," Don said.

There was no point in bandaging the wound because the dogs wouldn't leave a bandage in place, but we could clean and disinfect the area.

I went to get the pet first aid kit, and Don went to call Dr. Daniel.

Even though Malone had been pretty darn clear about what he thought of my investigative activities, I couldn't just sit around and do nothing. Since I'd told Mandy she had a day to let her husband know about her and Kevin, I thought it only fair to let her know the police now had that information. I headed to the Beenermans'.

Andy had not been home very often when I'd been at the Beenermans' working with Nietzsche, so I was surprised when he answered the door.

"Come in." He smiled in greeting but seemed distracted.

I stepped in and looked around for the dog. "How's Nietzsche doing?"

"From what Mandy has said, I think he's doing better."

"Has Mandy talked to you about Kevin?" If she had, perhaps I'd just talk to the two of them together.

"What?" His cell phone rang out a rock tune, and he pulled it from the pocket of his golf shorts.

It looked like Mandy hadn't had that talk with Andy.

"Sorry, I've got to take this." He stepped into the next room.

"Caro, we need to talk." Mandy appeared out of nowhere. She sported her requisite spandex but she looked as wiped out as I felt.

Grandma Tillie would have said she looked like she'd been rode hard and put away wet.

"We certainly do." I hoped my inflexibility was clear. She needed to know that I'd been serious about sharing the information about her and Kevin with the police.

She glanced around. "Where'd Andy go?"

"The study, I think. He got a phone call."

"Can you come into the kitchen?"

I followed her through the living room. Nietzsche was in his usual spot by the window. He seemed to be alright. His usual royal self. I resisted the urge to check on him. I wasn't there about the dog today.

As soon as we crossed into the kitchen, I pinned Mandy down. "Have you told your husband?"

"Not exactly, Caro. It's not what you think."

"Mandy, don't lie to me."

"Donuts," she blurted.

"Excuse me?" She'd gone off the deep end. "What's the matter with you? Are you on crack, Mandy?"

"Sugar donuts." Her turquoise eyes filled with big tears. "Kevin bought them for me. I'd go to his house to pick them up."

Oh, my gosh, she'd really meant donuts.

"Donuts? Like the pastry kind?"

"Yeah, the super sugary kind. The little ones with powdered sugar all over them. I've got a serious donut addiction, Caro." She covered her face with her hands and then looked up at me. "Please don't tell anyone."

Her eyes overflowed and tears ran down her perfect cheekbones. "Please don't tell Andy. I thought I could tell him but I couldn't do it. I couldn't bear to see the disappointment in his eyes."

I felt the burble of a hysterical giggle about to erupt from my throat. I swallowed hard to suppress it.

Seriously? This had been about a donut addiction?

I remembered the boxes of donuts in Kevin's pantry when I'd searched his house for Grandma Tillie's brooch. They hadn't been for him, they were for Mandy. As bizarre as it seemed, her story rang true.

She'd stopped sobbing but her eyes were still watery.

"How many donuts do you eat?"

"A couple of boxes a day, most days. Some days more."

"That's a lot of donuts." I didn't know what else to say.

"I've been having to drive all the way to Oceanside to get them. I'm so afraid of being seen buying them. Even then I wear a disguise just in case."

Again, that urge to let loose a snicker threatened.

"What kind of disguise?" I swear I couldn't help myself. If I was going to have the picture in my head of Mandy-Hot-Yoga sneaking into a grocery store in another city to buy donuts, I wanted to get the details right.

"Well, I put on jeans and a t-shirt, sunglasses, and leave my hair kind of uncombed."

Great, she disguised herself as me.

Suddenly, the thought wasn't quite as funny.

"If this gets out, Caro, my business will be ruined. I'm a role model, a fitness expert. I preach healthy food, clean eating."

I laid my hand on her tanned muscular arm. "Mandy, an eating disorder can't be dealt with until you acknowledge the problem. You need to get some help."

"I know," she whispered. "I'm just so ashamed."

It was still early afternoon when I left the Beenermans. I'd waved good-bye to Andy who was on another phone call. I'd given Mandy some names of potential eating disorder specialists (not local) she might consider contacting.

I'm afraid this latest revelation knocked Mandy and her husband out of my Murder Suspect Top Ten List. Still, there were plenty of others, and maybe their secrets were less hilarious. Oops, I meant more serious, of course.

When I arrived back at the office, Paris handed me a message from Jade at the Divine Dog Spa. What now?

Not Eleanor again, I hoped. I didn't usually do dog errands and had only agreed to pick up Eleanor the one time because I had time and didn't mind doing a favor for Lydia. I hoped she didn't plan on me doing it on a regular basis.

I called Jade and was surprised to find she wanted to know if I knew where Kendall was. He hadn't shown up for work that morning. They'd called his house and his cell phone. No answer.

Jade remembered me talking to Kendall yesterday and wondered if I had any idea what had happened.

"Do you think perhaps he had a family emergency? This isn't like him at all. He's a very dependable groomer, and quite well-liked by the staff and the clients."

I told her I hadn't heard from him. He'd arranged to meet me at the Sandpiper but hadn't shown up.

Jade said they'd just sent someone on staff to check his house and then if he wasn't there, they planned on calling area hospitals. If they didn't find him either of those places they would notify the police.

I told her I'd be sure to let them know if I heard from him.

My gut said Kendall's disappearance was related to Kevin Blackstone's murder. I just didn't know exactly how.

CHAPTER TWENTY-SEVEN

After a morning that had included a dead landscaper, a donut confession, and now a missing dog groomer, I was more than ready for a break.

I was headed home for a good long walk with Dogbert. The dealership had dropped off my car and picked up the Audi. I climbed in, started my car, and tried the window just to make sure it worked. Satisfied, I put the top down and pulled out of the parking lot.

The rain the night before had left everything washed clean. There were a few random palm fronds and leaves that'd been blown loose, but other than that, it was like it never happened. You've got to love southern California weather.

I'd just turned onto my street when my cell phone rang. I figured it was Diana calling to tell me she'd confessed, Malone calling to tell me I was about to be Diana's roommate, or my mother calling to say she was en route.

Lately phone calls had not brought good news.

"Caro Lamont." I answered more sharply than I should have. The phone call could be from a client after all.

"Caro." The voice was difficult to make out. "It's Kendall."

"Hell's bells, Kendall, where in Sam Hill are you? Everyone is looking for you. Even the police." I pulled into my driveway and put the car in park.

"Oh, no," he squeaked. "I was afraid of that."

"Tell me where you are and I'll come and get you."

"No! I can't be arrested, Caro. What would my Guido do?"

I didn't even ask who Guido was. I wasn't sure I wanted to know. "Why would you be arrested?"

"Because of what I did. What I asked Kevin to do." His voice quivered. "I am so sorry." He was sobbing now, and I couldn't make out all the words.

"Kendall," I said with some force. "I need you to buck up and tell me what's wrong, or I can't help you."

There was silence on the other end.

297

Mostly silence anyway. I could still hear a few sniffles.

"Tell me where you are, and I'll come there. No police, I promise."

"You swear?"

"I swear."

"Alright, meet me at the Beanies coffee shop in Dana Point. It's easy to find. I'll be there in five." He hung up.

So much for my walk with Dog. There was no way I could make it in five minutes, even if there was no traffic, and this time of day there would be traffic. I hit redial on my phone and tried to call Kendall back, but the call just went to voicemail.

Figuring I was going to be late anyway, I ran inside and let Dogbert out for a quick doggie break, and then got back in the Mercedes and headed toward Dana Point.

Kendall, hon, you had better show up this time.

I thought about calling Malone. I really did, but in the end I didn't. I didn't trust Detective Malone to handle Kendall carefully. I didn't know what he'd done or asked Kevin to do, but it had probably been illegal. It came through loud and clear that Kendall was upset and scared.

When I reached the back lot at Beanies, I looked around. Having no idea what Kendall drove, it was hard to tell if he was there or not.

I walked into the coffee shop and looked around. No Kendall.

Great.

I'd known it was a possibility after the last time. And it had taken me a while to get there. I wondered if he'd gotten tired of waiting and left.

I'd started back out the door when I heard a *pssst.*

I looked around again.

"Pssst!" A heavy-set lady in a bright red and black tiger-stripe caftan was waving at me. A tall black turban swathed her head and gorgeous dreadlocks fell to her shoulders. Her bright red lips smiled and she motioned for me to approach her table.

Did she want to talk to me?

I looked behind me. It was definitely me she was motioning to.

Maybe Kendall had left a message.

I was within spitting distance before it hit me. The "lady" wasn't a large woman but a man. Kendall, in fact.

In a wig and either a bodysuit or a lot of pillows.

Truth be told, I have to tell y'all there's a distinct possibility Kendall made a better looking woman than he did a man.

I sat down at the table. "Kendall. For cryin' in a bucket, hon. Everyone is worried sick about you."

"They are?" Tears welled up in his eyes and threatened his false eyelashes and very thick mascara. I hoped it was the waterproof kind.

"Oh shoot, darlin'. Don't cry." I reached into my bag for some tissues.

"I didn't mean to scare anyone, but I am in so much trouble."

"Yes, I believe you are." I handed him several tissues. "Now do you want to tell me what's going on? And why you didn't show up last night?"

"I did show up last night, but there was a suspicious man dressed all in black lurking in the alley," Kendall said. "I got a bad feeling about him, so I left."

"That was Detective Malone. He has that effect on people. Okay. So tell me how you knew Kevin."

"I met him at the dog park where I'd taken my Guido for a run. He's cooped up all the time, poor little guy, because I work such long hours, and so I brought him to work for a while. But he had to stay in the kennel while he was at the spa, so it really wasn't much better."

"Guido is?"

"My little precious Pomeranian pal. He's with a friend right now. I was afraid to go home." Kendall looked over his shoulder nervously.

That explained Guido at least.

"Kevin was really nice and easy to talk to and I was telling him about my friend." He stopped to take a sip of his frappuccino.

"Your friend, Carlo?" I urged him to continue.

"Yes, the hot and handsome Carlo Manolo. We were a couple at the time." His eyes welled with tears again, and he blotted at them with the wad of tissues.

"Your friend," I prompted again.

"I was blinded by love. That's my only defense." He hiccupped a sob. "What am I going to do?"

"Kendall, hon. Slow down." I patted his big hairy arm, which was adorned with large black and red bangle bracelets.

I had two thoughts.

One, how did I ever think he'd been a women? What the heck was matter with me? My observation skills were definitely in question.

Two, if you were thinking you were in trouble with the law, and maybe accused of murder, would you stop to coordinate your accessories with your outfit? Just seemed a little out of whack.

But then, overall, Kendall was a bit north of normal in the fashion department. Okay, maybe not just the fashion department.

I pulled myself back to the issue at hand. "What did Kevin do for you?"

"He got fake ID papers for Carlo."

"Carlo was here illegally?" I was beginning to get the picture.

"He told me he was here on a visa. Then his visa expired, and he just needed some time to get things all legally fixed up." He flipped his dreadlocks over his shoulder.

"What made you think Kevin could help you with fake identification papers?"

"It was Kevin who suggested it." Kendall had calmed down but still continued the periodic sniffle. "I'd run into him in Oceanside at a bar where he was with this guy who it turned out does the papers. Kevin approached me about Carlo, and said he'd help us. All I had to do was forget I ever saw him with that guy. I don't remember his name. See? I've forgotten it."

He barely took a breath before he continued. "So I took Kevin up on his offer, but then Carlo left me for Harry, this designer from San Diego who had the hots for him, and then Kevin was killed, and I wanted to tell the police about the guy, but I knew I'd be in trouble if I did. And then whoever killed Kevin might come after me. Or the police might put me in jail. And I don't know what I'd do." He'd begun to cry again. "Who would take care of Guido? He'd be an orphan."

Oh, good golly. The drama. There were soap operas with less convoluted storylines than Kendall's.

"Okay, first off, you have to tell the police."

"Oh, no, Caro. No," he wailed. "I'm not strong like the beautiful Diana. I'd never last in a jail cell."

The other people in the coffee shop were staring at this point. I had to get him quieted down.

"I'll call Detective Malone." I felt a bit of kinship with Kendall. He and I had both been keeping information from the police in an attempt to protect people.

"I'll explain. He'll be very understanding," I lied.

I called Malone on my cell phone. Lo and behold, he actually answered. I gave him the basics and asked him to meet us. You could have knocked me over with a feather when he agreed.

When he arrived, thank goodness he wasn't driving a police car. I'm afraid a police car might have sent our caftan-wearing dog groomer over the edge.

I had Kendall recount all he'd told me for Malone, who to his credit made no comment about Kendall's disguise. I could see the disbelief I'd felt on Malone's face, as well as the confusion.

Once Detective Malone had heard the whole story, we bundled Kendall into his Toyota, assured him things were going to be okay, and sent him to pick up Guido.

Malone leaned against his Camaro. He'd parked next to me. His car was spotless, the silver metallic finish gleaming in the late afternoon sun.

"I see you got your window repaired," he said.

"Yes, thank goodness it didn't take them long." I'd been surprised the repair had been quick.

He looked over the repair job and nodded approval. "Looks like they did a good job."

"Where is the book?" I asked.

"What?" He lifted narrowed blue eyes to my face.

"Kevin's book. Where is it?"

"In the evidence lockup at the police station. Where it belongs."

"Do you remember an entry about Kendall in it?"

"I don't remember seeing his name. Why?"

"I don't know. This just seems like the kind of dirt Kevin might have noted."

"Caro . . ." His tone warned. I'd dealt with enough bad dogs to know what came next.

I was better with dogs than detectives.

"I now know Mandy Beenerman's deep, dark secret," I taunted.

"And?"

"And it's not what you think."

"How do you know what I think?" One dark brow lifted.

"Because you're not all that hard to figure out." I leaned in to look him in the eye. "You probably think it has something to do with sex."

His expression gave him away. That was exactly what he'd been thinking.

"It has nothing to do with sex, and everything to do with donuts."

"Huh?"

I filled him in on Mandy's donut addiction, Kevin serving as her donut supplier, and my recommendation for eating disorder help for Mandy. "So, there you have it. One you can check off your list."

Malone reached out and took me by the shoulders, his strong hands warm against my bare skin. He turned me around and looked me over from head to toe.

"What are you doing?"

"Looking for your badge, Officer Lamont." He dropped his hands and stepped back. "You don't seem to have a badge."

"Point taken." I opened my car door and got in.

"I'll follow you home."

"I think I can find my way, Detective."

"I'm sure you can find your way, but can you stay out of trouble? That's the real question."

I wasn't looking for trouble, but I couldn't let sleeping dogs lie. I understood all too clearly Malone's point, but the police were taking too long. Meanwhile Diana was still locked up and they were no closer to finding the real killer. I would continue working my way through Kevin's list and try to figure out if anyone on the list had a secret worth killing for.

When I got home, I pulled out my copies of the pages from Kevin's book. After my car had been broken into, I'd put them in the safe with Grandma Tillie's brooch.

There had to be a note that referenced Kendall. Searching the pages, I finally located it. It said: *KR, cub gy dgr, frm SFB, so fk id, LB 2yr, rtr*

306

If KR stood for Kendall Reese, *gy dgr* could mean gay dog groomer or guy dog groomer. Who was I to say? I wasn't sure about *frm SFB* but it could be a reference to wherever it was Kendall was from. I could ask him.

And I was pretty sure *fk id* was fake identification.

Shoot, I'd missed the connection before.

People and their secrets. If everyone would be a bit more forthcoming, maybe we (I know, I still don't sport a badge) could figure out who had killed Kevin.

I had a sudden thought.

Why had Kevin been with someone who dealt in fake papers? I'd tried looking up Kevin before. There were Kevin Blackstones in nine states. I tracked down information on each one of them but none of them had lived in Ruby Point. In fact, none even had a California connection. At least not that I could find.

Kendall's friend, Carlo, had gotten help with a fake identity from Kevin. Was it possible Kevin Blackstone wasn't who he'd appeared to be? Nothing I'd been able to find matched with the Kevin I knew. What if I'd been looking under the wrong name?

I wondered about J.T. and if he also wasn't who he seemed to be. What if the brothers were hiding from someone, and whatever it was J.T. thought Kevin had given me had something to do with their secret identities?

I pulled out my laptop and settled in on the couch. Dogbert joined me and tucked himself against my side.

How do you start looking for someone when it seems everything you know about him is false?

I never oversleep. Generally an early riser, I set my alarm only as a back-up. However, the last few nights of fitful sleep must have caught up with me.

I rushed through getting dressed. Another warm, sunny day was on the horizon, so I opted for a yellow print Banana Republic sundress and my Ferragamo flats. I grabbed my bag, picked up my daily list, and headed out the door.

By noon I'd met with the caterer about the Fur Ball and visited with Katie at Tivoli Too, the facility where the event was to be held. When that was over I felt a little more caught up and decided to go by the office to pick up some client records.

Once there, I grabbed the files I needed and hurried past the reception desk. I could see Paris trying to get my attention, but I didn't want to get hung up when I'd promised Dogbert that walk.

"Caro." She followed me to the door. "Caro."

If she'd been a dog she would have nipped at my heels.

I turned. "What is it, hon? I'm kind of in a rush."

"I've been meaning to ask one of you about this, but I can't seem to catch anybody. You're busy with more and more clients every day. And Kay is busy because she's got this potential pending sale on the Mitford property. And Suzanne is, like, not very responsive at all. You'd think being a psychic and all she'd *know* what I wanted to talk to her about, and I wouldn't have to tell her. She should just, like know. You know? Maybe she does and that's why she won't answer me. She can't be bothered. All I know is she totally ignores me. How rude is that? And David, well, he's just David. You know. I don't take it personally."

Oh, my gosh, I didn't think she would ever take a breath.

When she finally did I broke in. "So you've been trying to discuss something with one of us about the office? What did you need?"

"Well, it's this mail." Paris lifted a stack of unopened envelopes carefully without using her fingers. Obviously her manicure hadn't completely dried. "I don't know what I should do with it."

"Whose mail is it?"

"I don't know."

"What do you mean you don't know?" I was about to lose what little patience I had left, whether it was her fault or not. "Who is it addressed to?"

"No one."

Now I was completely exasperated.

"I mean, no one person specifically. It's mail for Suite C."

Suite C was the empty office between the real estate broker and the psychic.

"It's addressed to 'ACME.'" She held up one of the envelopes to show me. "I don't know who ACME is."

"Well, who usually gets the mail?"

"A courier mostly." Paris restacked the mail. "This guy comes in once a week and picks up the mail, but he hasn't come for the past three weeks. So it keeps piling up."

"Contact the owners and see if the lease has expired. Who keeps track of the leases?"

"I don't know. I don't have anything to do with that." All of a sudden the stack of envelopes she'd been straightening collapsed and the mail began sliding every which way. She tried to catch it, but that just made things worse.

I lunged for it but couldn't move quickly enough. "Well, call the number we have to report building problems to. They should be able to put you in touch with the leasing agent or the owner."

"Okay. Thanks, Caro." The mail continued to cascade off the desk. "I knew you could help."

"You're welcome." I picked up a bunch of the envelopes that had fallen on the floor during the avalanche and handed them to Paris. The top one had been marked "Return to Sender."

Paris reached to take it, but something drew my attention. "Wait."

I pulled the letter back to look at it. The handwriting on the envelope was Kevin Blackstone's distinctive scrawl. I'd seen it on the checks he wrote to PAWS and I'd been looking at it every single day for the past two weeks trying to figure out his shorthand code.

"Let me see those." I put my files down and held out my hand for the rest of the mail.

I flipped through the envelopes. Most were addressed to "ACME Pharm."

"What is ACME Pharm?" I looked up at the blonde.

"I have no idea." Her pretty face was creased into a frown.

"I'll take care of these, Paris."

I probably shouldn't have butted in after Malone had told me in no uncertain terms to stay out of his investigation, but really, the police needed to see this. I knew it was borderline messing with the US Mail, which I'd always heard was a federal offense, but I wasn't going to open any of the letters. I would just deliver them to Detective Malone at the police station.

This time I didn't bother to call Malone. I stuffed the letters in my bag and drove directly to the police station.

Arnold and Gidget were at the desk. I now knew their names were Sally and Lorraine, but in my head I still thought of them as Arnold and Gidget. The two women had turned out to be great allies in taking care of Diana.

"Hi, Caro," Arnold greeted me.

"Here to see Diana?" Gidget asked.

"Not at the moment, hon. I need to see Detective Malone right away."

"I'll check, but I think he's gone to lunch." Arnold lumbered by to peer at an old-fashioned check-out board on the back wall. "Yep, out to lunch."

I let the obvious comment pass.

"I'll wait." I settled on the bench with my bag of letters. I resisted the urge to pull them out and look them over.

Malone walked in the door just then with a Shake Shack bag in his hand.

"Ms. Lamont." He nodded. "You here to see me?"

I thought we'd transitioned to a first name basis. So much for that. "I am."

"Come on back then." He pushed through the door and held it open for me.

I'd been in the police station more times recently than I'd like, but I'd not been to Malone's office. He led me down the hallway in the opposite direction from the holding cell where Diana held court.

"Have a seat." He shifted a chair from behind the door and offered it.

"Go ahead and eat." I pointed at his Shake Shack bag. "Don't let your burger get cold."

He set the bag aside. "What brings you here, Ms. Lamont? Another suspect? Some other piece of evidence you've withheld? Another theory?"

He didn't say "crackpot theory" but it was implied.

"There's no need to be rude, Judd." I used his first name with purpose. "I tried to reach you for several days about the notebook,

313

and you didn't return my calls."

"Shouldn't have taken it in the first place, Caro."

He was right, I shouldn't have, but I did try to return it. I chose not to respond to that. "And you continue to not answer my calls in a timely fashion. So I've brought you some more evidence that fell into my lap, which is not at all the same as either inadvertently violating a crime scene or withholding evidence. Are you interested?"

He waved for me to go on.

I may have tipped my nose up a bit as I continued. "At the office today, Paris, our receptionist, mentioned that the suite I always thought was vacant is actually rented. And the mail is usually picked up, but hasn't been for three weeks. It's been piling up."

"Go on."

"Well, she pulled out all of these envelopes, and I couldn't help but notice that several of the 'Return to Sender' letters are addressed in Kevin's handwriting." I handed over the bunch.

"You sure?" He picked one up and stared at it.

"You can compare the writing with his notebook to be sure, but I know it is. Kevin paid by check for his services from PAWS, and I've seen his handwriting." I didn't mention I'd also been staring at the pages I'd copied from his notebook.

"We'll check it out." His expression didn't change much but his sense of alertness did. He pulled out of his slouch and sat forward in his chair.

Finally, something had gotten his attention.

"You know, if Kevin helped Kendall's friend get a fake ID, it's possible Kevin wasn't who we thought he was."

"Not lost on me." He pulled his Shake Shack bag forward and stood.

Clearly I was dismissed. I pushed back my chair and left.

I took the opportunity to look in on Diana while I was there. She was busy doing an interview with *Entertainment Today.* The television cameras took up a lot of room in the holding cell.

She looked good. Bella must have dropped off her PUP (Protecting Unwanted Pets) t-shirt. She'd paired it with a long silk skirt, knotted the t-shirt at her waist and managed to look glamorous.

I caught her attention and mouthed, "I'll come back."

She smiled and nodded and then went back to her impassioned plea to the public to not take on animals they couldn't take care of, to spay and neuter their animals, and to lend support, either money or time, to their local shelter. She was a dream-come-true spokesperson for animal rescue, and I'd be willing to bet before the end of the taping, she'd work in a plug for the Fur Ball.

As I ducked out and headed toward the parking, my cell rang.

I knew from the caller ID that it was Mama. I could let it go to voicemail, but I'd decided I needed to put my big girl pants on and deal with her myself. I would just explain to her that now was not a good time for a visit.

"Hello, Mama."

"Hello, sugar." Her Texas drawl reached across the miles, and I felt my blood pressure climb a notch. "I can't believe what you're going through with this murder and all. How are you holding up?"

I took a deep breath. *She means well. She means well.*

It was my mantra. And she did mean well. It's just that we were like oil and water. More like Texas crude and champagne. She was the champagne, I was the crude.

At least in her mind. She saw me as strong, important, even valuable, but not always appropriate for polite society.

"I'm doing just fine. How are you? How is Daddy?" I didn't tell her I'd talked to Hub, and I was sure he wouldn't have ratted me out.

"We're all well."

"Glad to hear it." I waited for the purpose of her call. I knew there was a purpose. I only hoped the purpose didn't have a plane ticket and an itinerary attached. Or yet another potential date to spice up my social life.

"Carolina, sugar, I'm callin' to tell you I don't think I'm going to be able to come to stay with you right now after all."

"Re—eally?" I gulped.

"Yes, darlin,' it seems Hub has scheduled this big event, and you know he's completely inept at these things."

As Grandma Tillie used to say, "Well, butter my butt and call me a biscuit."

Hub, the lovely brilliant man, had pulled it off. I was safe, at least for a while.

"I'm afraid I'm stuck here until this shin-dig is over with. So much to do, invitations to get out, a decorator to hire. I've looked at several venues but none with the right ambiance for this very special event."

She was off and running. I have to admit, I tuned out just a bit at this point. I was so

317

relieved, and the occasional "uh-huh" satisfied my mother that I was listening.

Hub had saved my bacon. I was sending him a case of Glenlivet the minute I got off the phone.

CHAPTER TWENTY-EIGHT

You know the saying, "you don't always get what you want"? After sitting in Malone's office where I was teased by the smell of his food, what I wanted was a Shake Shack burger and a date shake. Date like the fruit, not like going on a date. I hesitate to say it's to die for, given all that's been going on, but suffice to say it's a unique delicacy.

I was on my way there, but as I was getting in my car, I noticed Shar Summers pull up in her white Thunderbird convertible. I waited until she parked and got out, then walked over to check on how Babycakes was doing with guests.

Okay, I confess I had an ulterior motive. After reading through the notes in Kevin's book again, I'd come up with a theory about Shar's secret, and I wanted to test it.

"Hi, Shar." She'd unfolded herself from the convertible, and tucked the Chinese Crested into her pink Juicy Couture dog tote that proclaimed "Will Beg for Juicy" in big letters on the side.

"Oh, Caro, you startled me." The girl and dog were attired in matching pink sequined tank tops and headbands. "I didn't see you walk up."

"I just wondered how Babycakes was doing." I pushed my sunglasses up on my head so I could see her better.

"Pretty good. Though she's still a nervous little girl."

The dog looked up at me with pleading dark eyes. She shook nervously, her whole body quaking. My instinct was to touch her, but I knew better than to reach into the carrier.

"You have to be firm, Shar," I told her. "That's the secret."

She nodded, her sparkly headband winking in the sunlight.

"Speaking of secrets." It was an awkward segue, but I didn't have time for subtle. "Kevin shared some secrets about his neighbors, and I wondered if you could confirm some things for me."

"Secrets about who?" Her voice was definitely squeaky now.

"Well, you for one." I took a deep breath. "Your real last name is Schwartz, right?"

"Sure. A lot of actresses take stage names.

320

Like Marilyn Monroe was Norma Jeane Baker and Doris Day was Doris Kappelhoff, and Greta Garbo was Greta Gustafsson and —"

I held up my hand to stop her. The kid knew her Hollywood history. I had to give her props for that. "My question is about your age."

Shar stilled. "M-my age?"

Bingo.

"Yes, your age. You're not seventeen, are you?" The entry had said, *nt 17.* And if it were true, she wasn't seventeen, but older, and word got out, the producers of her television show might have a problem with renewing her contract for another season.

What had clued me in to this possibility was her tendency to dress so young. Frilled dresses, flats, soft dewy make-up. It could just be that her taste ran to those things, kind of like her over-cute home furnishings. Or it could be she wanted to give the impression of being younger than she was.

Most teen girls, on the other hand, seem to want to dress like they're older. I had one thirteen-year-old cousin back in Texas who often dressed like she was thirty. That was if her daddy didn't catch her and make her change her outfit.

"I, uh, I . . ." Her voice trailed off.

"Shar, hon, if Kevin knew you were older than what your producer believes, and you had a fight with him about it, it would be better to tell the police about it than to let them find out from someone else."

Her lip trembled. "There wasn't anyone else around."

Ah-ha. I thought so.

"When was it you and Kevin fought?" I asked. Could it be the little bitty TV star had tased Kevin?

"The day before he died." Her quivering lip had turned into a full-body tremble, and soon she was shaking as badly as her dog. "He said he wouldn't tell." Her eyes filled and tears began to stream down her cheeks.

Seemed I was having that effect on a lot of people lately.

"It's okay, Shar. It's okay." I reached into my purse for tissues but I'd given them all to Kendall.

I finally got Shar calmed. Then I made her agree to call Malone and tell him what she'd told me. I was hoping he would take the information in Kevin's notebook more seriously if he realized how damaging some of it could be.

Then I went home, hoping Dogbert hadn't given up on me and moved in with the neighbors, and wondering what in the heck

Kevin Blackstone had been up to that had led to three people being killed.

CHAPTER TWENTY-NINE

Malone was parked in front of my house when I got home. What now? Had sending Shar to talk to Malone tipped him past the breaking point? Maybe he was going to try to arrest me for meddling. Whatever.

I waved at my next-door neighbor, Kitty Bardot, who was also just pulling in. She had her two Bengal cats in the car with her. Beautiful felines.

I could only imagine what she and the rest of the neighbors must think with all of the times the police had been to visit me lately.

I ignored Malone and hit the remote for the garage door opener. I pulled in, closed the garage door, and went through the house to the front door. When I opened it, Malone was standing there.

Black leather, five o'clock shadow, bad attitude. Too bad about that attitude thing. I didn't even know what I'd done this time. Except maybe question a suspect.

"Gosh, Detective, we've got to quit meeting like this," I said in my best Mae West voice.

As was usually the case, Malone had no sense of humor.

"Come on in, then." I held open the door. "Would you like a coke or a tea?"

"I'm good."

"Are you really?" I smiled my best don't-underestimate-me smile.

It seemed I'd gone over the edge. Maybe it was the lack of sleep. Maybe it was the worry. Maybe it was the craziness of donut addicted yoga instructors, dog groomers on the lam, and twenty-five-year-olds lying about their age. And three dead men.

Whatever it was, I was living on the edge and I couldn't seem to help myself pushing and trying to ruffle his feathers.

"Hmm." He still didn't smile.

"Alright. What have I done this time?" I pointed to the couch and sat in the chair. "I brought you the mail with Kevin's handwriting as soon as I was made aware of it. I opened nothing, I lost nothing, I kept nothing. I sent Shar to tell you her deepest, darkest secrets so you could judge for yourself what kind of information Kevin was collecting."

"I just have a few questions for you, Ms.

Lamont." He didn't sit.

"Dammit, Judd, stop with the Ms. Lamont crap."

There was a little flicker. Was he laughing at me?

"Did Kevin ever talk about what he did for a living?"

"He did not."

Malone stood in front of me arms crossed, feet planted.

"But that's true of most of my clients," I continued. "When I'm working with them, our only discussion is about their pet. How they make their living may come up in conversation related to how much or how little they're home, but other than that, we don't really talk about it."

Still silence from Malone.

"I assumed Kevin must either work from home, or have an independent income of some kind because he was home most of the time."

"Did you ever hear him mention any connection to the pharmaceutical business?"

"Never." I would have expected Kevin to be into sales or marketing if that were the case. He struck me as a people person. Not so much the science type.

"Alright." He moved to leave.

"Anything you'd like to share?" I stood

326

and walked him to the door.

Seemed like he could throw me a bone. After all, I'd been the one to cart all that mail to his office.

"No, and Caro. I heard from Shar Summers. Leave this the hell alone. Understand?"

"I understand."

And then he was gone.

Drug companies, huh? As soon as Malone left I headed for my computer. "Understand" and "obey" are two totally different words.

I stopped only to fix myself something to eat. The memory of the smell of that Shake Shack burger still haunted me, but I had to settle for warmed-up soup and a grilled cheese.

I searched the Internet until my eyesight blurred. It was like searching for a needle in a haystack. There were so many pharmaceutical companies. I tried every combination I could think of with Kevin Blackstone and most of the well-known corporate giants in the drug world. Then I tried just Kevin, thinking perhaps Blackstone was an alias.

Then I resorted to reading through websites detailing scandals, cover-ups, lawsuits, and case-action cases involving any sort of drug company. There were just too many.

I finally had to give up and go to bed.

As I fell asleep I told myself at least it seemed Malone had been open to taking the investigation in a new direction.

I prayed I'd wake up in the morning to a headline that said, "Hollywood's Sweetheart Set Free — Real Killer Behind Bars." Of course, it would make Diana happy if it also said, "Tickets still available for next week's Fur Ball."

CHAPTER THIRTY

I'd had enough of secrets. I'd had enough of lies. I'd had enough of everything in a muddle. So first on my list for the morning was cleaning up my own muddle. The boxes from Geoff, my ex, had arrived and I had stacked them in my living room. Maybe I couldn't straighten out all the secrets and lies today, but I could at least lend some order to my household.

Dogbert and the cats looked at me like I'd lost my mind when I tore into the boxes.

Two hours later I had a pile of books I wanted to keep, another stack to donate, and a garbage bag full of old mail, notices, and memos that hadn't been worth shipping.

Leave it to Geoff to let me sort it all out.

There were wads of unopened mail, mostly advertisements and outdated invitations to conferences. I smiled at the "Conference for Psychopharmacology and Treatment Modalities" in Barcelona, Spain. Then a drug company sponsored announcement about a new drug to treat sleep disorders. There were slick advertisements from all the big drug companies, including some of the ones I'd come across in my searches trying to find info about Kevin.

Wow, those drug companies spent a lot of money on advertising. I shuffled through the ads but practically all of them were outdated.

That had been my old life. It didn't really apply to dog psychology. I added the stack of paper to the recycling box.

My cell phone buzzed and I noted the number. Dr. Daniel Darling. I hoped it was good news on Kevin's dogs.

"Hi, Doc."

"Hey, Caro. Do you have a minute?"

"Sure."

"I contacted Don at the shelter, but I also wanted to let you know what was going on with Zeus and Tommy Boy."

"How are they? I wondered if the behavior could be grief related."

"Here's the deal. The spot where Zeus had the hot spot was the injection site for a microchip."

"Oh gosh, I gotcha. The identification chips the rescue groups use. We do them all

330

the time at the shelter. We check to see if they have one and then we scan it for the information. If they don't, we put one in."

"That's what I thought, too, at first. I had to take the one out of Zeus and this seems to be different. Or defective. My reader won't read it."

"That's odd." I continued stacking the papers to be disposed of.

"I've saved the one I removed and fixed them up. Both dogs are back at the ARL. One of the volunteers came and got them, but I knew you were worried, so I wanted you to know."

"Thanks, Daniel. I appreciate it." Something was nagging at the back of my thoughts but I couldn't quite bring it into focus.

"I also called Kevin's brother to let him know since, technically, he's the one responsible for them. I know you're looking at potential adoptions. It sounds like he's ready to sign release papers so adoption should be easier. And now that we've got this problem solved."

"Thanks, I'll look in on them later today." I hung up and added a note to check in on Zeus and Tommy Boy to my list of things to do.

Glad to be done with the mess of papers

Geoff had shipped to me, I stood and stretched. Wow, I was stiff. Those missed yoga classes were catching up with me.

As I carried the box of papers to the garage to place in the recycling bin, one of the flyers caught my attention. ZTB — Zeta Thomas Barnes. One of the big companies. They were as well known as Wyeth, Johnson and Johnson, and Pfizer. But it was the initials that made me stop and think.

I'd seen those initials recently.

I went and retrieved the copied pages from my safe. I was sure I'd seen ZTB in them. At the time it had made no sense relative to what I knew about Kevin, but now that Kevin had clearly had some connection to a pharmaceutical company, I knew it was too much of a coincidence.

I skimmed the pages. Sure enough, it was in the middle of all the Latin phrases Sam had translated for me.

Hidden in plain sight. ZTB.

I went back to my online search this time with a new objective. I looked for information on any scandals related to Zeta Thomas Barnes Pharmaceuticals. It didn't take long.

There it was. ZTB was in the midst of a government investigation related to the release of a drug found to have disfiguring side effects. The FDA had received complaints from many former patients who had used Poncé, one of the company's most popular and extremely profitable prescription-only products. It was an anti-aging serum.

There were stories with accusations of fraudulent clinical trials. They included shocking pictures of skin reactions after several treatments. Some sources claimed the government was in on the cover-up.

It was difficult to sort through which information was legitimate and which was not. In what seemed to be a reputable article, the author noted that apparently the company was on the verge on financial ruin if it turned out that the ZTB executives had been aware of the side effects.

It took a while, but I finally came across a picture of ZTB's executive marketing team. There was Kevin Blackstone. It wasn't a very clear picture, but it was him.

Except his name wasn't Kevin, it was Kirk. Kirk Blankenstein.

He had worked for ZTB and been one of their top-producing salespeople and then been promoted to a marketing director position. Guess what he'd been tops in?

Yup, sales of Poncé, the foundation of youth serum.

Wowza. That important secret hadn't been

in the list of Ruby Point residents' secrets in Kevin's book.

Kevin's secret was the biggest one of all.

The secret worth murder.

CHAPTER THIRTY-ONE

You know, it's funny how things work. If it hadn't been for my creep of an ex-husband and his timing in sending all the junk from our practice to me . . . if I hadn't been so angry he'd been too lazy to sort anything out . . .

And if I hadn't been so frustrated with everything else I couldn't figure out, I would've just let the boxes sit. Then I would have never figured out the right drug company connection. Not for a long while, anyway.

Once I made the drug connection, I still wouldn't have figured out where Kevin had hidden the information, if not for my "to do" list. When Dr. Daniel called about the dogs, if I hadn't written the note to remind myself about Zeus and Tommy Boy in such a hurry, I wouldn't have abbreviated their names.

As soon as I picked up my to do list and

saw my note — ZTB, the cogs in my brain made one of those slight turns and everything suddenly clicked.

ZTB.

The drug company, ZTB, Zeta Thomas Barnes.

The dogs' names, Zeus and Tommy Boy.

Daniel's call about the microchip.

Kevin's notation that ZTB was in ZTB. Good Lord, the guy had spelled it right out. I'd be willing to bet Kevin had put the information on a microchip and put the microchip inside the dogs. What was on that microchip? Incriminating evidence that would cost ZTB its reputation and bankrupt the company? Had Kevin been a whistle-blower?

If he had been, it made sense that someone might be willing to go to great lengths to shut him up. Like killing Joe, the regular Ruby Point landscape worker who'd been found beaten in the state park. Which opened the door for Spike, the new landscaper who wasn't really a landscaper, to be hanging around Kevin's house the day Kevin was killed. And who was now conveniently also dead.

If Spike killed Kevin, which seemed like a pretty good bet, the unanswered question remained: Who'd killed Spike and Joe? And more to the point, where was the killer now?

Holy guacamole, this was way bigger than I'd imagined. No wonder Malone kept warning me off. How much of this had he figured out? More than I had until just now, but maybe not enough.

My hands shook as I called Malone.

Shoot. His voicemail again. I left a scattered, cryptic message. I didn't take the time to go into detail. I wasn't even sure I understood it all yet. Mostly I just said I needed to talk to him right away. Right away.

I called the police station. Arnold/Sally answered and told me Malone had gone into L.A. to meet with some federal guy. That told me he'd figured out the same connection I'd come across. He was way ahead of me on that front.

I told Sally I needed to speak with Malone as soon as he was back. What I guessed he hadn't figured out yet was that Kevin had hidden the information in the dogs.

The dogs. Oh, God. I felt sick.

I had to keep Zeus and Tommy Boy safe until I could talk to Malone. I decided the only way to do that was to go to the ARL, pick them up, and keep them with me. The evidence would be safe, the dogs would be safe, and soon the people responsible for Kevin Blackstone's death would finally be behind bars.

And Diana could go home.

I drove as calmly as I could to the ARL. Don Furry was on duty, and he didn't question me picking up Zeus and Tommy Boy. He'd just filled their bowls and they happily lapped up water.

"The guys will be happy to get out after being cooped up at the vet's." Don handed me Zeus and Tommy Boy's leashes and the dogs bounded out to my car.

I drove around for a while trying to think what to do. Maybe I should simply take the dogs to the police station. They'd be safe there. I was just ready to turn back toward town when my cell phone rang. It was Malone.

"Thank God." I couldn't wait for hello.

"Caro, where are you?"

"Laguna Canyon Road," I answered. "Near the dog park."

"I'll meet you there."

It was a good plan because the amount of water the dogs had downed was making them antsy. That and they probably sensed my tension. We all three needed a break.

The dog park was minutes away and I scored a parking place up front. As soon as we were through the two gates, I turned them loose. They took care of business and then raced and romped and barked at each other like school kids out for the summer. I walked to the far end of the big dog area.

They were a sight to behold. German Shepherd dogs love to run. I leaned against the fence and watched and listened for Malone's car.

In my mind, I reviewed the facts as I thought I knew them.

Kevin Blackstone was not Kevin Blackstone.

He was instead Kirk Blankenstein, a former pharmaceutical marketing guru who had uncovered incriminating evidence about a ZTB drug with horrible side effects.

It was a drug that had been poised to save a company that was on the verge of bankruptcy without it.

Spike, the landscaper with the *Die Hard* fake name must have been sent to get the information from Kevin/Kirk. He may have killed Joe, the regular worker to gain access to Ruby Point.

The dogs in the gated community had known what the humans had not. There had been a predator in their midst. They were unsettled and in their own dog language they'd been communicating the danger. Too bad we hadn't understood sooner.

Spike may not have known about Kevin's

heart condition. Or maybe he had known. In any event, in what I figured was supposed to be an effort to convince Kevin to give up the goods, the torture had instead killed him.

That's when things got desperate.

I believed the company had then sent someone else in to take care of things, including Spike. But the clean-up man had been unsuccessful in finding where Kevin had hidden the incriminating evidence.

Kevin had trusted no one.

For good reason.

He was never sure who would turn out to be the enemy so he'd gathered dirt on everyone around him. Even me. Even Diana.

But there were two guys who Kevin had trusted completely.

And right now they were racing around the Laguna Beach Dog Park unaware that Kevin had placed the information the government authorities, the police, and Kevin's killer were seeking in them.

Now that information would put the real evil behind bars for, I hoped, the rest of his life.

That could only be the mastermind who was currently posing as Kevin Blackstone's half-brother.

I heard a car door and turned, expecting to see Detective Malone.

Instead it was J.T.

He moved with purpose through the two gates and toward me.

Malone was right. I should have left the investigating to the police.

I'd forgotten that Dr. Daniel had said he'd also contacted J.T. about the microchip.

I looked around for an escape route but there was none.

In my attempt to get the dogs out of harm's way, I'd left myself no options. The hills rose in front of me and I was surrounded on all other sides by high fences.

I wished I had a gun. Like many Texas girls who've grown up on a ranch, I'd learned to shoot at an early age.

No gun.

I looked around for my purse.

Maybe mace.

Dang it, I'd left my purse in the car.

No mace.

Maybe I could play dumb. Buy some time. Malone *was* on his way. "J.T., what brings you to the dog park?"

"No dice, Caro." His face, which I'd previously thought of as friendly, now seemed menacing. "I know you've figured things out. At least enough to be dangerous."

"How did —"

"Your friend, Don Furry, the guy at the dog place, told me I'd find you here." A derisive smile twisted one side of his mouth. "I'd just planned to pick up the dog, rip out the other microchip, and be on my way."

I cringed.

"It would have been less messy. But now you get to help me." He pulled a pistol from his jacket and aimed it at my mid-section. "I've already got the one chip. I picked it up from your friend, the vet. Nice of him to call me. Now, I need the other one."

I could sense, rather than see, the dogs come closer. Crap. I'd put them and all the other people and animals at the dog park in danger.

The brush of the two Shepherds against the back of my legs told me they knew J.T. was a threat.

"Tell them to stay back." J.T. ordered.

He still aimed the gun at me but his eyes dropped to the dogs.

Zeus growled deep in his throat. A primitive sound.

Tommy Boy nudged my leg and pushed against my hand.

"I said, tell them to stay back. I'll shoot them both."

I believed he would too.

"Too bad you couldn't leave things alone. Kind of like Kirk."

"I've called Detective Malone."

"Too bad. Now I'll have to take care of him too."

My money was on Malone. Too bad I wouldn't live to see it.

"You need to come with me." He reached out and took my arm, concealing the gun between us. "Walk slowly toward the exit."

If I resisted, everyone in the park was at risk. The people. The dogs.

The man was a lunatic.

The one thing I'd never do is use an animal to hurt a person.

I'm sorry, guys. We've got to try. Forgive me.

I heard the twin engines of their ominous growls. They were ready.

"Zeus. Tommy Boy. Fass!" I shouted. "Fass!"

I used the German attack command, knowing there'd be no hesitation. Kevin had trained them in German.

The two dogs lunged at J.T. taking him down and knocking me down in the process.

They went for his throat.

I crawled toward J.T. intending to wrest the gun from him and then call off the dogs.

In my peripheral vision I could see people

343

scatter in all directions.

I yelled. "Take your dogs and get out."

I tried to reach J.T.'s wrist but I knew better than to get into a fray with dogs in an aggressive state. I pulled my leg back, thinking I could kick the gun from his hand.

"Got it, Caro." I didn't know where Malone had come from but, boy, was I glad to see him. "Call them off."

"Zeus. Tommy Boy. Aus! Off."

They immediately obeyed and came to sit by me. One on each side.

Malone kept his weapon aimed at J.T. and reached down to flip him over. There was a lot of blood, but he seemed to be conscious.

"Thanks, guys." I hugged the two dogs. "I'm so sorry." I could feel the tears behind my eyes and buried my face in the dogs' fur. I'd been so afraid for them.

The wail of sirens broke in and in a matter of minutes there were paramedics, uniformed officers, and crime scene techs swarming the place.

J.T. was patched up, read his rights, and packed up.

Zeus and Tommy Boy were hailed as heroes, and taken to be checked over thoroughly by Dr. Daniel, who would also remove the other microchip.

I owed them an extra-special batch of

PAWS Good Dog Treats.

The paramedics insisted on looking me over, too. But I was fine. A little roughed up from my tussle on the ground, but nothing major. Malone insisted on taking my arm as he walked me to his car. But I didn't care.

The media circus, which had descended out of nowhere, demanded a statement. Malone offered no comment with a look that no one cared to challenge. I'd begun to shake. Having dealt with enough trauma victims, I knew it was shock, but understanding it didn't help me make it stop.

Malone helped me into the car, then got in himself, and shut the door. "Are you okay, really?"

"Please don't be nice. I'm afraid I'll do something stupid like cry."

"Fine." He laughed. "Are you an idiot? I can't believe you were going to kick J.T. when he was down. What kind of technique is that?"

I laughed too.

"Better?"

"Yeah."

We were quiet for a few minutes.

"What's J.T.'s real name?" I knew it would be a while before we knew everything, but I wanted a few things straight in my head.

"Rocko Lamberti." Malone shook his

head. "He's a real bad guy."

"Spike killed Kevin?"

Malone nodded. "We're still not sure if he meant to or not, but we know he killed Joe, the regular landscaper. Then he was sniffing around Ruby Point, trying to figure out a way to get to Kevin, or rather Kirk. The dogs made it difficult."

"Probably it was Spike's presence that made all the dogs in Ruby Point go a little crazy."

"Could be. Like I said, we're still sorting things out."

"One more thing, Detective." I turned to face him. "And then I want to go home."

"Okay, shoot."

"Why keep Diana in jail?" It had been bugging me. From what Malone had said so far, the police had been looking at J.T. as suspicious since he'd arrived.

"Well, that's a more difficult question than some of the others, Caro." Malone rubbed his jaw. "It kept her safe. It kept the real criminal complacent because he believed we weren't looking at him, and Diana wanted to stay."

"More than just the dogs went a little crazy."

"I agree."

"Want to go with me to release her?"

"Yeah." I buckled my seat belt, happy to see my hands were no longer shaking.

"Let's go then." He started the car.

I had an awful thought. "J.T. won't be there will he?"

"Nope. We take the real criminals to Orange County lock-up."

"What?"

Malone just smiled.

CHAPTER THIRTY-TWO

The Fur Ball was only two days away. Diana and I were back at Zino's. I was again in the seat by the window so I could enjoy the view of the vivid blue Pacific Ocean. We had notebooks and folders spread on the table so we could go over my list of last minute Fur Ball details one more time.

People kept stopping by the table and interrupting, so it had taken more than an hour to get through just the first page of my list. I thought if I had to say one more time how happy I was to be alive, I might just borrow Diana's Taser and tase myself.

Diana was a lot better at this than I was. She graciously smiled and thanked each person. Then we'd get back to our Fur Ball list, and then another person would stop by our table.

Our food was getting cold, and our list was not getting done.

"I think my face is stuck like this," Diana

said, her mouth turned up in an exaggerated grin as the person moved out of earshot.

I nearly choked on my iced tea. It was so incredibly nice to have her back. I'd missed her bubbly sense of fun and snarky good nature.

"There really isn't much to go over, Caro, honey." She picked up the second page of the list. "You've got everything lined up and ready to go."

"I think we have some great auction items." I handed her the sheet with donor names and the prize packages.

Some were actual items while others were experiences. "We've got a safari, two whale watching excursions, an Alaskan cruise, dinner with the Governor, several autographed pieces." I ran my finger down the list. "Your celebrity friends have been very giving. I think I might bid on the Sonoma get-away."

"We've already raised thousands in ticket sales." Diana patted the advanced receipts. "I hope Tivoli Too can hold the crowd."

"They've assured me they can."

"Well, I think you've just done a wonderful job, Caro. And I hope you'll make me a promise to be co-chair next year."

"I'll promise only if you'll promise to stay out of jail."

"Deal," she agreed.

We shook hands.

Diana was suddenly serious. "I do feel a little bad that I thought so poorly of Kevin Blackstone when here he was trying to do a good thing and let people know what that drug company was up to."

"No one knew." I touched her hand. "The information they were able to get from the microchips Kevin hid in Zeus and Tommy Boy will undoubtedly hold accountable several company executives. They may be sharing jail time with J.T."

"What will the police do with Kevin's book of secrets?" Diana asked.

"I don't really know. Malone's not saying. But I did want to tell you one more thing." I leaned forward and lowered my voice. "I dropped off some more dog cookies to Ollie. I'm afraid he may not be sharing them with the dogs."

"You might think about selling those," Diana said. "Mr. Wiggles and Barbary love them. And Abe, the goat, too. Though he's not very discriminating in what he eats."

"It wasn't the dog treats I wanted to tell you about." I sighed. "Ollie was the one who tore the missing page out of Kevin's book. But it turns out it wasn't anything about him or his family. The page he tore out was about you."

"Caro, like I told you before, Ollie is a lovely man." This time the smile reached all the way to her dancing blue eyes. "I might have to marry him to keep my secrets safe. How do you think I'd look in black leather?"

I actually snorted iced tea at the thought. Not very lady-like, so don't tell my mother.

"Now," Diana said, packing away my lists and folders. "Let's talk about the important stuff. What are you wearing to the Fur Ball?"

CHAPTER THIRTY-THREE

Dammit!

Please excuse my bad language but that girl is beyond polite language. I didn't even know the brooch was gone until I was getting dressed for the Fur Ball.

I'd chosen a red Valentino. There's nothing like a high-quality classic design to give a girl the confidence she needs. And I was already feeling great.

I could tell Mama I'd been on two, count 'em two, honest-to-goodness dates. With two very eligible men-folk. Okay, one of them was an afternoon Shake Shack rendezvous with Malone for a burger and a date shake. It still counted. Maybe the news would keep Herself in Texas where she belonged.

Diana was out of the clink.

J.T., or whatever the heck his real name was, was in the clink. Zeus and Tommy Boy were all healed up, and had applied to police dog school. All should be right with the world.

Emphasis on *should.*

Then I'd opened my safe and reached in to get the box where I'd oh-so-carefully placed Grandma Tillie's brooch. I knew the minute I picked up the box that it was empty.

Damn.

Okay, not very creative, but I was beyond mad.

I was fiery mad.

I was whatever *beyond* fiery mad is.

I was foaming at the mouth, rabid, bite-anything-in-sight mad.

Damn.

Grandma Tillie would have threatened to wash my mouth out with soap for those damns. But I felt justified. Besides, I'd heard the occasional damn out of her mouth. Usually it involved Grandpa Montgomery or my mama.

I didn't know how Mel had known to look there. I didn't know how she'd figured out the combination. Wait a minute. I *did* know.

I hadn't used the obvious. Not my birth date, my address, my wedding date nor my divorce date. Those were all too easy to find out, even for a stranger who didn't really know me.

The date I'd used only someone truly close to me would know or realize the significance of.

That was the date of my freedom, the date I'd walked out of the Miss Texas pageant and told them I was done. That was the date I'd told my mother, no more. It was the date I'd stopped being everything everyone else wanted me to be.

That was the date I became me.

Mel had broken into my home and robbed my safe.

Worse, she had used what she knew about me to do it. Intimate cousin info.

There was going to be hell to pay.

CARO'S PAWS
GOOD DOG TREATS

Preheat your oven to 350° F.

In a big bowl, combine all the ingredients with just enough water to make it the consistency of cookie dough.

You'll need:

1/2 cup of creamy unsalted peanut butter
1 cup oat flour
1 cup brown rice flour (Caro uses organic)
1 egg
1 tablespoon of honey
1/2 cup finely grated carrot (Dogbert loves carrots and so does Abbey)

Optional: You can also add cooked bacon, a bit of grated cheese, or other ingredients for flavor, but don't add too much or it will mess with the consistency of the dough, and cause your treats to fall apart.

Once you've got your treat dough all stirred up, put it between pieces of parchment paper and roll it out to about 1/4 inch thickness. Then cut the dough with a cookie cutter. You can use whatever shape strikes your fancy. Caro often uses dog bone shapes of different sizes. Next, put them on a regular cookie sheet and bake them between fifteen and twenty minutes or until they're Golden Retriever brown.

Let them cool and then put them in an airtight container. You can store your PAWS Good Dog treats for about a week (or you can freeze them for later use) but keep an eye on them. There are no preservatives, so watch out for spoilage.

This makes a couple of dozen treats so there's plenty to go around. Please share them with your dog.

ACKNOWLEDGEMENTS

We'd like to acknowledge our husbands and our families. Thank you for your stalwart support, your incredible sacrifices through the years, and most of all your unwavering belief in our dreams.

Also, huge thanks to our critique group. Your input, your suggestions, your encouragement is always above and beyond. Cindy, Christine, Laura, and Tami, we could not have done it without you.

And to Alex and the crew at Starbucks Fleur (who know us as the Skinny Hazelnut and the Chai Tea Latte) thanks for always being ready with a table, a hot beverage and a friendly face. And thanks for being so polite when you have to let us know we've stayed past closing — again.

We are also grateful to the wonderful people

in Laguna Beach, CA who spent time answering our multitude of questions. Any errors are ours alone and we apologize for the creative license we've taken with your community, such as (among other things) creating a homicide division where none exists.

Finally, to the amazing publishing team at Bell Bridge Books who believed in Team Pets and the Pampered Pets mystery series, you rock! We are so blessed to be part of you endeavors. DebS and DebD we are grateful for your guidance, your advice, and your amazing industry knowledge. Lynn, our editor extraordinaire, you made this a much better book. The whole team at BBB is an absolute class act and we appreciate all of the energy that has gone into this project every step of the way. Thank you from the bottom of our hearts.

Sparkle Abbey
aka ML and Anita

ABOUT SPARKLE ABBEY

www.sparkleabbey.com
The authors love to hear from readers.
sparkleabbey@gmail.com

Sparkle Abbey is the pseudonym of two mystery authors (Mary Lee Woods and Anita Carter). They are friends and neighbors as well as co-writers of the Pampered Pets Mystery Series. The pen name was created by combining the names of their rescue pets — Sparkle (Mary Lee's cat) and Abbey (Anita's dog). They reside in central Iowa, but if they could write anywhere, you would find them on the beach with their laptops and depending on the time of day either an iced tea or a margarita.

Mary Lee
Mary Lee Salsbury Woods is the "Sparkle" half of Sparkle Abbey. She is president of Sisters in Crime — Iowa and a

member of Mystery Writers of America, Romance Writers of America, Kiss of Death the RWA Mystery Suspense chapter, Sisters in Crime, and the SinC internet group Guppies.

Prior to publishing the Pampered Pet Mystery series with Bell Bridge Books, Mary Lee won first place in the Daphne du Maurier contest, sponsored by the Kiss of Death chapter of RWA, and was a finalist in Murder in the Grove's mystery contest, as well as Killer Nashville's Claymore Dagger contest.

Mary Lee is an avid reader and supporter of public libraries. She lives in Des Moines, Iowa with her husband, Tim, and Sparkle, the rescue cat namesake of Sparkle Abbey. In her day job she is the non-techie in the City of Des Moines IT Department. Any spare time she spends reading and enjoying her two sons and daughters-in-law, and four grandchildren.

Anita

Anita Carter is the "Abbey" half of Sparkle Abbey. She is vice-president of Sisters In Crime — Iowa and is also a member of Mystery Writers of America and Kiss of Death the RWA Mystery Suspense chapter.

She grew up reading Trixie Belden, Nancy Drew and the Margo Mystery series by Jerry B. Jenkins (years before his popular Left Behind Series). Her family is glad all the years of "fending for yourself" dinners of spaghetti and frozen pizza have finally paid off even though they haven't stopped.

In Anita's day job, she works for Manpower Inc., of Des Moines, in sales and marketing. She lives in Des Moines, Iowa with her husband and four children, son-in-law, grandchild and two rescue dogs, Abbey and Chewy.